Chapter 1

Colors explode in my mind, their corresponding emotions a sucker punch to my brain. Red anger, gray sorrow, and then Will Wunderliech, our top ER doc, moves his hand from my bare arm, releasing me from his tumultuous thoughts.

Despite the lack of contact, Will's wife continues to scream at him—at me—her voice bouncing through my brain like a ball in a pinball machine. I gulp in a breath, squeeze my eyes shut, force the voice into hiding.

Being an empath is a curse.

Whoever thinks it fascinating needs to live my life. Then maybe they'd stop calling me crazy.

Will's wife fades into nothing, her voice and image disappearing into the dark recesses of my mind.

I take a deep breath. *Steady now*. I should be used to the flashes, to the glimpses of people's thoughts and emotions, but nope, I'm not. At least it only happens with skin-on-skin contact. But I don't have on my scrub jacket, and he touched my bare arm.

"You okay, Gin?"

I look into the pair of blue eyes featured prominently in my dreams since high school. Who would've thought we'd end up working together years later at Blue Forest Hospital in the Emergency Room. This time, though, I'm not the school freak. I'm a

1

kickass ER nurse staring into the eyes of the local Dr. Dreamy. My old friend.

Who needs lying to about my empath ability. No use in him thinking I'm still a freak.

"Yeah, sorry. Lost my balance. How are you?"

"Eh." His hand floats in the air, twisting back and forth in a so-so motion. "I've been better."

"Is it the wife?" Or as I've always thought of that trashy blowjob queen, a ho.

He pauses, blinks, clearly weighing past friendship with professional pecking order. When he sighs, I know friendship wins. "You must be psychic or something. Yeah, we got in a big fight this morning." Pain-filled eyes meet mine then look away. When he replies his voice softens so only I can hear. "I think she wants to leave. Maybe it's for the best. I don't know." He clears his throat, offers a lopsided grin. "Anyway, I've gotta get busy. There's a new patient in number one. Stomach pains. Those are always fun." The intimate glimpse into his thoughts disappears, leaving me with a bitter taste in my mouth.

He waves and hightails it away from where I stand. I sigh. It's not meant to be, obviously. I mean, sure, I see what's going on with him and his wife, so I could easily say something to encourage him to leave her. But how likely was it that he would come knocking on my door?

Unlikely to not. And I'd feel bad about it.

Guilt sucks.

Almost as hard as being an empath.

Since Blue Forest doesn't pay me to stand in the hall and stare at Dr. Dreamy's buff bod, I might as well check on the dehydrated patient. Putting the fantasies of us lying tangled in silk sheets into the review-before-going-to-sleep section of my mind, I push open the door to the patient's room and reach for the glove box hanging on the wall.

"Hello, Mr. Talley, how are you feeling?" Snap, snap, and the gloves sheath my hands.

"A little better. Still not right."

And he thought he would be all right with one liter of saline? The man walked, or more like shuffled, into the ER after several days of pooping and puking. He thought he could rehydrate himself at home. Oops. Faulty logic there.

"Well, Mr. Talley, we're going to need to pull a bit of blood out of you. Is that okay? I'll access the needle we already have in your arm."

"Sure, sure. Whatever you need to do."

Protected by the gloves, I grab a needle and get to work accessing the catheter in his arm. With gloves on, I can touch patients and not have to worry much about their thoughts and emotions intruding on me. Only if they're broadcasting loudly, and I do mean loudly, will it bother me. Mr. Talley is too out of it to project anything but pain and illness.

Being a nurse might seem an odd career choice for an empath, but occasionally I can help someone. Touch them and know where their illness comes from. What will help them feel better. Or if they're too far gone to ever feel better, as the case may be. And those rare instances make the unwanted flashes of memory worth every minute.

"Okay, I got it. I'll go take this—" I hold up his tube of blood "—to the lab and see what you have in there. Then I'll come back to check on fluids." I point to the bag dripping a rehydrating solution into his veins.

He chuckles and closes his eyes.

I drop the blood off at the drop station for the hospital lab to pick up and am about to return to the nursing desk to make my diligent notes in the patient's online chart, when I hear what sounds like coughing coming from Room 1. Dr. Dreamy's stomach pain patient.

In an ER coughing is par for the day, but this cough sounds different, inhuman. The sound stops me mid-step, a live statue in the hallway. A fine tremor captures my spine in its grasp. The intuition buzzer wails like a tornado siren in a hailstorm. The coughing, so normal in here, and yet, clearly not right, precedes a dull thump, a light shake of the wall missed, in the bustle of the ER, by all other ears but mine.

My vision narrows, blocks all the noise, the rush, of medical staff, focusing on Room 1 like light shining at the end of a tunnel. As if pulled by invisible strings, I walk to the exam room, heart double-timing a crazed beat. What's wrong? Why do I feel this way? Why doesn't anyone else hear the coughing, the unusual thud?

My hand reaches for the handle on the door, only to hit air as a nondescript man barrels out of the room as if chased by the hounds of hell. Before I can move, he runs right into me, and I almost fall over.

His thoughts, oh my god, his thoughts. Tangles of dark strands mesh together, piling upon one another in a jumble of terror. Anger, revenge, disappointment. What he wanted wasn't here. A body, blood running down its chest, over its white lab coat.

And then he steps away from me as the door clicks

closed.

"Excuse me." The melodious tone of his voice doesn't jibe with the web of thoughts dashing through his mind. I look into his eyes, into vast pools of empty obsidian and a cold shiver consumes my being. My muscles tense, shaking a jitterbug. I can't move, can't flee, can't scream.

"Where's my sister?" my twin T's shout booms down the hall as if fired from a canon. "I need to see her now! Where is she?"

And just like that T's voice breaks the communion I'm having with the scariest thing I've ever met. I say thing, because his thoughts, his emotions aren't human. Or not totally human. Or maybe it's just I've never met a human that evil.

For that's what the tangles were, evil.

My muscles relax enough with the sound of T's voice for me to glance over my shoulder toward the waiting room. Why was T here? T only showed up when bad things were about to happen to me.

And what could be worse than that evil thing?

I turn my head so fast it's like I'm Linda Blair. But the evil thing disappeared. I glance up and down the hall only to see my co-workers going about their business.

T continues to yell at Sally Ann, our intake coordinator, to let him pass. If she doesn't, he'll give up on being polite and shove his way through the doors. It doesn't matter if they are locked to the ER. T has no problem with making locks disengage.

I ignore T's outburst. Room 1 calls me, my intuition shrieks a warning as my skin erupts in tingles. I take a breath, push open the door, and step inside. The coppery scent of blood assails my nostrils. Fresh blood. I'm standing in it.

Will is slumped against the wall, blood streaming out of him from gunshot wounds in his chest and abdomen. His eyes flick to me, pleading for help, for relief, while his lips form words I can't hear.

I do not keep a cool head like I've been trained to do in emergencies. I'm standing in a pool of blood from my friend, and everything goes blank in my brain. I scream, realize I'm screaming and shut myself up.

"Doctor down! Doctor down!"

A loud shattering sound streaks down the hall, but I'm inside the room and slipping to Will. I grab his hand because lucky for him all I need is a touch to see what happened, to get into his head.

I want you to have it, I want you to have it, I want you to have it.

His thoughts hit me first, and then I'm pulled past them, into his memories.

Will walks into Exam Room 1, but the man is not doubled over, is not having stomach pains and he looks familiar. Where does he know him? Unease scratches across his skin and into mine as I relive his experience.

The man stands and tries to smile, but it's a hideous imitation of a welcome.

Will takes a breath, tension spreading to his muscles. He's two steps into the room and going no further. "I'm Dr. Wunderliech, what seems to be the problem?"

"You have something I want."

"I don't know what you mean."

The man's eyes look black, cold as space and as welcoming as an out of control eighteen-wheeler headed his way. Must be an addict looking for a hit. But even as he thinks it, he realizes that's not true. An addict's stare lacks the cold calculation and spark of glee this man's possesses.

Like a stone-cold killer's dark gaze.

Will steps backward, toward the door.

"Oh, no you don't." The man stretches out his hand and catches Will by invisible strings, each strand a frozen length cutting into his flesh, forcing him to stand against the wall.

He fights, but to no avail. How can he free himself if he can't even see what's holding him? Nothing moves except his lungs working overtime.

"Where is it?" The man takes a step closer. "I've spent years tracking it down. And back to you. I killed her trying to get it, but never could find you."

Thoughts blossom in Will's mind, thoughts hidden for years, remembrances of when he was a child, the last night of his mother's life.

Terror blossoms in his throat, an acrid scent wrapping him like a blanket, a threat of death in the guise of comfort. He hid under a bed, hearing sounds of a fight, hearing the thuds of fists as they struck his mother, over and over until nothing but silence remained. His breath echoed loudly in his ears, even as he tried to relax the see-saw of air raking in and out of his mouth. He clutched a silver-link bracelet in his hand, held it so tightly it cut into his skin.

Please don't see me, please don't see me, please don't see me. Don't hurt me, don't hurt me, don't hurt me.

The phrases ran through his mind, circling around, until they were all he heard. The bracelet felt hot in his palm as if it tried to fuse with his skin. It burned now, he felt blisters forming, smelled his skin burning, but didn't make a sound, didn't move. He was a good boy. His mother said so. She said to hide under the bed, to hold the bracelet, to not let it go. She said everything would be okay, she said so, and yet he knew it wasn't.

Footsteps creaked on the floorboards, each step bringing someone closer. Not his mother, though. Her steps weren't so heavy. He pressed himself against the wall, trying to make himself tiny.

Please don't let him see me. Please don't let him hurt me.

The comforter of his bed was thrown back, a bland face peering underneath.

Please don't...

The comforter dropped into place, as the man walked around the room. Doors opened and shut, opened and shut. Drawers were pulled out, their contents dumped on the floor.

The boy huddled against the wall under the bed, clutching the bracelet, whispering over and over for the bad man to go away, to leave him alone. The silver links hurt his hand, burned his palm, but he gripped it tight like he had his mother's hand on the Ferris wheel at the state fair. He was still gripping the bracelet, hiding under the bed, when the police found him hours later.

And now the man, the one who had killed his mother, the one whose face was seared into his memory, who scarred his life, was at the hospital, pinning him to the wall with an invisible hold.

"Where is it?"

Will knows what the man wants, knows but refuses

to tell him. His mother died protecting that bracelet. For whatever unknown reason, she considered her life a fair trade to keep the silver links safe from this man. How could he honor her memory by doing less?

"Don't have it."

"Where?"

"I. Don't. Have. It."

The man growls, a low rumbling threat and pulls out a gun. Panic ricochets through Will's limbs as he tries in vain to escape his bonds. He's not ready to see his beloved mother again, but the choice is taken away on what sounds like a string of soft coughs. Pain blooms throughout Will's chest and stomach as the man laughs with no sound.

A hand shakes my shoulder, pulling me away from a now unconscious Will. His pain still pings around my chest and abdomen, traveling throughout my limbs. I taste terror in the back of my throat, threatening to choke my breath, Will's terror, not mine, but I can't differentiate between the two. Doctors stream in, nurses hurrying around, but I stay slumped on the floor, my brain slowly turning over. I'd never touched another person in that manner for that long before, never been that deep into their thoughts, their remembrances. Blood soaks through my scrubs, soaks right into my skin, like the remains of Will want to become a part of me.

"Gin!" T bellows from the hallway, blocked by the frantic motions of the ER staff working on Will.

I'm okay.

T and I can talk telepathically. Maybe all twins do this, I never bothered to ask one.

What the fuck did you think you were doing?

Going to work?

Don't be a smart ass with me. I saw you in a pool of blood up here at the hospital and dropped everything to get to you. You think I like seeing shit like that?

I look out the doorway, straight at my twin. He stands in the hall, fists balled at his side, a muscle twitching along his jaw. It takes a lot for T to come to a hospital.

The dead walk at hospitals.

Or so he says.

I wouldn't know, having never met a ghost, but T says they're here and I believe him.

I'm sorry. It's not my fault Will got shot, but it seems like the thing to say in the face of my jaw-twitching, fingers-clenching twin.

T sucks in a deep breath and shakes as if throwing off his anger. Which is good. Anger and T—

I'm thrown from my thought by a touch on my arm. A touch with a glove, thank god. No emotions.

"Are you okay?" Laura, another nurse, peers at me from where she squats in Will's blood.

By okay, does she mean, am I physically hurt? Because emotionally I bounce around, unable to focus. My friend has been shot. He might not survive. Will I ever be okay? But as she expects an answer, I decide she means physical and answer accordingly. "Yeah. No. I mean—" I gesture to where the doctors are trying to stabilize Will "—I lost it seeing him like that."

She does the little rub on the arm thing people do to show support. It feels nice. "I know. I can't believe it. Did you see the guy who did it?"

I shiver and close my eyes. When I open them, T stands in front of me, staring down, his brown eyes full of concern. Laura glares at him.

"How did you get in here?"

"It's okay," I say.

"It's not okay. He's not supposed to be in here. How did he get past Sally Ann?"

He has this thing with locks. "He's my brother."

"I'm taking her home." T reaches for me, but before he makes contact, the huddle of doctors around Will moves.

"Out of the way! We need to get him to the OR!" They shove the gurney across the room, and T hops back to avoid being hit. The wheels streak lines of blood through the doorway and down the hall, crimson reminders of death. We watch them run down the hall to the elevators, a huddle of shocked faces, exploding into excitement.

"Let's take you to a room." Laura rises, pulling on my hand. "I think you're in shock."

Yeah, ya think? But the shock she thinks I'm in is not the only shock I'm experiencing. Not only am I dealing with the emotional trauma of seeing my friend shot and lying in a pool of his blood, but a million questions about the shooter rush through my mind. Who was that evil man? Why did he want Will's bracelet? Really, what was so important about a bracelet? Couldn't he have just broken into Will's house and stolen the thing instead of shooting Will?

I rise to my feet, my head swimming, and put a hand out to T for support. He grabs my palm and squeezes, and instantly I feel better. Laura grabs my other arm and together we walk down the hall toward an empty room.

Something rattles in my pocket, hitting against my

work cell phone, a metallic clink. Odd, nothing but the phone should be in my pocket. I shake loose of Laura's grip and stick my hand in my scrubs.

One phone. One...I pull the object out and stare. Gulping in a deep breath does nothing to calm my speeding heart. My stomach makes a pit and shoves my body into the gaping maw.

"What's that?" Laura and T ask simultaneously.

Silver links shift, catching the light. Something's carved into the metal, words, runes, a recipe for disaster, who the hell knows. I'm too busy staring at the thing as if it's going to bite me. Which, judging from what happened here today, it very well might.

How the hell did it get into my pocket?

Will's special bracelet lies in my palm, the links glowing under the florescent lights and the cold bite of metal against my skin makes me...*happy*.

Chapter 2

But not nearly as happy as what I sense from the bracelet. Since when do bracelets have emotions?

The thought prickles my scalp. I try to shake it off, to no avail.

"It's a bracelet."

"Duh. Did you hit your head?" T gives my hand a squeeze, a little joke, and yet not.

"No. I just sat in blood. Which is all over my pants. I need to change. Would you please get me a spare pair of bottoms?" I turn to Laura, trying to forget it's Will's blood soaking my skin.

"Sure. You feeling better?"

"Right as rain." I'm such a liar. My hands shake like a Parkinsonian patient.

"You look better."

That's because T holds my hand. Touching each other helps calm us. Always has. And not something I share. "Yeah. I need to change and then go check on Mr. Talley."

"Sure. I'll be right back."

T and I slip into the empty room as Laura hurries away to fetch me a pair of pants. I take a couple of deep breaths, willing the hand tremors to disappear. T's touch calms me enough for my mind to stop whirling and focus on the oddity of having Will's bracelet appear in my pocket.

"What the hell is that?" Still holding my hand, T points to the bracelet.

"It's a bracelet."

"Aren't you fucking Sherlock?" The muscle under his eye twitches.

I squeeze his hand tighter. "What is it?" Usually my touch helps him to not see the spirit world. But he's acting as if ghosts are standing in the room.

"It's not working," he hisses. "There's one that won't leave me alone even with you holding my hand. And others keep floating by. I need a drink."

"Why don't you ask him if he knows who shot Will."

The eye twitch becomes more pronounced. "I. Don't. Talk. To. Them."

"You have before. You can do it again."

His go to hell glare sparks a memory best left forgotten. But Will was shot and the ghosts can help catch the shooter. You know you have a messed up life when you can think that thought in all seriousness.

"Whoever shot Will is evil. I need to know who it was." So I can tell the police about the evil man.

"Are you fucking nuts? Who do you think you are? Nancy fucking Drew?"

I stare at my twin, open my mind and let Will's memories pour into him. He sucks in a breath, his eyes flying wide.

"That bracelet? It's his?"

"Yep. And T. It's happy."

He glances to where I'm clutching the bracelet. "What happens if you put it on?"

"I become a beacon for Mr. Walking Evil?"

"Maybe it fights evil."

I stare at the silver links. They seem to be waiting, hoping, desiring...me.

"There're more of them now. Like the whole freaking cemetery is standing outside the door." A fine sheen of perspiration beads on his forehead, slides down his cheeks, bleeding color from his face.

"Ask them if it's okay to put on the bracelet." I hiss back.

He clears his throat. "Can she—" The rest of the sentence dies on his lips as his eyes widen. He turns to me and the look in his gaze sends chills chasing through my limbs. "Put it on." The voice is not T's and my chills multiply.

"T?"

"They say do it." This time it's his voice.

I obey, dropping his hand, fumbling with the catch. He helps and the bracelet settles against my forearm, slightly above my wrist. I turn my wrist back and forth.

"Nothing's—" Pain shoots through my arm, traveling up to my neck, ricocheting into my brain, settling along my nerves. I want to scream, but the noise dies in my throat.

And as suddenly as it came, it vanishes.

I blink a couple of times, trying to clear the pain-tears from my eyes and clutch T's hand. Blurry figures cluster in the doorway. Blurry see-through figures.

"Are those ghosts?"

T shivers. "You can see them?"

Laura uses that moment to walk right through the shadow figures, bursting through the door holding a new pair of scrubs. "Sorry it took so long."

"Not a problem. Thank you."

She turns to go and holds the door open, looking

over her shoulder at T. As if my twin will walk through a cloud of ghosts. Judging by his coloring, I'm surprised he's still standing.

"I think he needs to sit down. It's all right."

Laura raises a brow, clearly not approving of brother watching his sister undress.

If she only knew.

Once the door snaps shut behind her, I shimmy out of my ruined scrubs and into the fresh pair. Oddly enough, despite seeing Will shot and bleeding out, I feel happy. Ecstatic. Like I've found a long lost friend and been reunited.

Questions ping through my mind, a repetitive chase of who, what, when, where, all swirling around the bracelet and the evil man. And then my mind stutters back to Room 1. Were the doctors able to save Will?

Oh god, Will. My poor friend. What if he doesn't make it? What if he dies? Why him? Who would want Will dead?

A sense of calm sweeps through me, a sense all will be made known, all will be okay.

Oh, wonderful. To top the day off, not that it needs a cherry on the whipped cream, the bracelet seems to have infiltrated my thoughts.

How much worse could the day get?

"Are you having some sort of communion with that thing?" T glares at the bracelet, snapping me out of my thoughts.

"It's like it speaks to me."

"Okay, that shit right there just freaks me the hell out. Take it off."

I give it a half-hearted tug. "It won't come off."

"That's bullshit. You put it on—"

"At your insistence."

"You would've done it anyway. What goes on can come off."

"Except this time."

He grabs my wrist and tries to unfasten the hook. Or what was the hook. The silver links join together without a trace of the clasp, prohibiting the thing from ever being removed. Not that I want it removed. It makes me as happy as I make it.

Where's a psychologist when I need one? Happy should not be on my feelings list right now.

"Fuck. It won't come off." He punctuates each word with a jerk on the bracelet.

I yank my wrist back before he tears the thing off. "I told you that. Come on, you need to get out of here. You're getting pale." Not to mention sweating.

"Best idea I've heard today." T grabs my hand, yanks open the door, and pulls me through the opening.

Blue-suited men swarm through the hallway like bees on pollen, speaking into their wrists, their voices a buzz of energy. Wires spiral from their ears down their necks, disappearing under their collars. Security. Now they show up. A bit late for the shooting party, but I guess none of them possess psychic abilities and therefore can't be held accountable for allowing a would-be murderer onto the premises.

Letting said would-be murderer escape is another matter.

I'm being dragged toward the exit by the equivalent of a twitchy human train, when I spot Laura talking to a security guard at the same moment she spots me. One finger points me out, and the guard marches in our direction.

"Hey, T. I need to stay." This is the ER after all. Just because you see your friend shot and bleeding out is no reason to leave before shift end.

Not to mention I'm the star witness. Plenty of people wanting to hear my story.

"Nope. I'm getting you out of here."

"I'm pretty certain that guard wants to talk to me."

"I don't care."

"Ms. Crawford?" Mr. Security Guard stops T's frantic bid for the exit.

"Yes?"

"May we have a word with you?"

"Of course." I try to remove my hand from T's grasp of steel and get nowhere fast. *Let me go.*

No. You need to get out of here.

No. You need to. I have beer in the fridge. Go help yourself and I'll be there when my shift ends.

Beer. The ambrosia of tatted, ghost-seeing auto mechanics.

Curses fill my brain, but he releases my hand, bids adieu to Mr. SG, and darts out the exit as if the place wasn't on lockdown. I watch the doors snap into place, sealing us in and T out, before turning back to security. Soft brown eyes hold a quizzical expression as the guard glances to the closed exit doors and back to me.

"He doesn't do well in hospitals. They kinda freak him out." *Don't ask about it, don't ask about it, don't ask about it.*

Security ignores T. Doesn't even bother to ask him to come back, to stay for an interview, to give his side of things. Weird. T's talents might include talking to ghosts and breaking through locks, but he's usually hard to miss. And yet the security guard continues to look at me as if I've been caught muttering to myself. But I'm not complaining. The less T hangs out at the hospital the better.

"I hear you found Dr. Wunderliech."

And with the guard's words my mind flashes back to Will lying in a pool of blood. *Dying.*

I wrap my arms around my torso as a tremor shakes through my body. Are the surgeons able to save him?

The guard's hand hovers behind the small of my back, not quite touching, but still a guide. His other arm gestures toward Room 2, where it quickly becomes apparent the room has been turned into an interview room. Operation Central.

I force myself to not look at Room 1, to not look at the blood trails screaming down the hall toward the elevator. Focus on Room 2, on the blue suits packing the room like a football team. I clasp my trembling hands together hard enough to hurt.

The guiding hand settles me into a chair. "Tell us what happened."

So I do. Minus the evil tangles in the man's mind or the way the bracelet suddenly appeared in my pocket. Speaking of what I saw when I touched Will, how his remembrances slammed through my mind, fusing to my memories was a no-brainer—not to be mentioned or even hinted at.

They'd lock me up at Blue Shores Psychiatric Institute quicker than I could say uh-oh. Been there, done that. The less people know of my little ability, the better.

"What made you check in on Dr. Wunderliech?"

Didn't I already tell them? Granted, I've had quite

the shock today, but still. I know I've told them why. Why are they asking again? Surely they don't think I shot him?

"I heard what sounded like coughing but not. So I checked it out."

My questioner nods, brown eyes aiming for sympathetic but falling short of the goal. I'm sure he means to inspire trust. It's not working.

"May I go now? I have a patient to tend to." I tap my fingers against my leg. Is Will still alive? How long until they let us know the outcome of his surgery? I really want to go check on him instead of sitting here answering questions.

"Just don't leave the ER until the cops talk to you."

"Yes, sir."

I'm out the door faster than a champagne cork shooting out of a newly opened bottle. And promptly slam into what feels like a mountain of muscle.

Strong hands grip my upper arms, the skin of his palms resting fully against the sleeves of my scrub top. Not an ounce of his skin touches mine, yet zingers of heat race up my arms, hitting my nervous system like mainlining adrenaline. My heart races while my core goes into overdrive, heating up, getting wet.

As if we're about to throw down for a sex-fest.

Which, oddly enough, sounds like the best idea of the day.

What the hell is wrong with me? After being drowned in Will's memories while sitting in a pool of his blood, sex should not be on my mind. And yet one touch from this giant and I'm ready to get it on.

Maybe security needs to haul my hormone-ridden ass to Blue Shores.

The mountain man drops my arms as if they crawl with scorpions and shakes his hands, flexing and curling long fingers as if he's been stung.

"Are you ok, ma'am?" His voice sounds like melted chocolate, warm with a hint of sweet in the tone.

I drag my gaze up his body, from eyelevel at his chest, across wide shoulders to his face. Black stubble grazes his chin, the look of a man whose morning shave ceases to be effective in late afternoon. Piercing blue eyes stare out of a tanned face surrounded by short black hair. A study in contrasts.

Apparently running into him renders my voice non-existent. I clear my throat, taking a step backward. Distance is my friend.

"I'm sorry." I try to step around him, but he moves with me. I take a step back, he follows, and we fall into that little dance two people stuck in the same place at the same time do. I giggle. He doesn't.

"I need to see my patient."

"I need to talk to you." His voice sends another round of zingers zipping through my system to lodge in my core.

So this is what it's like to star in a romance novel.

"I'm Detective Smythe. Please clear the room so I can interview this witness." One hand slips into his navy blue sports jacket pocket, pulling out a badge which he proceeds to flash, a quick open-close motion.

The security guards look at each other, back to Detective Smythe and shrug. The good detective moves out of the way, and the guards file past, joining their blue-suited brethren and the now-arrived police. A regular party out there and I'm trapped in here with Mister Fuckalicious.

And I'm complaining—why?

Click. The door snaps closed, and Detective Smythe crosses the room. It might not be professional, but I check out the view, pleased to see the back end looks as good as the front. Muscles roll under khaki pants, the clench and release of thick thighs leads my thoughts away from attempted murder toward how all that flesh would feel against my skin.

"Please sit."

His voice snaps my mind out of the sack and back to the room. Busted. Heat splashes my cheeks, disappearing as I suck down a breath. No reason for embarrassment over simple biology. This type of thing plays out in bars all over the country every night.

Although, admittedly, the almost overwhelming urge to do a little booty-bumping in a public place after experiencing a tragedy is a new one for me.

Talk about having issues.

He gestures to the chair, a subtle reminder to stash my hormones in the deep-freeze. Easier said than done. The hormones apparently like raging through my veins. But that doesn't mean I can't comply with his verbal request.

I sit, crossing my legs at the ankle, hands folded in my lap, one hand covering the silver links circling my wrist. Just because I want this man to fuck me senseless, doesn't mean I want him to check out the bracelet.

Go figure.

"Gin Champagne Crawford?" One black brow rises.

How did he know my full name? No one up here knows my middle name since I left it off the application. The police department must have a super-computer to figure out that one.

"Yeah?"

"What kind of a name is that? Were your parents drunk or something?"

"Or something." Oh, right. As if I'm going to go into my parents' drinking habits. It's bad enough they named their children after their favorite drink, Gin and Tonic. At least I got the name Gin, which can be a diminutive of Ginger or Genevieve or even Jennifer if you overlook how it's spelled. Once we graduated from high school, very few people ask what Gin is short for.

T on the other hand. Poor T. Tonic Scotch Crawford. Talk about enduring years of teasing. It was clearly a WTF moment when we were born. Good thing we weren't ice skaters. Announcing, Gin and Tonic Crawford!

I grin at the good detective, who looks like he wants more of an answer. I hope he doesn't mind disappointment.

After a moment of staring, he clears his throat. "Tell me about the man who shot the doctor."

Memories slam into my mind, hurtful in their intensity, diminishing my libido. I swallow, shove the memories into a dark recess and focus on helping the good detective. "He was rather nondescript. I didn't get a good look at him." Which is true. I got a good glimpse into his corrupted mind, but the tangles of evil and ensuing shock prevented me from getting a good look at his face. "When he opened the door, all I saw was Will. Dr. Wunderliech."

"On a first name basis with the doctor?" His eyes narrow, as if hearing me say 'Will' makes him jealous.

Right. My imagination is clearly hanging out with my hormones in overdrive.

"We went to high school together."

"And that bracelet." His gaze hits my wrist like a laser beam before bouncing to my face. "How did you get it?"

The bracelet reacts to his words. Surprise. Fear. Or maybe those are my feelings. It's becoming hard to tell.

I definitely need a trip to Blue Shores. Stat.

"It was a gift." A surprise gift. Big on the surprise.

"May I see it?"

I hold out my wrist for his viewing pleasure. The bracelet is not happy. It does not want to be seen, does not want to be noticed. I pull my wrist back before he gets a good look. "May I go now?"

"How long have you had it?"

"Isn't this an interview about how Will got shot? What does the bracelet have to do with that?" I can't keep the hitch out of my voice, or the indignation.

"That bracelet has everything to do with it. That bracelet is the reason your friend got shot. I need to know why you have it and when you'll give it back."

"I don't know what you're talking about. It was a gift." Are the walls moving closer? Walls don't move. Really. They don't. Maybe in an earthquake, but Dallas, Texas is not exactly earthquake prone.

No matter, I want out. Out of this room, away from the detective with his animalistic stare, the way he makes me feel as if I'm prey to his predator. All those hormones pinging around my system morph from lust to fear and catching the fast horse out of Dodge becomes imperative.

I stand, backing toward the door, willing my

shaking limbs to function, to make good my escape. Detective Smythe moves faster, one strong hand grabs my wrist, right above the silver links.

Flesh on flesh.

And nothing happens.

No flashes of insight, no reading his thoughts. Maybe he has no thoughts?

Oh, right. Everyone experiences thoughts.

Clearly, this man knows how to block his from people like me. Which is unheard of.

And damn fucking frightening.

I twist my wrist and yank it toward me, breaking his grasp. "Who the hell are you?" I take another step toward the door, but it seems far away. I take another step and he follows, once again trapping me into an unwanted dance complete with panicked breaths and racing heartbeats.

Blue eyes narrow. "You don't know what you're involved in. You need to return the bracelet to me."

"I don't think so." The door handle hits my butt and I reach back, step to the side and yank it open.

Noise slashes through the air, police talking to security, to staff, photographers snapping pictures of the pool of blood, patients milling around. I step into the cacophony, limbs shaking, adrenaline giving fuel to my motions. Not bothering with closing the door, I fast-step into the crowd.

I hope he doesn't see me, hope he doesn't follow me. *Don't follow me, don't follow me, don't follow me.* Loud cursing starts, the chocolate of Smythe's voice turning into bitter darkness. I turn to see him standing in the doorway, head pivoting as he looks up and down the hall. For me.

Darting around people, I yank open the first door I see and slip into the room.

"Who's there?"

"Mr. Talley, it's me, Nurse Crawford."

He screams, high-pitched and frantic, ending in a gasp. Shit, I just scared the bejeezus out of the poor old man. Forgetting about the gloves, I race to his side and pat his arm. Not long enough to get much of a reading, just a few flashes of sleepy thoughts.

"Shh, shh. It's all right."

One hand clutches the blanket to his chest. "I heard the door close, but didn't see anyone and then you spoke and there you were. Right there. Appeared out of nowhere. Liked to have scared me half to death."

Diagnosis: hallucinations as a result of fluid loss. I needed to find the attending and get another bag of saline into the old fella.

"It's all right. I'm sorry to have scared you."

"What's all the ruckus?"

"Someone shot a doctor." My voice hitches, forcing me to clear my throat. "It's a mess. How are you feeling?"

"You think they'll come shooting in here?"

"Of course not. No one is coming after you. I need to check on your orders. I'll be back."

Don't let the Detective see me, don't let him see me. I slip into the hall, inconspicuous in the crush of sound and color. The no-longer-sexy detective is standing with his back to me, hands on hips and I crouch down, weaving until I arrive at the nursing station, away from his line of sight.

"Are you okay?" Laura raises a brow at my crouched state.

I straighten. "Sure. No problem. Just stretching."

Her raised brow informs me she doesn't believe my words. "Really, Gin. I wouldn't be okay if I were you. Maybe you should've left with your brother."

"Yeah. Probably. But I needed to talk to the police, and that detective started asking weird questions so I ducked out of there."

"What detective?"

"Big, tall as the door, looked like a walking mountain. Kinda cute until he started popping questions."

She steps out of the station, into the hall crowded with the frantic voices of too many blue-suits and looks in the direction of Room 1. Her brows crease in puzzlement as she turns to me. "What detective? There's no one down the hall like that."

I step out beside her. She's right. No tall, mountain of a man anywhere in the hall.

"I think you need to go home, Gin."

"Maybe you're right. Where's Ruth?"

Ruth is my supervisor. Nickname, Nurse Hatchet. I go out of my way to avoid her. But Laura is right. Seeing Will shot and bleeding replays through my mind, each repeat bringing a shock of tremors to ice the lining of my stomach. An emotional imprint on my memory. Detective Smythe's questions add to the mix an unwanted wave of panic.

How did Detective Smythe know about my bracelet? Why did he think he should have the thing? It belongs to me now. It wants me. I want it. Enough said.

"Ruth is talking to one of the security guys." Laura points in the opposite direction of Room 2. Thank god. "Go ask her. Good luck."

Chapter 3

An hour later I sit on the couch in my living room, beer bottle in hand. At the other end, tangled up like a ball of Christmas lights, curls T and his girlfriend Jackie, the double-D wonder. I take a soothing sip of beer and let the liquid slip across my tongue and slide down my throat, while I watch Will's face splash across the evening news.

Not even beer cures the emotional chills shaking my core. Nothing in my training as a nurse prepared me to see my friend and coworker lying in a pool of his own blood, dying. And no class exists to train one on the aftereffects of looking too deep into another's mind. I still hear the ragged breathing of a young boy listening to his mother die, knowing he's the next victim of her killer.

Another swig of beer washes away the lingering taste of terror lodging in my throat. Not that the disappearing act will last. It takes a lot more beer than is in the fridge to get rid of terror's acrid taste.

At least that's my assumption, which is about to be put to the test.

One beer down another twelve or so to go.

I go to the fridge, get another cold one, pop the top, and return to my seat on the couch. A wet chill seeps into my hand from the brown bottle, and I shift the thing to my other palm. It's been years since drinking half the case in a night made for a viable escape option. I've been good. No hard booze. No hard drugs. No excessive beer. And yet as I stare at the brown bottle leaking condensation onto my palm, it becomes evident the good run is not going to last.

Unless I come up with a better option.

And what better option is there than a good romp between the sheets? One, it saves me from getting my drunk on, thereby ending my good run of responsible alcohol imbibing. Two, it makes me think of something besides Will's blood and memories. And three, it has the benefit of not frying the ole liver.

And on that thought, my mind returns to the detective, to my first impression of him, to how my body reacted. Damn shame he started popping questions that scared me. More like he scared the bracelet.

Okaaaay. I need my head examined. Bracelets don't think. They don't talk. They definitely don't possess feelings. I did not hit my head. I do not smoke pot or drink excessively when I have to be at work. That left shock. Why didn't I think of it before? I'm in shock.

Shock would explain thinking I know what the bracelet feels, thinking I know what it wants. Shock. Not a one way trip to Blue Shores. Thank goodness.

I take another swallow from my longneck. Good thing that's settled. The knowledge should make me feel better. So why doesn't it?

Maybe since shock failed to explain the bracelet's sudden appearance in my scrub pocket?

Whatever. Bracelets don't appear out of thin air either. Someone had to physically put it in my pocket.

But who? And how?

Will might have wished me to have it, but really, come on. I wish for a million bucks, and I don't see any cash stacks hiding out in my living room.

"We're hitting the bedroom. You gonna stay home tonight?" T's question snaps me out of my thoughts, returns me to the reality of life in the living room of Casa de Crawford. He's looking at me, for all appearances concerned I might leave the house drunk and streak nude down the street.

But I know the question beneath the concern, the question he refuses to voice aloud or in my thoughts, and shake my head. His eyes blink a slow open and close, his way of acknowledging my refusal. I take a swallow of the beer, keeping the end of the longneck in my mouth while I watch T stand, quite the feat seeing how Jackie hangs off him like a stripper on a pole.

She slaps his arm, a feeble whack from an inebriated woman. "Silly. Of course she's not leaving. Right?"

Pulling the bottle out of my mouth with a pop, I level a stare at the happy couple. "Right. I'll be in here. Watching TV. Keeping the beer company."

T winks at me. "Enjoy."

"Have fun." I wave them away and slouch back on the couch, drawing my legs up to my chest. His bedroom door clicks shut, muffling a feminine giggle, and my white-knuckle grip on the beer bottle eases.

For a moment.

Like a dam bursting, images of finding Will lying in a pool of blood replay on an endless loop. Red blood blossoming on a white labcoat. A shiny red puddle smothering the white linoleum.

The scent of copper rides a wave of suffocation, thick, like a smothering blanket. I gulp down the beer, tilting it back and swallowing it in a constant stream of fizz. So much for being good. The memories refuse to leave me alone, continuing to replay on a constant loop like a rolling video. They need to go away before they rouse deeper, scarier ones.

I shake my head. Inhale. Draw my thoughts back to the present, back to my current freak-out session.

The news continues to cover Will's shooting. Really? Didn't something else, anything else, happen today? Listening to the anchorwoman talk about how Will is currently still in surgery, struggling to survive, makes me want to drink.

Lucky me. Beers are in the fridge.

As I haul myself off the couch, I ignore the little voice inside my head howling not to get another beer. Until that little voice comes up with a way of obliterating my memories, beer it is.

But even beer won't stop the questions haunting me. Would Will live? How could he? Multiple gunshots to the torso and stomach tended to kill a person. What if I had gotten to him faster? Would he have a better chance of surviving?

Silver links on my wrist reflect the waning sunlight creeping through the kitchen window, sending bright lights to bounce against the wall, catching my eye. Questions about Will stop parading through my mind as other questions take their place. What was so special about this bracelet that everyone wanted it? How had it gotten into my pocket? Why, why, why?

Wasn't I the toddler tonight?

Setting the fresh beer on the cabinet, I bring the

bracelet closer to my eyes to check out the dark lines etched into the metal. What language is this? At least I'm assuming it's a language. For all I know, it's pretty designs etched into the silver, not a whole new writing system.

Ms. Indiana Jones I am not.

Discovery of new languages might befuddle me, but one thing I know: if I want a cold beer instead of a warm one, I need to pick that bottle up and start drinking instead of focusing on unsolvable thoughts.

What a shame all problems weren't as easy to solve.

Grabbing the beer with a shaky hand, I walk to the couch and park it, bringing my legs up to sit cross-legged. The pictures on either side of the TV start to rattle. *Thump, thump, thump.*

What in God's name was I thinking to invite T and Jackie back to the house? Oh, yeah. I wasn't.

Months ago this was a daily routine, back when T lived with me and brought over a string of sketchy girlfriends for the night. Then he met Jackie and moved in with her and rattling walls became a thing of the past.

Until today.

I take a sip of beer and crank up the volume on the TV in what proves to be a vain attempt to drown out the bedroom noises. A little hard to ignore the wall shaking, but I give it the good ole college try.

'Breaking News' flashes across the TV in orange and yellow and red, electric colors to catch my eye. The newscasters sit in front of their desk, wide-eyed and trembling with excitement.

"Earlier we brought you the story of Dr. Wunderliech's tragic shooting at Blue Forest Hospital.

We have just learned that his wife, Lara Wunderliech, has been attacked and killed in the house they shared in Highland Park. Our reporter is on the scene now."

From someplace far away comes the crash of a glass bottle against a wooden floor, the release of liquid lost in the rhythmic thumping of a bed against the wall. My eyes lock on the TV screen showing Will's house, on the flashing emergency lights reflected off the windows. Reflecting morbidity and horror. Lara was dead?

Sure, I never liked the greedy, blowjob-queen bitch, but to wish her a savage death?

I am not that cruel.

Not even if it meant for certain Will fell into my arms.

The news segment ends, and my gaze drops to the broken bottle, to beer splattered across the floor. Life is like that bottle. Fragile. Breaking into pieces by accident. And as I do with the broom and paper towels, someone needs to come along and clean up the mess. Although in real life, that someone is yourself.

Deep thoughts of a semi-buzzed nurse. I need to write that down and publish it. I'd make a million bucks.

Yeah, right.

After dumping the broken shards of glass in the trash, I return to the couch sans beer. Breaking one is a sign from above to keep to the straight and not quite so narrow. Finding another way of forgetting the day's work heads up the to-do list. But how?

Rhythmic thumps continue to shake the wall, sparking jealousy and desire, reminding me of a better option than a drunken stupor.

Getting laid.

Guess I need to call Blake again.

****

Blake is my friend with benefits. No commitment. No jealousy. He does his thing. I do mine. We see others. Well, okay, he sees others. Touching people presents somewhat of an issue with me. I've known Blake for years, since we met in college at a frat party, back when I did things I'm a bit ashamed of. He knows about my touch-and-see problem, but doesn't let it bother him.

The main reason he holds the top position on my extremely short friends with benefits list is he's learned how not to think about much of anything when we have sex. I would say this is quite the accomplishment on his part, but the reality is, during the act itself, most men don't think about much other than how being inside you feels.

With that being said, I could use almost any man for carnal purposes, but Blake fits me like a well loved sweater. And I don't have to worry about a guy who doesn't get lost in the sex and starts thinking on other topics. It can, and does, happen, and is downright unpleasant. Who wants to hear how you aren't pleasing your partner? Or worse, how he's some sort of sick bastard and dwells upon disgusting future plans for you. Talk about a mood killer. At least Blake tries to concentrate on the task at hand.

And it keeps me on the mostly straight and narrow road of being good.

Before Blake took the top position on my FWB list, experiencing carnal pleasures presented difficulties. The only way I can touch another without getting into their thoughts and feelings is to be falling down drunk or stoned out of my head. I'm sorry to say I used to do both quite a lot and not always for sex. Coping mechanism and all that.

Then I met Blake. I could fall for him—and sometimes I swear I have—but it's not worth it. He expects his girlfriends to behave a certain way, to look and act toward the expectations of his family.

Blonde, rich and hiding behind the door when the good Lord passed out brains.

Brunette, in debt and semi-intelligent don't qualify. And even if they did, his mother doesn't like me. Thinks I'm white trash. Thinks I'm not good enough for her highfalutin' lawyer son.

She's right.

But damn it, I can't stay away from him. Don't want to even try. And despite how his momma raised him, or maybe because of it, he prefers hanging out with me. A secret addiction is a dangerous thing to hide. Even more so for him. Rich lawyers steeped in family money fall further than in-debt nurses. Harder too.

But I need him to save me from this emotional free-fall, to kiss me and make it all go away, if only for a few minutes. Maybe that makes me a bad person, to only think of myself, to not think of the position I'm putting him in.

If he doesn't want to come over, he won't. In which case, I need a contingency plan.

Thump! Thump! Thump!

The wall shakes and my eyes squeeze shut.

Blake or beer are the only ways I'm getting through this evening.

I hit speed dial on my cell and wait as the call goes through.

"'Lo?"

Like a shot of valium, his voice relaxes me, tension bleeding from my shoulders as I drift in a sea of calm. I love Blake's voice. Smooth and rich, like chocolate cake with ganache icing. Which is probably why he makes such a good lawyer, people love hearing him talk.

"Hey. Whatcha doing?"

"Gin! I'm just sitting here watching your hospital on the news. Were you there?"

"Unfortunately." The calm sea turns choppy as memories start replaying. I close my eyes on a long blink. "You wanna come over?"

"You know I'm dating Jordan."

"Yeah. Sorry." I suck in a breath. I need him tonight. Not his voice on the phone. Him. "I'm just...just a bit strung out over today. You know?"

"Yeah." A pause. "Jordan's out with her friends. Dinner. Getting high at some club. And to think, Mom prefers her over you."

"Don't get me started. You coming over?" My breath hitches as I wait for his answer. Say yes, say yes, say yes.

A pause. An audible swallow. "Yeah." I hear the smile in his words. "Wait. Is T there?"

"Yeah. Why?" But I know why. It's a redundant question. Perhaps his answer is not what I'm thinking. It could happen.

"It's not going to be the same as last time, right?"

I close my eyes and grimace. He apparently remembers things better forgotten. "Nah. Jackie's over.

You remember her? Bleach-blonde hair—"

"Big tits?"

"Yep. That's her. He's in with her."

"Okay. I'll be over. Whatcha got to eat?"

"Pick up a pizza, why don't you?"

"See you in thirty."

Cha-ching.

Chapter 4

Twenty minutes later the doorbell rings. Blake's early. Odd that, but why complain? Pizza and sex coming up. I place my glass on the coffee table, straighten my tank top, and pull my short shorts and thong out of my crack. Who knew pulling my undies out of my crack in elementary school every day would prepare me for the adult version of pulling the thong out of hiding. Things women do to look sexy.

I check out my appearance in the mirror behind the door, smoothing down a fly-away strand. Good enough for a romp in the sheets. Swinging the door open is the work of a moment and it dawns on me I should've looked through the peephole first.

The evil man-thing stands on my porch, his lips turning in a menacing smile of death. I don't need to touch him to know he wants me dead. Muscles freeze, trapping my breath in my lungs. Like a rabbit in view of a wolf, I'm immobilized, waiting for death's blow. Time slows, his gaze locks on mine, trapping me in place.

Move, move, move! My mind screams as the man's fingers twitch.

But the spike of adrenaline explodes into my limbs too late to stop the backhand blow slamming across my jaw.

I superman it halfway across the living room. Land

on the hardwood floor in a thud of pain-ridden limbs. My jaw morphs into a screaming ball of nerves. My head no sooner hits the floor than I hear the bracelet scream, a high-pitched wail quivering through my skin like vibrations from a tuning fork. The bracelet tightens around my wrist, cutting off the circulation, and then it loosens with a pop at the same time I hear the door click closed.

Ohgodohgodohgod, I'm going to die. I don't want to die. No, no, no, no, no. Pain and terror hold me crumpled on the floor as my mind crawls backward in time.

But I'm no longer a child, fearful of fists and words, cowering on the ground.

I'm a fighter.

My head spins, but I refuse to lie on the floor waiting to be killed, so I attempt to stand. Evil Guy laughs as I ass-plant it. Laughs as a moan escapes my lips. He takes a step toward me, right arm drawn back for a hit. His fist hurls toward my face, but I manage to block it with my left arm. My right arm, the one with the bracelet, shoves forward, slamming into his chest.

His black eyes widen, mouth open in surprise, his hands fluttering to his chest before dropping. I stare at my hand, stare hard, for I'm as surprised as Evil Guy. The bracelet had become a sword, a long, thin spike of metal extending from the silver links, straight into Evil Guy's heart.

A sword?

Definitely a sword. The flat of the blade rests against the back of my hand, cool metal heating from the warmth of my skin. Small silver links circle around my palm, lending stability to the two-foot long sword.

I'm not sure which scares me more, Evil Guy paying me a visit or the fact the bracelet performed a morphing trick.

Life seeps out of Evil Guy's eyes as I watch, still seated on the floor, and he sags forward, held upright by the sword. A gray mist crawls out of the sword wound, sizzling when it touches the sword blade, the metal answering with a cry like a vengeful Valkryie. The mist coalescences into a ball, which hovers above the sword as if watching me, as if taking the measure of my soul. Shudders rack my body, but I hold the sword steady and snarl at the ball of mist. I get the impression the thing laughs before it flies toward the door.

What the holy fuck? Where's a priest when I need one?

Heavy footsteps pound on wood, vibrations echoing into my skin. I stare at Evil Guy, who is standing only because he remains impaled on the sword-formerly-known-as-my-bracelet.

"Get down, Gin!" T hollers and I move fast, rolling back onto the floor, the sword vanishing at the same time the shotgun roars.

Bang! My hearing disappears, lost in the blast of T's shotgun. Evil Guy flies backward, slamming into the door, the gunshot wound obliterating the stab mark left by the sword.

Well, that was one way to get rid of evidence.

"Take that, fucker!" T pumps his arm in the air, one knee rising in a celebratory semi-dance. He's dressed in a pair of red-striped boxers riding low on his hips and a shotgun slung over his shoulder. He takes one peek at my face and snarls. "Fucking bastard." Swinging the shotgun off his shoulder, he levels it at

Evil Guy. *Bang!*

I slam my hands over my ears, but it doesn't help, they continue to ring. The door now contains a hole, through which the gray mist escapes, and T is aiming at Evil Guy's face. "T he's dead!" I spit out a mouthful of blood and run my tongue over my teeth. All present and accounted for. Thank god.

"Bloody fucking bastard. He fucked up your face." He kneels beside me, hand hovering over the skin of my face, eyes wide with a frantic energy.

"T, call 911."

"You're hurt."

"Call the damn police."

"Going, going. Don't get your panties in a wad." He grabs the phone yelling over his shoulder as he punches in the numbers. "Jackie, it's all okay now! Um, yes, I'd like to report a shooting. Uh-huh. I shot the bastard that broke into our house and fucked up my sister's face. You need to send the paramedics over now. And the police. Don't forget about them."

I listen to him giving our address, but my gaze is on the bracelet. Which is once again a bracelet. Did I imagine the sword? Maybe I hallucinated the entire thing. Bracelets did not shapeshift into swords. No way.

And yet, I know what I saw.

Welcome to the Twilight Zone, Gin.

T returns to the living room, ice pack in hand, and places it against my jaw. I wince and bite back a whimper. "Want me to shoot him again?"

"Once did the job. How am I supposed to clean up the mess?"

He looks at the body, meets my gaze and shrugs. "Don't they have people who clean messes?"

"Probably. Thank you." I take over holding the ice pack, blinking back tears.

"Nobody messes with my sister."

"Oh my god!" Jackie screeches as she walks into the living room. "Are you okay? What the hell happened?"

It looks pretty obvious to me, but I guess when you're as intelligence challenged as the double D wonder, it might be hard to understand.

"The bad guy—" I gesture to the body "—is now dead."

"Well, duh. What do you think I am? Stupid?"

I refuse to answer her question. She doesn't really want to know my opinion on the matter. Instead I focus on T's sudden white-knuckled grasp on my forearm. Beads of sweat ring his forehead, run down his cheeks, drip onto my skin.

What? I ask.

Ghost. Bad one.

I look around the room, breath hitching as my aching head turns, trying to find the ghost as sirens sound in the distance. After seeing shadow figures at the hospital, I wonder if wearing the bracelet gives me T's gift of seeing the spirit world.

Apparently, the vision at the hospital was a fluke. The only thing out of place in the living room is the dead evil guy.

I don't see it.

By the door. He jerks his head in that direction.

The thought of Evil Guy haunting my house transforms my spinal fluid into a staff of ice.

Emergency responder sirens wail as vehicles screech to a halt outside the house. Reflections of whirling blue lights chase around the walls of the room. T's hand shakes, his grip threatening to cut off the circulation in my lower arm.

"Baby, what's wrong?" Jackie sashays over, placing a hand on T's shoulder, her gaze turned away from Dead Guy to focus on the kitchen.

Car doors slam shut and T's grip loosens.

It's gone.

Thank god. Evil Dead Guy wrecked enough havoc when alive. Being haunted by his ghost is not my idea of a fun time.

Bam, bam, bam! The pounding on the door grows stronger with each strike. "Police!"

"In here! Come in!" T yells.

"We're coming in!" Police shove open the door, and Evil Guy flops to the side from the force. A gun comes through first, followed by a navy-blue clad officer, who takes one look at the body and gestures to others behind him. Two cops search the house, securing the premises, before hollering to the crew milling around outside. Within seconds my living room resembles an episode of Law and Order minus the TV cameras.

Paramedics and firefighters follow the cops and since my blood is escaping the confines of my skin and trickling out onto my lip, they snap on gloves to avoid infections. Lucky me. No extra thoughts or emotions. Good thing too, as enough thoughts run through my mind to fill a library.

Ouch! Their gloves might prevent unwanted thoughts from intruding, but they do nothing to make the exam less painful. I clutch T's hand and squeeze for all I'm worth, splitting my attention between the paramedics' exam and T telling a detective his side of the events.

The paramedics shine a light in my eyes, state they don't think I have a concussion, but should get checked out at a hospital to verify. I decline. You don't spend as many years as I have in the ER without learning a thing or two about injuries.

My jaw aches, but my teeth remain in place. Nothing feels broken, no concussion, only what would eventually become a huge nasty bruise crossing my jaw. Not pretty, but not life-threatening either.

Convincing the paramedics of that takes some doing, but I manage, once a release form is signed.

Besides, I know enough to realize they sit outside for a while in case the idiot patient is rendered unconscious due to their injuries. Where upon they rush in and take said idiot to the hospital. A safety net of sorts, in case I guess wrong about my injuries.

But I'm never wrong. Hardy-har-har.

"Ma'am." The next thing I know, a stout man in a faded brown sports jacket, no tie, stands beside me, his hard brown eyes a contradiction to his soft voice. "I'm Detective Williams, and I need to ask you some questions." The detective pulls out a notebook and waits, his eyes focusing on me like I'm the candy prize and he's the winner.

I sit up. Not smart. The room spins, and I stick my head between my legs, sucking down deep breaths like I've told countless patients to do. Note to self, be more sympathetic next time a patient threatens a fainting episode.

T rubs my back in little circular motions, and the spinning sensation disappears, replaced by a lot of oh-my-god-the-pain. I want to whimper, to crawl into my bed and hibernate, to forget about walking evil and bracelets that turn into swords. Instead, I have to tell the good detective about what happened without mentioning such obvious things like the sword coming out of the bracelet and how said sword stabbed Evil Dead Guy thereby releasing floating gray mist.

Geesh, I'm not going crazy, I've already arrived.

Might as well get the interview over with so I can get on with the whimpering, moaning, and pain-pill popping part of my evening. Taking a breath, I blow it out slowly through my nose and raise my head. My jaw throbs, but at least the detective remains motionless.

"Yes, sir."

"Tell me in detail what happened."

I start with the doorbell ringing, end with T's shooting spree and leave out the reason for my skimpy clothing choice.

"Why did you open the door to this fellow?"

"I thought he was my friend. I mean, my friend is supposed to come over so I didn't bother to look when the bell rang."

"Have you ever seen him before?"

"Yes, sir. I ran into him today at the hospital. He's the one that shot Will, I mean Dr. Wunderliech."

The detective's eyes pop wide. "Really? The same doctor whose shooting is all over the news?"

"Yes, sir."

"And you're saying this is the man who shot the doctor?"

"Yes, sir. I ran into him at the hospital as he left Will's room. Guess he decided to kill me since I'm the witness. Good thing my brother was home or else I'd be dead now." Chills dash across my limbs and I wrap my arms around my legs, putting my head on top of my knees, trying to get them to stop. Almost dead. The realization sends a shock of adrenaline through my veins, starting a trembling deep within, as if my innards shake with a cold fear.

"Would you hold on a minute?"

"Sure." What else am I going to do? Run a marathon?

He grabs his cell, walks into the kitchen, and starts talking. Only bits and pieces of his conversation drift to me, and I don't pay much attention, focusing instead on the pain in my jaw.

It's been a long time since I've been hit this hard, and it's difficult to process. My whole body feels like one aching lump of throbbing pain. And I've only been hit in the jaw.

Although I suppose landing on hardwood floors after attempting a flight might tend to make a body ache.

"Ma'am." The detective has returned and squats beside me. "I had my sergeant call the Dallas PD about this guy. The detective on the Wunderliech case wanted to speak with you before you left the hospital, so he's coming over now."

"Huh?" I stare at the man, convinced my aching jaw makes me deaf. "What do you mean talk to the detective? I talked to Detective Smythe at the hospital before I left."

"I don't know a Detective Smythe. Maybe he's new. Peterstown and Dallas departments talk, but I don't know everyone there."

"Even if he were new, wouldn't he have mentioned

to someone that he interviewed me?" If you could call it an interview. More like a questioning about my bracelet instead of asking what I knew about Will's shooting.

"Hmm. Hold on." With a grunt, he stands up straight, presses a button on his phone, and sticks it next to his ear. "Yeah, George. The nurse here says she spoke to a Detective Smythe at the hospital. Would you call Dallas PD again and tell them that...Yeah, I'll wait." His fingers drum a tune against his slacks as he stares at the photos hanging on my wall. After a long pause he snaps to attention and presses the phone closer to his ear. "Uh-huh. Really? You sure? Okay, then. We'll wait here." He presses a button and slips the phone back into his pocket. Grabbing hold of the pants material above his knees, he lets out a grunt and squats by my side.

"Ms. Crawford, there's not a Detective Smythe with the Dallas PD. I just checked."

My head pops up and it takes effort to close my mouth. "Then who did I," lust after, "talk to?"

"I don't know, but we'll figure it out."

"Why would someone interrogate me if he wasn't from the police department?" But even as I ask the question, the answer comes to me. Smythe, if that was really his name, didn't want answers to Will's shooting, he wanted answers about the bracelet appearing on my wrist.

I glance at the thing. It seems...pleased. Happy. As if it just found its true calling. I should want to take it off. Want to find Smythe and give the thing to him.

But the weird thing is, the bracelet makes me as happy as I make it. Even if it has a propensity for turning into a sword and stabbing evil intruders through the heart.

I must be going insane.

Blake shows up in the middle of the crime scene photos, raising a ruckus until the cops let him in. Seconds later he kneels on the floor beside me, arms wrapping me in an embrace, his thoughts frantic, laced with fear. It's one of the few glimpses into his inner being he's allowed in years and makes me realize how frightening my appearance must seem.

The thought barely forms before the door on his emotions slams closed, replaced by the generic mountain scene he usually remembers when touching me.

"Sorry about tonight."

He pulls away and cocks a brow, staring at me as if I've grown another head. "All that matters is you're okay."

Thank god he's not disappointed tonight turned into friends with no benefits. Despite my earlier need of good escapism sex, all I want now is to lie in the comfort of his arms. To feel cared for and dare I say, loved.

What better way to end this emotional rollercoaster of a day than in the embrace of a friend?

Chapter 5

I can't sleep. The air conditioning cranks away, whining a protest at the Texas heat, the sound a dull rhythm in the darkness. Each heartbeat brings a throb of pain to my jaw and the weight of Blake's arm across my stomach traps warmth like a smothering blanket. His breath falls in moist puffs of air against my shoulder and neck, the even rhythm more of an annoyance than a comfort.

Part of his arm rests against my skin, but the only reading I get from him comes in scattered flashes of dreams. When his arm first touched me, before he fell into the deep sleep of exhaustion, I felt his comfort in lying beside me, how it differed from his boredom with Jordan. Then the scene switched to a beach, complete with the roar of waves crashing over the sand. Good way to avoid the issue of me reading his mind.

Which is unnecessary considering how well I read his body language. His romance with Jordan is nearing its end.

Nothing new there. And nothing to concern myself with either. Unlike the rest of my day.

Questions run through my mind in a continuous stream of babble, but the answers remain elusive. I want answers. I want to know why that evil man attacked Will, his wife, and me. I want to know why the bracelet turned into a sword. I want to know why

Smythe lied about being on the Dallas PD, which led to the real Dallas PD detective driving out to my house for an interview. I want to know if I am going crazy, if my mind splintered into the wild and unbelievable when I saw Will lying in a pool of his blood.

I want an ibuprofen.

That one I can do something about.

Slipping free from Blake's arm, I ease out of bed and pad down the hall, my feet cool from walking on the wood floors. The only light in the kitchen comes from the streetlamp three doors down. Enough light to tell where the cabinets are, but not enough to pick out the ibuprofen bottle. I pat around on the wall until my fingers find the light switch. One flick and the room explodes into a dull glow as the fluorescent bulbs spring to life.

I take a step into the room and freeze, unable to draw in a breath. Oh shit. Not again.

My heart pounds, a staccato drumbeat locked in the confines of my chest. He's in my house. Smythe is in my house. Suddenly the ibuprofen no longer seems important.

I turn, and he's on me before my feet take a step. A strong arm cinches my waist. A broad hand covers my mouth. Pain shoots from my jaw and I wince and let loose a whimper. Breath fans my ear.

"Shh. I don't want to hurt you. I need to talk to you. If I let you go, will you promise not to scream?"

And just like at the hospital, my blood boils. Electric zingers bounce through my veins, sexing me up, readying me for this man.

What the hell? At a time like this, all I can think of is sex? What kind of sick freak am I?

Yet another question I don't know the answer to. Right up there with why he can touch me and not elicit a trip into his emotions. I nod in response to Smythe's question, and he releases me slowly, as if I'm a frightened mare and he's the horse whisperer.

The heat from his body disappears as he retreats to the kitchen table. I turn, still locked in place, willing my pesky hormones back to wherever they came from. I stare at him, running my gaze from the top of his short black hair, down his muscular body, over his relaxed fit jeans, ending at his black shitkickers. He's dressed like he's auditioning for the role of how to look sexy and still be lethal. I stop staring and meet his blue gaze, amazed at how fast he moves, wondering how he got into the house.

As if he read my mind, he gestures toward the living room. "Door was open."

I take a few steps into the living room, look at the closed door, and walk back to the kitchen. "It has a hole in it. That doesn't mean it's open."

He shrugs. "We need to talk."

"So you said."

"It would help if you'd come have a seat with me."

Yeah, right. As if we're on a date, carrying on a get to know you conversation. As if he hasn't broken into my house and scared the bejeezus out of me.

Men.

As soon as he realizes I'm going nowhere fast, he clears his throat, patting the chair next to him, his black T-shirt pulling tight against what has to be steroidal-induced muscles. "I need to talk to you about the bracelet. I don't think I can take it back now."

A leap of joy emanates from the silver links, jolting

up my arm into my brain, filling me with happiness. The bracelet's happiness. I get the impression if the thing had a body it would place its fingers in its ears, stick out its tongue, waggle the whole lot and say, 'niener-niener.'

I stop my hands halfway to my ears. Not going there.

Taking a breath, I walk to the counter and grab the ibuprofen bottle out of the cabinet. A big glass of water followed by a swallow and the pills slide down my throat, smooth as honey. It gives me time to think. Despite my guest's uninvited entrance into my home, he doesn't seem bent on harm.

Giving him a sideways glance, I notice his gaze locked on the colorful bruise covering my jaw. His lip turns into a snarl and something shifts in his eyes, as if he fights a battle against righteous rage and loses.

Okay, small modification there. He's not bent on *my* harm. His eyes state he'd like to grab Evil Guy and kill him again—inch by torturous inch.

It makes me feel...safe.

Where's a mind-altering pharmaceutical product when I need one?

Should I trust Smythe? The bracelet isn't reacting to him. Well, okay, the bracelet isn't turning into a sword and trying to kill him. Which I interpret as a good thing.

What's the harm in hearing him out? Maybe he can explain why I have some new wrist jewelry. And if it really turned into a sword. I doubt he knows whether or not I'm on the express train to Blue Shores.

I walk to the table and sit beside Smythe. One corner of his lip turns upward, the expression erasing the glint of murder in his eyes. Good thing he doesn't smile more often. I might melt into a state of obsequiousness.

"Talk."

One black eyebrow skims upward. "We can't figure out why the *justitia* has attached itself to you."

"The what?"

"*Justitia.* The sword of justice. That bracelet you're wearing."

"It has a name?" I drop my gaze to my wrist, the glow of the kitchen light absorbing into the silver. Of course it has a name. It wants me to learn it. Wants me to learn about it. Wants me to use it the way it was made to be used.

I'm not going insane. The thing really has invaded my thoughts.

"It has more than a name. It has a history. We don't understand why it wants you."

"Who's 'we'?"

His fingers drum a rhythm on the table. "We're the good guys. Protectors from evil."

"Really? Did you know the guy who came here tonight?" I touch the bruise, formerly known as my jaw. "Because I think he fell under the evil category, and that was before the gray mist came out of him."

Was that a hint of a blush on his cheeks? Must be a trick of the light. "We didn't realize he'd come here. At least not as soon as he did."

"Oh? So you knew he'd come and left me unprotected?"

His brow does another meet-the-hairline as his gaze glances off my bracelet, oops *justitia*. "You are far from unprotected."

"You are far from having answers. What is this? A lesson in how to be cryptic? Because I hate to tell you, but I excel at hiding things."

That half-turned lip appears, but instead of looking attractive, it makes him seem condescending. "So you do. Does anyone at the hospital know about your trip to the psychiatric ward as a teenager? No? What about the, shall we say, extra-curricular activities you partook in? It's a wonder you didn't get arrested."

"Lots of college kids do things they regret." I shrug, hoping to pull off nonchalant. Where did he get my, what I thought was hidden, information?

"True. But most of them aren't empaths. They don't touch another and know that person's immediate thoughts and emotions, do they?"

Heat flushes through my system, slaps into my cheeks, slams a ball of writhing snakes into my stomach. I try to swallow and come up short. How does he know? "What do you want?"

"When the *justitia* turns into a sword and kills a minion, then it cannot be removed from the wearer, barring death. That means no matter what you want, you are one of us now. You must learn how to fight the minions."

"Whoa, fella. I'm a nurse, not a fighter. Go find someone else."

"You have no choice. Once the *justitia* bonds with the wearer, your die is cast."

And I thought insanity knocked at my door? I have nothing on this guy. Chances are good he won't want to convince me I'm not crazy, seeing how his plans include me joining him in insanity-ville.

"Well. This was a nice conversation." I stand and

gesture toward the front door. "You can go out the same way you came in. I'm going back to bed."

"Wait. You can't ignore us."

"Watch me." I push in the chair, waggle my fingers at him, and head for the light switch. "Consider yourself ignored."

What a waste of—

I hear the chair hit the floor at the same time a muscular arm bands about my waist, trapping my arms to my side. One hand locks around my wrist, covering the bracelet, and his breath rustles hot against my neck.

"I am your guardian. I watch you. I protect you while you protect the innocent. For millennia it has been so and for millennia it will be thus, until the darkness falls from the land. Heed my words. Join your lifeforce with this vessel and together you shall conquer the forces of evil."

Can we say flair for the dramatic? What did he expect me to do? Get all patriotic and sing the Good Guys anthem?

Before I could show this fool my idea of the two-step—stomp on instep, kick out knee—the bracelet begins vibrating, an excited hum that reverberates through my skin. The damn thing is ecstatic over Smythe's words. *Ecstatic.*

I fail to share its joy.

Heat follows the vibrations, pulses of energy igniting every pleasure receptor in my brain. Ohgodohgodohgod, it's like the biggest orgasm of my life, coupled by the high rush of illegal substances, a lethal combination. My heart races a marathon, my skin tingles, my body hums with an unholy fire. I feel on fire. I am the fire. Burning. Alive. More alive than I ever experienced.

Whatever his words did, I want more. I need more. I will do anything for more.

The pleasure expands, filling me, invigorating me, pulling me into a vortex of desire. A desire whispering freedom from self, escape from reality. And then as sudden as it came, it shrinks, dissipating, leaving me alone in my body, alone with only myself for company.

Trembling sets in, rattling my joints, my limbs, a physical response to the loss of desire's demand raging inside.

"Please." I beg. I want to be lost in the pleasure, consumed by the fire.

"Please?" Smythe sounds confused. "Please what?"

"I want it back. The feeling. Please."

His curse sears. Hurts. I don't care. I want to lose myself in an ocean of pleasure, to drown in a current of desire. I need the escape.

"I hate working with goddamn addicts." He mumbles something, his thumb stroking the links of the bracelet and my cravings vanish, leaving me relieved.

And yet, disappointed.

I sag against him, trying to catch my breath. It's been years since I've craved pleasure above all else. Years. I've done well since I realized fleeing from myself is an exercise in futility. No matter where I go, there I am. The temporary escape of a high is a false illusion, one I craved for many years before pulling my act together.

Looking death in the face made me realize little things, like empathic abilities, aren't so bad after all. Once I came to that realization, I've been fine. More or less.

I don't appreciate him reminding me of my failings.

"Don't ever do that again." My voice comes out as a hiss, my throat ragged.

"Do you always react that way?"

I ignore him. "What was that? That feeling?"

"The bonding." Warm air brushes my neck on a sigh. "It wanted you, for whatever reason, so I told it to join its force to yours. You two are mated. You are part of the Agency now."

Agency my left ass cheek. I belong to no one, least of all some mysterious agency who sends a hotter than hell man to do its bidding. Although that's not such a bad thing, is it, a little voice inside my head asks.

I squash the errant thought.

"Gin?" T's voice sounds a second before his body comes into view. "Are you—"

His voice trails into nothing as he stares at Smythe, who still has an arm around my waist and a palm on my wrist. T goes from sleepy and concerned to pumped and ready for a kill in a nanosecond, the air around him sizzling with anger.

"Gin?" His eyes narrow, as he tries to judge whether or not Smythe has a weapon, if he can take him down.

"I needed an ibuprofen."

"That is not an ibuprofen."

"Meet Smythe. Smythe, my brother, T."

Smythe moves, dropping his arm, his palm, as he steps to my side. Air hits my back, brushing against the beads of sweat running down my spine. I shiver.

Are you okay?

Mostly.

Do I need to kill this guy?

I wouldn't advise it.

"Aren't you the detective that's not really a detective?" T crosses his arms, biceps bunching, his expression a palette of barely contained anger.

"Who says I'm not a detective?" Smythe shifts his stance as if he expects to go a round with T.

Smart man.

"The police force. So if you aren't a detective, then who are you? And what are you doing in my house?"

It's no longer his house, but I let the comment slide. Aggression saturates the room like the stench of spilled gasoline, two testosterone filled males primed and ready to punch. I try to take a step to the side, but Smythe grabs my wrist, his large palm encircling the thing as if I'm some sort of anorexic model. Unlike at the hospital, I'm unable to get out of his grip.

"Let go of my sister!" T takes a step forward and his body seems to grow, expand. Air crackles, little pops pinging around his head.

"My apologies, but I need to borrow your sister for the evening, perhaps longer." Smythe starts speaking, his words a roll of unintelligible mutterings sounding suspiciously like Latin and dripping with age.

To his right, a slash of light forms in the air as if cut by an invisible sword, widening into the shape of a door. In the glare of the light, I see T's eyes pop wide, his lip lift into a snarl.

"Like hell you are!" He leaps, but Smythe is faster, stronger, more determined.

Smythe jumps through the slash of light before I can resist, my arm, and consequently my body, yanked into the opening against my will. I reach a hand toward

T, the skin of my palm sizzling as the supercharged air surrounding him hits my flesh. His fingertips brush mine, reaching, missing.

"Gi—" His panicked cry cuts off as the slash of light seals shut.

Terror ricochets through my veins, my breath a frozen ball of ice in my chest. I attempt to read T's thoughts, attempt to use our telepathic language to tell him I'm alive, but fail. For the first time in my life, I cannot hear my twin.

Chapter 6

I'm lost in a sea of colors, of panic-filled swirls dancing in erratic lines. No air exists here, wherever here is. Or maybe I'm too scared to breath. Right when I'm about to pass out from lack of oxygen, the colors stop flashing, settling into forms, into shapes, into non-moving objects.

A room. People. I sway. Smythe yanks me against his body, supporting my sagging frame.

Giiiiin!! T's voice slams into my head, the scream a welcome relief from the silence.

T! I don't know where I am, but I'm okay. I think.

He curses an unrepeatable string of words. *Let me see.*

No. Another oddity of being twins, we can hop into the other's mind, see out of each other's eyes. Other twins might be able to telepathically communicate with each other, but I'm pretty certain we're the only set with this ability.

I'm so engrossed in dissuading T's incursion I don't realize someone is speaking to me until Smythe shakes my arm.

"Gin!"

With a mental thrust, I manage to block T from gaining my sight. The effort exerted coupled with however I arrived wherever I am, leaves my legs wobbly, my stomach woozy.

Nausea and unsteadiness fail to stop a good dose of what-the-hell-just-happened and its twin you-did-not-just-take-me-here.

I twist my arm from Smythe's grip and slam both hands against his chest. "Where the hell am I, Mister Kidnapper?"

His lids pop wide, brows touching his hairline. "Mr. Kidnapper?"

I slam my hands against his chest again in hopes the pain made a point. "Where," slap, "am," slap, "I?" His hands encircle my wrists before I get in the last slap, his gaze delves into mine as if he sees inside my thoughts.

Small tremors shake my muscles, and I try to yank my hands free, to no avail. It's sobering to realize he let me go a minute ago. So much for thinking I know some self-defense. Or possess my own thoughts.

The black of his eye seems to expand, grow, swallow me whole. Little yellow specks in the blue of his irises catch my gaze, and I stand transfixed, anger and fear forgotten.

Someone clears their throat, causing Smythe to blink and the spell he wrapped around me vanishes, leaving behind a sense of calm, a feeling of purpose.

The knowledge we aren't the only ones here. This time when I pull against his grip, he releases my wrists, allowing me to turn. I notice several things all at once. White light shines from overhead recessed lighting, bathing the room in a brightness never before seen this side of the sun. Or maybe it's so bright because the white paint on the walls reflects the overhead lighting. We stand next to a white marble fireplace, another glowing object in the over-lit room. The door, aka the avenue of escape, stands on the other side of the room. And, last, but not least, every person in the room stares at me.

Smythe's induced calm gives way to panic. How bad do I appear? I pat my bed-head look and pull down my shorts. Or try to. Rather hard to do with shorts meant to be worn for foreplay and then removed. They did not make for good first impressions.

Unless auditioning for a hooker.

The only sound in the room comes in the whisper of a dozen computers humming a merry tune. A long desk sits to my left, filled with computers, each manned by a hue of different colored faces, all of whom stare at me as if they've never seen a woman in short shorts. Which judging by their age, might not be too far off the mark.

Heard of child labor laws, anyone? Last time I checked, employing high school students after midnight was frowned upon.

A rule clearly ignored here. Wherever here was.

"Ahem."

My gaze snaps to a man and woman standing several feet in front of us. The man is older, late fifties, early sixties, tall and straight like former military with short steel gray hair and piercing blue eyes. Rather like Smythe's, come to think of it. He wears black trousers and a white long-sleeved shirt with the top button undone and the sleeves rolled halfway up his tanned forearms.

The woman next to him sports sun-bleached—or was that bottle-bleached—blonde hair, which hangs straight around a bronzed face sporting evidence of one too many sun exposures. Clearly she missed the sun tanning is bad for you lecture, replacing it by doubling up on the gym workouts. Not an ounce of fat on her, damn her to hell. Her black pants and white tank mold to her body like spray-paint on a fence, leaving little to the imagination. I'm willing to bet her ass looks better on display than mine. Probably warmer too. All those computers must require enough cold air to make Antarctica seem hot. I shiver, cross my arms over my chest and attempt to rub the goosebumps away.

The woman's eyes narrow, obliterating their color. Glaring doesn't help the fine lines creeping through the skin around her eyes. Someone needs to tell her that little tidbit of info, but it's not my lucky day. Even the bracelet grows quiet in her presence. Watching? Waiting? Her fingers flex, a distracting curl and uncurl. I drop my hands to my sides, fingers tightening and releasing, mimicking her movements. The air surrounding her snaps with energy.

Correction, make that anger.

"Why is she here?"

"If she is to believe, she needs to be shown." Smythe takes a step forward, the air around him pulsing in rhythm to the woman's, a volatile mix of testosterone and righteous anger.

"So you pulled her out of bed and brought her here? What were you thinking, Aidan?"

Aidan? Aidan? What did I know about this man? Not his name, for starters. A cold frost steals through me that has nothing to do with the room's temperature. What else has he hidden from me?

"He was following my directions, Samantha. Something you should try to do on occasion."

At Military Man's words, red suffuses the

woman's face. Her fingers crank into fists as she sucks a breath in through her nose. The pulsing energy surrounding her ceases its sizzle as she releases her held breath with an audible whoosh.

"A *justitian* should not look like a washed up prostitute. Unless she isn't a *justitian*?" Hope shines in her eyes until Smythe—or should I say Aidan—shakes his head.

"They've bonded."

"You've got to be kidding me. How can that be, David? Why is she here?" Her glare turns to Military Man.

Note to self. Next time Smythe tries to convince me of something, believe him. Not believing him leads to my sudden appearance as the focus of a disagreement.

"She knows nothing of us. She needs to learn."

"How can the *justitia* bond with her? She's not from a gifted lineage."

The insult grates against my psyche like a whip on flesh, a reminder of things better left forgotten. Allowing her words to bother me borders on the ridiculous. Obviously my lineage is not what they look for when trying to find someone for their precious bracelet. But then two falling-down-drunk abusive alcoholics rarely make anyone's hottest lineage list. Nothing new there.

Logic and reason cease to stop my proverbial hackles from bristling.

"Excuse me? Are you dissing on my momma?" I've always stood up for Mom, a defense started in elementary school when she'd pick us up wobbling from one too many afternoon gin and tonics. Mom's form of alcoholism never bothered me the way Dad's did.

Which isn't to say I condoned her behavior.

Samantha raises a brow. "Truth is not dissing. Your name does not show up on our bloodline chart."

I wave a hand. "Well, la-di-da." So she didn't know about my family. Whatever Smythe discovered about me, he seems to have kept to himself. Whew. The less they know the better. Especially about my lovely little emotion-reading talent.

Speaking of. Wonder what said talent would turn up if I touched Little Miss Appalled? I've never used my gift this way before, never purposefully touched someone, but the urge to slap my hands against her muscular flesh is overwhelming. For whatever reason, I want to see inside her snotty little mind.

I stride over to Samantha, whose eyes widen as if I carry a weapon of mass destruction aimed right at her. My hands slam against the firm flesh of her upper arms and unlike Smythe, her thoughts and emotions flow like a waterfall, rushing into my mind, filling me with visions of her essence.

Rainbows and roses she is not.

Her dislike of me bursts through first, my touch on her arms repellant. Red tinges the emotion, anger I wear the bracelet, anger I threaten her, anger at my lack of awe over being gifted a *justitia*. That last one I file for later review and continue rummaging through her thoughts.

I don't get far. One, I'm so used to avoiding meddling in others' minds I'm not sure what to do; and two, a strong arm bands around my waist, lifting me off the ground and breaking my contact with her skin.

It's unnecessary to look over my shoulder to know Smythe's arm encircles my waist. My body reacts as usual to his touch, the unwanted hum of attraction sings through my veins. Traitorous hormones. Despite them telling me to throw him down and sex him up, I slam my airborne feet into his shins. Or try to.

Right when I gain some momentum, he pitches me to the side, toward David, who lets me stumble into the white marble fireplace as opposed to catching me. Jerk. My hands sting from slapping against the stone, but at least I stopped myself from hitting my bruised face.

"What the hell were you thinking? She's a fucking empath! She gets readings by touching you!" Smythe's hands ball into fists, and once again the air crackles around him like an ominous thunderhead.

Instead of emulating him, Samantha pales, turning her popped-wide gaze to me, fear written in the lines surrounding her eyes. "Impossible." Her whisper blends with the background hum of computers as I straighten, pressing the cool marble against my now-warm back.

"Are you sure, son?" David keeps his gaze on Smythe. Son? Smythe has a father?

Well, duh. Everyone has a father. Even those of us who refuse to admit to one. It surprises me to realize his is standing in the room. Could his father jump through doorways of light, too?

Did that doorway even exist or am I still lying in bed next to Blake having a crazy dream?

I pinch my arm.

Nothing happens.

It's unnecessary to continue to pinch the hell out of my arm on the off chance I'd wake. I'm not going to wake. This room, these people, are real. My life went from a bit off-key to totally insane in a matter of hours.

At least I have company in the land of insanity. Not sure if I like the company, but it's better than sitting alone.

Things. Have. Changed.

My heart pounds an erratic beat as the realization settles in. Things I never knew existed, exist. My brain runs in circles, believing, denying, believing, denying.

Is this the definition of crazy?

Maybe.

Am I going to have a nervous breakdown in a strange white room with people who think worth is based on bloodlines?

Hell no. I'll fall to pieces later, in the comfort of my own home.

A sense of wrongness scuttles across my flesh. About time my mind got in touch with my current situation. As Smythe continues his impression of a pitbull defending its territory, I realize it's not my mind issuing the Danger-Will-Robinson command.

It's the bracelet's.

The silver links fear something or someone in the room. As the fear turns to puzzlement, I take a look around. Nothing seems out of place, no Evil Guy look-alikes, but how would I know if the room was normal? It's not like I have experience with this level of oddness. All the computer operators gawk at the trio, namely Smythe who appears as if he's going to explode.

Part of me wants to run out of the room, but I don't know where I am. Nix that idea. And I hope someone here will tell me what the hell is going on. Just when I think my life is under control, when I've conquered the demons inside, I realize I'm really living in a snafu situation.

Situation normal this ain't.

And why am I paying my newest jewelry addition any attention? Well, that question is easy to answer. It's the only thing in this room I trust.

"Sir!" One of the computer operators, who looks barely old enough to shave, let alone man a computer, jumps up, vibrating with energy. Nice to see certain energy drinks really do give one wings.

As if on cue, the room goes silent, all eyes on the operator as he points to the computer screen. "Demon outbreak! It appeared in Austin, Texas just now."

Aha! Guess that meant our governor really was a spawn of Satan.

"Where exactly?" David snaps.

"I'll send it to your phone."

"What the hell would I do with it? Send it to Samantha's. Her ward is closest."

Samantha's eyes widen, and then she shuts them for a long blink. She sucks in a deep breath, follows it with a nod. One hand whips a phone from a hiding place. How she hid a smartphone in the rear pocket of skin-tight pants remains a mystery.

Her fingers flash across the screen, her eyes narrow as she reads the directions. "As you wish," she speaks to the screen before focusing her gaze on Smythe. "But this conversation is in no way finished." One hand gestures to encompass my body. "Cheap looking tramps should not be brought here."

Her words flay across my skin like a whip. Fighting words. And yet, I give her nothing but a glare. Fact of the matter is, I do look cheap. But what do they expect when a certain detective impersonator grabs me out of my house without letting me change out of my do-me-now shorts?

Bottom line: Samantha will get her due. In time.

"Don't call my ward a tramp."

Samantha throws out her hand, four fingers pointing to the same corner Smythe and I arrived in. "You left out cheap looking."

A growl erupts from Smythe, and I fully expect him to attack the sun-worshiping blonde bitch. He moves forward, hands cranked into tight fists, but David steps between the two.

"We fight demons. Not each other. Cool down." His blue eyes focus on Smythe, who sucks in a deep breath and shakes like he's a wet dog trying to dry. David turns to Samantha. "Do you think holding your hand out makes you look pretty? Open the damn portal already."

Aaannnd the temperature drops another couple of degrees from the glare Samantha throws David's way. He holds her gaze as if drinking in her anger, draining her to fuel him, but that's a ridiculous thought. He's doing what I call the dominant dog act, letting her know who's boss, informing her she's not it. Her lids shutter, snap open, and focus on the wall where Smythe and I arrived.

Like earlier in my living room, a slash of light appears mid-air, growing into the size of a door.

Marching past us, she hisses at Smythe, "Try not to let this one die." Smythe stiffens, but instead of a retort, he pales the color of the marble pressed against my back. Was she referring to me?

With a final glare my way, she steps into the

swirling colors of light, disappearing as the "door" shrinks into nothing, the white wall returning into view.

Who laced my ibuprofen with acid?

"What—" I point to where the slash of light appeared, words evaporating off my tongue. Just because I arrived here through one of those light slashes, doesn't mean I understand what happened. Or am able to get a sentence out to ask.

"Wormhole." David mimics my gesture, waving at the wall.

"We use portals to travel from place to place. It's quicker and cuts down on airfare." The corner of Smythe's mouth quivers as he turns toward me, the attempt at a smile overshadowed by the angry glint in his gaze. At least he's no longer the color of snow.

He offers me his hand. Just like a gentleman.

A pissed off, blue-eyed, about to explode gentleman.

Not that I'm complaining.

I place my palm in his, still marveling how his touch elicits a pleasing nothing, no visiting emotions, no glimpses into his thoughts. Nothing but exciting me with an unwanted blast of lust. How does he do that?

As if seeing me for the first time, his father's eyes widen as he takes in the bruise on my jaw. "What the hell happened to her?"

"Minion. She killed it." Pride suffuses Smythe's voice like warm chocolate drizzled on cake.

"With no training?" Demon-finding computer operator chimes in, mouth agape.

Neither Smythe nor David pays him any attention.

David's eyes narrow, his gaze raking me from head to toe. "Were you there?"

I can't stop a brow from rising, but as Smythe answers, it becomes apparent I'm not the one he asks.

"No. It was before I came."

I do not like the way Smythe's father continues to stare at me. As if I'm a thing, not a person. If it was sexual, that would be one thing, but it's not. The look in his eyes creeps me out and makes the bracelet uncomfortable. But when he speaks, the odd stare goes away, replaced by concern. Maybe I'm imagining things.

Yeah, like this whole evening. One huge nightmare.

I wish.

"We need to discover why the *justitia* chose her. Have you traced her lineage?"

"Not yet. Only got to her history before I saw a minion tracked her down."

"Wait a minute." I interrupt. He'd mentioned the term at my house, but at the time, I had been more concerned with him informing me wearing the bracelet—or should I say *justitia*—meant I needed to fight. "What's a minion?"

"What attacked you."

And here I thought I was the epitome of evasion. "Way to answer the question without answering the question."

Smythe's eyes laugh, corners crinkling, a second before his lips turn in a grin. "Minions are a demon's workers. Demons can give a bit of their life's energy to a human in order for that human to do their bidding."

"Why don't they just do things themselves?"

"Demons don't like to appear in the world in their normal form."

"But I thought computer genius over there saw one appear in Austin."

"They don't like to appear. That doesn't mean they don't. And that's where you and others like you come into play. *Justitians* fight the demons and their minions. Minions are not hard for a *justitia* to kill. Demons on the other hand take training to kill. They're much tougher."

"So you invented these bracelets to kill demons?"

David answers. "They were invented millennia ago to fight the thirteen known demons. One bracelet per demon. Unfortunately the demons multiplied. Our organization came into being around the time of the first Romans as a response to the excess demon activity."

"Is that why the bracelets have a Latin sounding name?"

"Justitia was the Roman Goddess of Justice. Lady Justice. The same as portrayed in courts around the world even to this day."

I glance at the *justitia* with a new respect. "What were they called before Roman times?"

"We don't know." He shrugs. "The original name has been lost."

"But why was your agency even formed? Don't we kill these demons?"

"As I said, demons multiplied. Our agency was formed to protect the *justitians*."

"Uh, not to be bullheaded here, but if I'm the one that wears the *justitia*, and therefore has the sword, then how can you protect me?"

Smythe gives my hand a squeeze. "We're mages. If it looks like you're losing the fight, we can get you out.

You've already seen how."

"And a demon can't jump into a portal?"

"Oh sure. Just not our portals. They have to form their own."

Who knew? Demonology 101 really does exist.

The chuckle dies on my lips. Demons. Really. Exist.

And it's my job to fight them.

I am not crazy. The thought slowly seeps into my mind, growing stronger the deeper it goes. This evening really happened. Evil Guy was just that—evil, but evil can be killed.

I'm not up to the task. I believe Smythe now, but how can they expect me to fight? Even with the *justitia*. I want to be a nurse, to heal people, to help people.

Isn't fighting a demon infestation helping people?

Was that my voice or the bracelet's?

Tingles shoot across my nape, almost as if a nerve suddenly became pinched. Which is ridiculous. Standing around does not cause pinched nerves. By the time I realize what the tingling sensation means, it's too late.

My vision dims as T stares out of my eyes. Dammit. And here I thought my mental barriers would keep him out.

What the hell, T?

What the hell? Are you kidding? I had to know you were okay. You stopped answering me.

I squeeze my eyes shut, throw both hands over them, and squat on the floor.

"Gin!" Smythe drops beside me. "Are you all right?"

"Headache." To put it mildly.

Open your eyes!
Get out of my head!
What the fuck is going on?
See for yourself. I give him access to my memories, my remembrances of what happened since Smythe took me from my house.

While T's taking a look-see around my mind, I jump into his. He sits on the couch in my living room, hands resting on his knees, palms up. Like a yoga meditation position minus the crossed legs. Blake and Jackie hover in the periphery of his vision. I could make him look at them, but then they might try to talk to T and that would prove weird.

Letting others know about our body switching abilities would lead to an extended, if not permanent, stay at Blue Shores.

So I pull back into my own mind, leaving T sitting on the couch.

The first thing I notice is a hand on my back, patting me like I'm a hurt pet. Smythe's. Amazing. It appears he has a gentle side. Who would've thought?

The second thing I notice, which really should have been the first thing, is T's presence. He's not a happy camper.

Demons? What the fuck?
Don't ask me. I just put the bracelet on. Didn't mean for it to lead to a superheroes episode.
Can you take it off?
You saw my memory.

"Gin? Do you need an ibuprofen?" Smythe asks.

"I need a different life." Did I really speak that out loud?

Yep. I heard it.

It was a rhetorical question, T.

Sorry. Couldn't help myself.

"No. You need to adjust to the one you have."

"Quit mollycoddling the chit, son. Give her an assignment, and she'll get used to things soon enough. Or die." I drop my hands from my eyes and stare at David in time to see him shrug.

I don't like that guy.

A wave of anger sweeps over me, and I'm halfway to my feet before I realize it's not my anger, it's T's. Word to the wise, do not make my twin mad. I know this, and yet I'm unprepared for the pure force of the rage that shoots through my limbs.

It's all I can do to straighten and stand still. I want to hit David, want to beat him bloody, want to let him know I don't appreciate being thrown to the demons to sink or swim, so to speak.

I shove the anger back into T's presence, shove until my body shakes with the effort. David's eyes widen in a split second, his nose wrinkling, his lip twitching like it aches to snarl.

Taking a deep breath, I glare at David, while talking to Smythe. "Take me home. Now."

Smythe doesn't move so I turn the glare on him. He glances at me before focusing on David. "Do you disagree with how I'm treating my ward?" The chill in his words drops the temperature in the room another degree. Or ten. Unlike when he spoke to Samantha, where his anger ran hot as lava, this time the tone of his voice reminds me of steel, cold and unmoving.

David must sense it too since his gaze narrows on Smythe. "I'm just saying, son. She needs to be taught, not coddled. Never does any good to coddle 'em."

Smythe relaxes, tension bleeding out of him like water exploding from a balloon. He nods. "I'll start her training tomorrow. She's hurt and needs her rest."

"Will you come back after you return her?"

"No." He walks over to the long desk, stepping behind the thing and squatting to pick something up. A black laptop backpack hangs over a shoulder when he rises.

David watches his movements, jaw tensing and releasing, as if he needs to say something and can't get the words out. Smythe grips the older man's arm as he walks by, that guy gesture of support women don't often give. David pats him on his back. As if they didn't almost come to blows. Over me.

The bracelet isn't the only one puzzled by their exchange of words and underlying tension.

You've really fallen down the rabbit hole, Gin.

You need to get out of my head, T. That portal cuts off our contact, and I don't want you hurt.

Good point.

A second later he's gone, leaving me alone with my thoughts. Okay, not entirely alone. The bracelet continues to give a puzzled outlook on the whole situation. Best I can tell, it doesn't like this too-white room. I knew the thing possessed intelligence.

Smythe grabs my hand, his other hand held outstretched toward the wall. Murmured words reach my hearing. Unlike Samantha, he needs to speak the spell words aloud. Does that mean she's a more powerful mage?

A slash of light appears in the wall before us, the glow almost blinding me. I squint as Smythe pulls me into the fissure. This time I'm prepared for the nausea-inducing swirls of color, the wintry air, the fear of breathing in this space between places. It's still unsettling. I doubt if I'll ever adjust to taking trips this way.

And then we're in my living room, three sets of eyes focused on our appearance.

T stands before Jackie and Blake, arms crossed, eyes narrowed. He takes a deep breath and points a finger at Smythe. "Lucy, you got some 'splaining to do."

Chapter 7

The reference to the old sitcom rolls right off Smythe, who cocks a brow and enters into one of those male glaring matches with my brother. A pale-faced Jackie stares at me like I grew an extra appendage. One hand points to the wall behind me and I turn, expecting something or someone to be there.

Nothing.

When I face her, her lips are moving, but no words escape. I really don't blame her for being shocked. If I had seen someone appear out of thin air, I'd have the same what-the-fuck look on my face, too. Blake steps around Jackie, ignores the show of too much testosterone going on in the middle of the room and walks to my side.

His arms grab me in a hug, pressing my face against his red Texas Rangers T-shirt, the shirt he always sleeps in. He's got to be the only man alive who has sex with his woman then puts on a shirt and undies and crawls back under the covers.

Not that I'm complaining. He's so damn hot in bed, if it makes him happy, he can wear *my* undies.

"You had me worried." The whisper of his breath brushes my cheek while his arms tighten, his touch eliciting his favorite mountain picture. Strands of fear and concern weave between the snow-covered peaks. For once the emotional images don't bother me. It feels good to be missed.

"It's a long story."

He takes a step back, hands on my upper arms, his narrowed gaze meeting mine. "Did he," his eyes flick to Smythe, return to me, "hurt you?"

"No." I shake my head for emphasis. "Just dragged me somewhere else."

"How? T said you were gone. Then there was this flash of light and you appeared?" He's still whispering, apparently not wanting the others to hear.

Speaking of, what were the guys doing? I glance over my shoulder and check out the glares and balled fists. The air reeks of aggression.

Men.

I focus back on Blake. "You wouldn't believe me if I told you."

"It can't be as bad as you touching me and getting inside my mind. I believe that. What's worse?"

"Do you really want to know?"

His gaze flicks to the testosterone saturated males and widens. "You might want to stop them."

I turn. Both guys have shifted positions, one foot back, fingers waggling at their sides, waiting for the other to strike. Geez Louise.

"Hey, now. Let's calm down." I wade into the middle of the dominance pissing match and hold my hands out. As if that's really going to stop them if they decide to throw a punch, but it makes me feel better. They'd at least think before swinging since I'm standing in their way.

I hope.

"You—" I point to T "—take Jackie to bed. She looks a little surprised to see me. And you—" I point to

Smythe "—you can sleep on the couch. It makes out into a bed."

Neither man moves. Figures. They haven't finished marking their territory. That territory apparently being me.

"Are you deaf?" I look between the two of them, decide the answer is a yes and give T a little shove toward Jackie. I know he won't lay a hand on me, which is why I push him.

I can't say the same about Smythe.

For a second I fear I made the wrong decision. T's eyes narrow on me, lip turned in a snarl, an about-to-explode-like-a-certain-green-comic-hero look written across his face. I swallow, but his anger dissipates as he glances over his shoulder at the still shell-shocked Jackie and then back to me. He points a finger at Smythe.

"This isn't over."

I don't see Smythe's expression, but I do catch the infinitesimal widening of T's eyes, the tensing of his jaw. Air brushes my arm as Smythe walks by us, stopping in front of Jackie. His back blocks my view of her face, but I see his hand wave between them.

"What are you doing?" T's at her side, truce with Smythe forgotten.

"Nothing."

"Why's everyone in the living room?" Jackie looks at T, brows wrinkled. "It's late."

Smythe wiped her memory? Maybe not, but it sure looks that way. Then why wasn't he wiping out T's? Or Blake's?

Jackie giggles as she notices everyone staring at her. "What? It's late. Come on, honey." She tugs T's hand, walking backward in the direction of their room.

T allows her to lead him a couple of paces, then stops, turns, points a finger at Smythe. "Tomorrow." Jackie gives another yank, and he follows her into the room, clicking shut the bedroom door.

"Let me get you some sheets." I gesture to the couch while staring at Smythe. "Blake, I'll meet you in bed in a minute."

Blake shrugs, passes Smythe, and pops me on the butt as he walks past. I can't help watching his sexy black boxer brief covered ass stride into my bedroom. Maybe my jaw doesn't hurt so badly after all.

Smythe clears his throat, and my gaze snaps back to him. His arms are crossed, biceps bunched, one brow cocked as if he knows what I'm thinking.

"Sheets. Right." I scurry down the hall, out of his sight, and grab a spare set of sheets and pillow from the linen cabinet in the bathroom.

Back to the living room, where I push by Smythe and flop the sheets and pillow on the couch. "What did you do to Jackie?"

"Relaxed her."

"You mean you wiped her mind."

"I found that to be a little hard to do."

I might be wrong, but it seems like Smythe has a sense of humor. Although maybe he just had a moral twinge over blanking out Jackie's mind. I'm betting on the humor.

"Why not T and Blake?"

He shrugs. "It didn't seem to bother them."

By that I assume he means our sudden appearance through a slash of light and not the fact he kidnapped me out of my house. "Good. Leave them alone."

His head tilts to the side. "As you wish."

I take a step away from him. My traitorous hormones need the distance. "You know where to find me. But I hope you don't need me." I make it to the hall before he speaks.

"Good night, Gin."

Not turning, I raise a hand and walk toward my room, running my tongue over my cut lip. It stings a bit, but the ibuprofen worked wonders on my no-longer-aching jaw. Which is a good thing, seeing how Blake lies on his side, head propped on his hand, facing the door wearing nothing but his birthday suit and a happy-to-see-you expression.

My gaze sweeps over his chest, continues lower, then raises to meet his eyes. "Are you happy to see me or is that a potato in your pants?" I kick the door shut and put a bit of a swing in my hips as I saunter toward the bed.

"I'm wearing pants?"

"Ah. Silly me."

"Shut up and come here, Gin." One hand reaches for me, palm up, fingers waggling, a beckon for pleasure.

I don't care if I see every bad thought he's ever had. I crave his touch like a desert craves rain. Stepping forward, I place my palm in his outstretched hand and steel myself for his rush of emotions.

A beach greets me, sand warm under my feet, the waves breaking in a relaxing rhythm. I've always wanted to have sex on the beach.

Sometimes wishes really do come true.

Chapter 8

When I wake, Blake is gone. Sunlight slips into the room under small gaps in the slats, the victor in the blinds' battle to keep it out. I shut my eyes against the intrusion, willing myself back to sleep. To no avail. I'm usually awake by now and despite the fact I pretty much got no sleep, my body still thinks it's up and at 'em time.

I sigh, eyes squeezed tight, and touch my jaw. It feels swollen, but not as much as I expected, and oddly enough doesn't hurt. I run my tongue over my lip and touch a scab. No pain.

How long did I sleep? My injuries should be painful, an aching throb worse than last night. Instead, it feels like they've had days to heal.

The surprise sends me rolling over, meaning to get out of bed and take a peek in the mirror. Instead I gasp and sit straight up, sheet clutched to my bare chest. T leans against the door, arms crossed, lips flat.

"What the hell are you doing in my room?" I hiss, clutching the sheet tighter.

"The door is fixed."

"Huh?" What does that have to do with him watching me sleep?

"The front door is fixed. No hole. And the blood splatter is gone."

I swallow. "And that requires you to lurk in my

room?"

"He did it." A muscle tenses in his jaw, releases.

"Again. Why. Are. You. In. My room?"

He shrugs. "Thought you wanted to know."

"Sure. But you didn't have to wake me."

"What if he does something else?"

"Like what?" Form another portal and haul my resisting ass through it?

"You don't think he's going to come in here? I've seen the way he watches you."

"No, I don't." Because Smythe might be a lot of things, but I'd bet good money rapist isn't on the list.

"Really."

"Don't you have someplace to be? Like work?"

"You think I'm going to leave you alone in the house with him?"

Sit him on the front porch if it worries you that much. I stop myself from saying the words. Knowing T, he'd throw Smythe out the door, or attempt to, and the ensuing fight would break some of my hard-earned furniture.

"T. You need to go to work. You can't hang around here all day and lose your job. I'm fine. Smythe won't hurt me."

"I'm not so sure about that."

"Well, you can't watch me all the time." But it's nice to know he tries.

He runs a hand over his shaved head. "I know."

"Which isn't to say I don't appreciate the gesture."

He grins. "I know."

"I'll be fine. Just lock my door when you leave and he won't be able to get in here." Right. Smythe can wave his hand and go anywhere in the world, my bedroom included, but maybe T will overlook that little fact.

"If you're sure."

"Yep. Sure as sugar's sweet. Now get on with you."

He walks over to me, gives me a big hug and a kiss on the cheek. "I can't help it."

"I know."

One hand gives me a noogie, and then he's out the door, the lock turning with a click. Fancy trick he has there. I get the emotion/thought reading specialty, but T possesses the really cool abilities. Locks? No problem. Ghosts? Okay, that's often a problem, but only because he refuses to speak to them anymore, and they refuse to leave him alone.

We're the poster children for why mothers shouldn't drink during pregnancy.

I listen to the A/C whine a complaint against the heat, the only noise echoing in the house. The smell of hot coffee wafts in through the rattling air vent. Either T left the coffeepot on again, or Smythe wanders around my house, spying.

Guess I need to discover what's going on. And I want to check out the ole jaw.

Dropping the covers, I head for the robe pitched over the extra kitchen table chair sitting by the dresser and slip my arms into its sleeves. Then I peer at myself in the dresser mirror.

What the...? Instead of being the bright colors of a fresh bruise, faded yellows and grays brush across the skin of my jaw as if painted with a light stroke. The cut on my lip is healed into a scab, a thin line barely noticeable. A tad of swelling rounds out my jaw, but if you didn't know me, you might not realize those weren't the normal contours of my face.

Bruises don't heal that fast.

Ever.

Did I play a Rip Van Winkle and sleep for a week? I dash the idea almost as soon as it appears. T didn't mention my excess sleeping habits, so it must be the day after All Hell Broke Loose.

Well, looky here. First thing in the morning and I already have a question for Smythe's weird and wacky expectations list.

Wonder how many more will join it by the time I actually see the man?

Grabbing a T-shirt out of the closet, shorts and under-things from the dresser, I carry the load into the bathroom and do my morning ritual. Then back to my room where I deposit the robe on the chair, make the bed, and dump last night's outfit into the clothes hamper.

Activity helps keep the shock at bay. Too much has happened over the last day, and my mind whirls along too many paths, all vying for top position.

I rub my fingers over the bracelet, warmth seeping into my skin from the silver. Tiny black etchings mar the otherwise smooth surface. I hold my wrist close to my eyes and try to read the writing. No such luck.

Guess that's another question for my dear friend Smythe.

My mind continues its disbelief over yesterday's events. Am I really supposed to hunt demons? The bracelet sends a jolt of happiness into my nervous system. Oh, yeah. Definitely supposed to hunt the baddies down.

Who the heck came up with that brilliant idea? Me? A demon hunter? I appear to be having issues grasping the concept. Mainly since I always put demons in the same category as angels, a nice mythology to explain good and evil things in the world.

Expecting them to really exist never crossed my mind. However, believing the bracelet turns into an evil-destroying sword doesn't present a problem. Odd, eh? Or maybe not odd at all. I saw it change, transform into an instrument of death. Its emotions permeate my thoughts. All I've seen of a demon is a minion.

Which was bad enough.

And what about that gray mist escaping out of the minion's body? Did I ask Smythe about it? Nope, don't think I did. Easily remedied.

Another item on my list.

My jaw pops when I yawn. No wonder I'm yawning. I've been ignoring the scent of fresh made coffee since T left. Maybe Smythe is up and can be peppered with questions.

Quiet whispers through the house as I step out of my room, the wooden floors protesting my weight, squeaking until I step onto the kitchen tile.

Someone, I'm assuming T, grabbed the paper off the sidewalk and stacked it in the middle of the table. A pot of fresh coffee sits on the coffeemaker, steam circling around the machine. Manna from heaven.

I pour myself an extra-large mug and take a sip. Ahhh. Nothing like coffee to greet the morning. Now that important things are taken care of, I mosey into the living room to check out the door.

First thing I see is Smythe stretched out on the couch, head flat on the cushion, feet hanging off the arm. He looks peaceful in sleep, young, less intimidating. His black laptop backpack rests against his chest, arms crossed on top, as if he fears it'll be stolen.

T and I are a lot of things, but thieves aren't on the list. I should feel insulted, instead I stifle a laugh.

Is he afraid we'll steal the computer? Or what's inside?

Oh. Deep thoughts for another time.

It's hard, but I manage to stop staring at Smythe and focus on the door. The new front door. Completely. New. And the entire living room has been cleaned of blood splatter.

He could've been nice and cleaned. But the new door?

How the hell did he get that in place without me hearing it go in?

And where's the old one?

I peer out the window into the front yard. No old door. It's not in the house either, unless he hid it in T's room, which is unlikely on so many levels. Maybe in the backyard?

When I get to the kitchen, I walk outside onto the porch. Nope. Not in the backyard.

What did he do with it?

Part of me wants to go wake him and ask another part wants to sit and drink my coffee. As I'm usually a better person after coffee, I listen to voice number two.

The paper splashes Will's face across the front page, a dedication to him and Lara and their assault. I swallow, hoping extra saliva stops the burning in my stomach. My mind flashes back to his memories, his emotions. His blood pooling on the white linoleum.

Shaking my head, I flip the page and swallow. Nothing like a good trip down a bad memory lane to start off the morning. Is he even alive? I make a mental note to call the hospital later and ask. Or maybe Smythe knows the answer.

And another question gets added to my already long list.

My attention turns back to the newspaper, back to a different attention grabbing article. I waggle my jaw in hopes of getting it to relax and suck in a deep breath. Despite the breathing exercise, my veins imitate a pressure cooker, jacking my blood pressure into the outer atmosphere. A headache forms behind my eyes, a warning to find a bottle of chill pills and swallow them whole.

I did not just read what happened. And why wasn't this on the news last night? A doctor shot in a hospital full of people, only one of whom see the attempted killer, deserves a spot on the news. This story, however, deserves the entire broadcast dedicated to finding the asshole perpetrator.

My hands shake as I read the article. Who would do that to a kid? A clerk at a convenience store took a smoke break behind the store, but instead of getting a nicotine hit, he discovered a teenager naked and stabbed, bleeding to death. Security cameras caught a man yanking her behind the store, and she came to enough to describe her attacker to the police, but so far they haven't found the man.

Teenager lies unconscious in the county hospital, fighting for her life.

"Whatcha looking at?"

I let loose with a squeak and bang my knees on the

underside of the table, splashing coffee over the edges of the mug to puddle on the paper. "Dammit, Smythe, look what you did."

"Learn to listen even when you're concentrating."

I shove him out of the way and reach for a paper towel. "Don't sneak up on me when I'm reading." I blot at the spill, trying not to tear the newspaper.

One hand grabs my wrist, while the other takes the towel out of my grasp. "Sorry." He dabs at the newspaper, each touch removing the coffee stain. "But you need to learn to keep your senses open at all times. You never know who is going to sneak up on you. They aren't all as friendly as me."

I watch as the paper towel soaks up coffee, until the paper looks as pristine as it did coming off the printing press. "How'd ya do that?"

He picks up my palm and drops the wet paper towel onto it. A grin breaks across his face like the dawn, his eyes twinkling blue diamonds. "Magic."

I fail to stop the eye roll as I push around him, opening the cabinet under the sink. "The trashcan is behind this door."

He looks at it, back at me, holding on to his grin like a child holds a balloon. "That's good to know."

"Coffee?" I gesture to the steaming coffeepot, which has yet to auto-shutoff.

"I'm more of a tea drinker, if you have any."

"I'm big on caffeine in whatever form. What's your poison?"

He selects the English Breakfast tea, and I nuke him a cup of water, place it and the bag in front of him, and return to my chair.

"Did you see this article?" I point to the one about

the teenage victim, not caring if he sees my fingers shake.

He takes the paper and reads the story, his jaw tensing. "I hope they catch the asshole." He starts to lower the paper, but then picks it up, his eyes scanning the page. "Is this neighborhood in east Fillmore?"

"Yeah. It's not the greatest area, but still. This kind of random violence doesn't normally happen there."

"I need to find out who the girl was." When he lowers the paper to the table, his lips press together in that determined way I often see on my twin's face.

"They don't publish victim's names."

"Don't worry. I'll find out." Getting out of his chair, he heads to the living room.

"How?" I know ways, none of which I mention. I like my nursing license just fine and don't want to lose it by doing something stupid like impersonating an employee at a different hospital and sneaking up to the victim's room.

He takes his laptop out of the black bag and tucks it under an arm before striding back into the kitchen. Putting the thing on the table, he pops the top and eases himself into the chair next to mine. His fingers fly across the keyboard as he pulls up a browser.

T won't be happy once he realizes he and Smythe share the character trait of determination against all odds. But it gives me the warm fuzzies to know they have something in common.

Silly me.

"Okay. I'm in."

"In where?" Leaning sideways, I peer at the screen. The angle is wrong so I get up and, coffee mug in hand, stand behind him. No sense in releasing my grasp on my morning addiction, ahem, I mean medicine. The substance needs to get into my system somehow and mainlining the liquid doesn't work.

Or so I've been told.

Fillmore Police Department flashes across the top of the laptop screen, disappearing in a rush of data. I lean closer. "Holy shit!" Case files march in columns down the screen, blurring by as he scrolls down the page. "Turn that thing off! What if they track you here?"

"They won't."

"How do you know, Mr. Confident?" I eye the power button, but his hands lie between me and the off-switch.

"I do this all the time. How do you think I found out about your past?"

I stop eyeing the power button. Trying to breathe takes up all my energy. "How..." I clear my throat, gulp a swallow of coffee and try again. "How much do you know?"

His fingers stop their flight of the bumblebee over the keys as he turns to face me. One brow raises a question as his eyes search my face. "I would say everything, but nothing I found should generate your reaction, so maybe my search wasn't as thorough as I thought." He shrugs and turns back to the screen. "Or you're hiding information that wasn't in your file."

Okay. My brain kicks in, rushing through my past, determining what he knows, what he doesn't. He knows about the empathic abilities and about my stint in a psychiatric hospital as a teen. I remember last night when he mentioned it along with certain extra-curricular activities as he called them. Neither of which my employer would look favorably on, but plenty of teens do stupid things and manage to turn their lives around afterward.

While I don't like people to know those past facts about my life, it's not as bad as the other things I fear Smythe might discover. Things no one should know. Things T and I will keep to our graves.

"Which is it?" Smythe's voice snaps my attention back to the present, out of the wretched past.

I shake my head, raise my mug to my lips and burn my throat swallowing the hot liquid. No pain no gain. "Want more tea? I'm going to have another cup of coffee."

After a glance at his full mug he shakes his head. "Nope. But thanks."

My hands tremble as I walk to the coffeepot. Whether from my trip down memory lane, the story in the paper or caffeine, I don't know. Maybe all three. I will not think about the distant past. I will not. Focus on the present. Remember Will.

Fear of discovery bleeds from my muscles, replaced by the pain of loss, the fear of the unknown. I'd rather deal with Will's attempted murder, with minions and demons and strange agencies than dwell upon things best left dead.

"Ah! I found it." He pauses, clearly reading, while I pour myself another cup.

Focus on the present. On. The. Present.

"Goddamn it! That's what I was afraid of!" He shoves the chair into the wall, popping up to stalk around the kitchen, fingers curling and releasing, curling and releasing.

I back against the counter, watching his anger grow

like an expanding balloon before releasing into a deflated mass of muscle and bones as he sinks into his chair. My breath releases on a sigh, relief his anger remains self-contained. My fingers stop clutching the mug like it's a weapon, but they still tremble.

I clear my throat. "What were you afraid of?"

He points at the screen. "She's one of ours."

I walk toward him until I stand beside his chair. "One of ours?"

"A descendent. One of the minor bloodlines able to wear the bracelet."

Chapter 9

"Minor bloodlines?" Fear disappears under the onslaught of curiosity.

"Okay. Looks like I have a lot to cover in a short amount of time. Sit." He gestures to my chair, and I oblige, parking my butt on the wood. "The makers of the bracelets cast some sort of spell over the metal so that only descendents of their lineage could wear the bracelets."

"Some sort of spell? Don't you know—"

"No idea what it was. And quit interrupting."

"Sorry. Go on."

"As I was saying. The gift of the *justitia* went to the first-born female—"

"Why not a male?"

He growls. Literally. Growls. "I don't know! Didn't I just say—"

"Yeah, yeah, yeah. Sorry." I wave my hand in a circle. "Go on."

"Whatever the spell said explains why only females wear the *justitia* and not males. We haven't been able to crack it. Okay?"

"Okay." I play the obedient student and keep my opinions to myself.

"So. The gift goes to the first-born female. Best case scenario is the female gives birth to a girl before she dies, passing on the *justitia* and the gift. That's happened with six of the bracelets. Direct descent from the original wearer through the female line. Primary bloodlines. Okay?"

"Got it."

"Now, it gets tricky when the first-born female dies prior to giving birth. In theory, all descendents of the original makers have the ability to wield the *justitia*. When the oldest dies, sometimes her sister is able to take her place fighting. Other times the gift skips a generation. In those cases, the *justitia* is taken into the Agency and kept until the next wearer appears."

How do they know when that happens? "Do you have tryouts or something?"

"Something like that. Yeah. That's what happened to your *justitia*. The line died. Completely died out. It was one of the strongest lines, lasted until 1940. The wearer was young. Thought she could kill Hitler on her own." He shakes his head. "Hitler was one strong-ass minion. But even minions can be killed by bombs. Remember that."

"Hitler was a minion?" I'm fairly certain my mouth gapes like a hole in the earth. Since Smythe doesn't need to examine the back of my throat, I make an effort to press my lips together.

"You don't think he got that evil on his own do you?"

I shrug. I really have abso-fucking-lutely no idea, since I never took Evil Beings and Their Penchant for Destruction 101. All I can say is I'm glad he died, the evil bastard.

I blink away my surprise, eager for the lesson to continue. "And the minor bloodlines?"

"Oh. Sorry. As you can imagine, in the millennia

since the bracelets were forged, the descendents of the makers have multiplied. Not all of these descendents know about the *justitias*, but we track them. Julia," he touches the screen with the tip of his finger, "was one of those."

"What about me?"

"I don't know." He shakes his head. "I didn't get far enough in your bloodlines to see. I don't even understand how you got the bracelet."

"Will gave it to me. Yesterday." The words escape my mouth before I realize what happened. Way to go, Gin.

"How?"

I pause. Should I tell him? Trust is a two-way street. Along with sharing information. He's shared with me—granted, the question list I made for him remains a mile long despite all his sharing—so I should come clean and tell him about the bracelet. Besides, I can tell by that determined tic in his jaw my escaped words tantalize his curiosity, which means he won't rest until I tell him the answer.

"It appeared in my pocket."

His eyes narrow. "Come again?"

I tell him. About touching Will. About delving into his memories. About the weight of the bracelet as it appeared in my pocket.

Smythe curses.

"Yeah. It's weird, eh?"

He shoves back from the table and stalks around the kitchen, punctuating each step with the f-bomb. Clearly he thinks it more than weird. He slams both fists onto the counter to the side of where I sit and glares.

"What made you put it on?"

Holding his glare, I run my fingers over the silver links, committing each groove and etching to memory. "It wanted me to. I wanted to. It's hard to explain."

"That I understand. How Will got it...I have a theory."

"Care to share?"

His eyes narrow. "More research is needed."

"Fine." So much for the share game. "Then how did you fix the door?"

"Huh?" He blinks, clearly thrown out of his thoughts into a different direction. Men don't do well when you redirect their thoughts.

"The front door. I see it's fixed. I don't see the old one."

He waves a hand. "The Agency has a crew that cleans up messes."

"You generate a lot of messes?"

One brow raises, and he stares me down. I swallow, but refuse to drop his gaze. His lip twitches.

"We need to find Julia's attacker."

What do I look like? Sherlock Holmes? "That's the police's job."

"They don't know what they're doing."

"Hey, now. I admit they've had their problems, but they are perfectly capable of tracking down a would-be killer."

"Sure, if the killer wasn't a minion. That's where you come in. You need to be shown the ropes, and this is the perfect situation. Low risk."

"Are you crazy? It's my day off. I go to the gym and run errands on my day off."

"It'll be like going to the gym. Just a bit more

strenuous."

Yep. He's crazy. Bona fide.

"Whatever. I didn't do so well against the minion last night." I point to my almost healed jaw.

"You killed it didn't you?" A touch of pride sparks the ice-blue of his eyes. "And *justitians* heal fast. As I'm sure you've noticed."

Ah. That explains the almost healed bruise. Nice to know.

"What about mages?" Will he be able to protect me if another minion attacks?

The lip twitch grows into a full-fledged predacious smile. "We have our own set of skills." He walks back to the table, leaning over his chair to pull up a map on the screen. His eyes scan the page before turning to me. "Ready?"

"I haven't finished my coffee." I take a sip, looking at him over the rim of the mug.

"Bring it with you."

I should argue the point. Insist he wait. Not allow him to think I'll do whatever he asks as soon as he asks it. Show a bit of steel backbone.

But the bracelet hums with excitement, a beckoning to hunt, to destroy. I want its excitement, its joy to permeate my senses like an extended high. So yeah, I'll do what Smythe asks, let him think I'm the obedient mentee. Why do I need to tell him the reasoning behind my action?

I smile, taking another sip of my happiness liquid. "Only if you'll answer my questions."

"Haven't I already?" One brow pops a query.

"I have more."

"I'll answer whatever. Just move your ass."

"Aye, aye, master." I bury my lip twitch behind another sip of coffee.

"It's mentor, not master."

"What about Aidan?"

He glares at me, thrusting his outstretched hand toward the wall behind the table, murmuring words under his breath. A slash of light forms where the wall stood, a warm breeze drifting out to allure the unsuspecting journeyer into believing the passageway resembles the temperature of a beach. I know better than to fall for its charms.

"I changed my mind. Leave the coffee." He flips the laptop closed, grabs my hand, and pulls me into the swirling colors of the deceptively warm portal.

Chapter 10

This time, the trip between places takes no more than the speed of a blink. For once, the thought 'I'm going to pass out before exiting' doesn't occur. Dare I say the trip was pleasant?

Okay, I won't go that far. I'm chilled, but not bad, more like walking under an air conditioning vent during the heat of a Texas summer.

We're standing in the deserted area behind a store, materializing behind a dumpster. No one is back here, thank goodness. Try explaining that one to a homeless guy.

Really, sir, we didn't appear out of thin air. We've been standing here the whole time. Right.

"Where are we?"

"By the crime scene." He gestures toward yellow police crime tape waving in the air like a broken antenna.

I jump, banging into the metal gang symbol decorated dumpster. Standing in the same spot as the victim gives me the creeps. And the chills. Can't forget about those.

Rubbing my hands over my upper arms, I look around, spotting bloodstains not far from where I stand. I take a step away from the discolored concrete. Will flashes through my mind, a pool of red encircling his torso, his eyes pleading with me for help.

Flashbacks are a bitch.

I swallow and face Smythe. "You think the attacker is around here?"

"No. But a clue to his identity is, and you're going to track him."

Oh, great. "What do I look like? A bloodhound?"

"Are you always this much of a smartass?"

"Only to people who don't let me drink a third cup of coffee."

"I'll keep that in mind." His hand touches my bracelet, the remnants of a smile fading under his mask of serious determination. "Your *justitia* can track minions. You just need to activate it."

"Okay, oh, wise mentor. How do I do that?"

He scratches his head, licks his lips, stares at the cracks meandering through the brick wall of the building. "My last *justitian* just did it when asked."

"Last *justitian*? Did she graduate and no longer need you as a mentor?"

"I'd rather not talk about it." His hand grips my wrist, a painful tightening sure to leave a bruise. For the first time since we met, a crack forms in the shield he locks over his emotions, allowing me a glimpse into a world of orange pain and gray sorrow overlaid with red anger. The twisting colors ball in my stomach, bile fleeing into my throat, saliva flooding my mouth. And then the crack seals, throwing me out of his mind, shaking me to the marrow. He drops my wrist like it's a snake, his eyes narrowing, fingers curling and releasing.

Despite the heat bouncing off the concrete like white-hot lasers, I cross my arms, rubbing my hands against my goosebump-covered flesh. No wonder he keeps his emotions locked down like Fort Knox.

Their bitterness threatens his sanity.

What the hell have I gotten myself into?

A rush of calming thoughts sweeps through me, dispelling the ice freezing my blood, leaving me warm, happy. Able to manage the confusion threatening my sanity. Maybe one day knowing an entity living inside my bracelet managed to fuse to my nervous system and control it will bother me. Alien, anyone?

Smythe sucks down a deep breath and focuses on my bracelet. "Try talking to it."

Oh, right. After that insight he wants me to strike up a cheery conversation with the links of silver? I'd rather discover what happened to his former mentee.

Instead I hold my wrist up, bracelet level with my nose. "Go track a minion."

I'm not sure, but I think the thing laughs. It wants to hunt, but needs something else from me. What?

It can't, or won't, tell me.

I shrug, lower my wrist, and stare at a no longer seething Smythe. "Nothing."

"Try again."

I'm pretty sure this will turn into an exercise in futility, and it gives me no pleasure when after three more tries, I'm proven correct.

"Why don't you ask someone?"

His eyes widen. Apparently, it's not only driving directions men refuse to ask about. "We'll figure it out. Why don't you try closing your eyes and communicating telepathically."

I fail to stop the eye roll. "Fine."

Closing my eyes, I picture strands of nerves running through my arm, down to my wrist, connecting to the bracelet. Visualizing my nerves attached to the entity helps me imagine my thoughts connecting to it. Asking for its help.

Electricity shoots up my arm, deep tingles rolling into my brain on a wave of pleasure. My eyes pop open. But instead of seeing the world as it normally appears, I see colored lines overlaying everything.

It reminds me of a tactical display.

The target in this case being minions.

Lines fill the crime scene, colors intersecting, only to shoot off in different directions. Not different colors. Shades of the same color. Variations.

And the darkest, strongest, colors lay over the blood-stained concrete like a suffocating blanket.

I point at the nearest red strand. "Here."

"Really? Never would've guessed."

I turn to him, giving him my best go-to-hell look.

His eyes pop wide, his lips turning upward in a grin that pulls years off his expression. "You did it! Good job! What do you see?"

"Strands of colors. Different shades of red."

"Where do they lead?"

"Here."

"No. Where away from here?"

It takes me awhile to discern the trail leading to my left. The colors closest to the dumpster glow stronger, more vibrant, than either color-strand leading into and out of the area.

"The trail to the right is slightly stronger than the one to the left. And I know from reading the paper he came from the street to the right, so," I point to the left, "it looks like he went thataway. Why are the colors over here so much darker?"

"Because the evil is so much stronger. It'll fade

after a day. That's why we need to track it now before it goes away."

An overwhelming sense of urgency breaks through Smythe's words. The bracelet telling me to get the lead out and start tracking.

I'm nothing if not obedient.

I gesture to Smythe and start walking in the direction of the lighter colored strand, following it onto the sidewalk of a busy street lined with stores and cracked asphalt parking lots.

I hook a left at the stoplight, continue walking down a busy street, then hook another left leading to my old stomping grounds. Smythe follows like a stalker. Not that I mind his stalking. Nope. He can stalk me back to my house, where we'd...what the hell am I thinking? I just had sex. Mind-blowing damn good sex, too. Why on earth am I fantasizing about Smythe?

I glance over my shoulder. Face forward. Okay. So I understand the appeal of the fantasy. But understanding why doesn't stop the hormones from pinging around my veins like balls in a pinball machine. *Bing, bing, bing*, the buzzers lighting up at a touch.

Or a glance.

Dealing with obnoxious hormones makes me feel like a horny teenager. Not a decade I wish to return to for a myriad of reasons.

Obviously I need to make more of an effort to ignore whatever horny spell he's cursed me with.

And if ignoring my overactive libido doesn't work, a hike into the neighborhood I grew up in will do the trick. Lust slides away, revealing memories of pain, fear and resolve best kept hidden. Please tell me the strands don't lead to my old house. Please.

A higher power I no longer pray to for once hears my pleas as the colored ribbon crosses over my childhood street, continuing toward the high school. Unease skitters across the damp flesh of my nape. My heart beats a terrified rhythm as my mouth turns into what feels like the Sahara desert. The fear becomes a fist squeezing my insides into a tangled mass. I refuse to look down the street, not wanting to glimpse the house where...

No! Not remembering. Not going there. If I don't think about it, then it didn't happen.

Sounds from the past refuse to obey, creeping around my mental barriers, pulling me backward in time.

Screams.

Thuds of fists on bruised flesh.

The deep voice of an enraged bull.

No! No! No!

I'm not listening. Am. Not. Listening.

I'm hunting minions. With my shiny, new bracelet.

Focus on the strand. Focus. Focus.

But the strand disappears into the dappled shadows of overhanging tree branches. Despite wishing to focus on the colored ribbon, my mind stutters in an effort to block out memories, to keep the remembered terror at bay.

A multi-tasker I am not.

Smythe runs into me when I come to an abrupt stop.

"What's wrong?"

"It's gone." Hopefully he won't ask why.

"Hmm. Where exactly?"

I stand by the last place I saw the thread of color

and point. Don't ask why, don't ask why, don't ask why.

Smythe raises a brow, but keeps his curiosity to himself. "That's not half bad for your first time. It goes up one more block and then crosses the street."

"You mean you can see the strand?"

"Of course." His tone implies I possess half a brain. Which at the moment I do, so getting mad at him is out of the question. "Let's go." Now it's his turn to lead my addled ass on our minion-finding journey.

I glance behind us at the street sign. The voices in my head fall silent, fretful entities waiting for another chance at freedom. Terror sits on my tongue like the taste of spoiled milk. I need a bottle of Jack to wash it away. Instead, I shake my head and start walking after Smythe. The taste fades the farther I walk, disappearing with a swallow.

Thank goodness.

Oak tree shade covers the street, branches reaching toward the opposite side. A relief from the hot Texas sun. Cicadas sing a symphony, the vibrations of their wings an accompaniment to the heat of the day.

And it was only morning.

As we walk farther away from my old house, I begin to see the colored strands indicative of a minion. It goes without saying if I want to learn how to use this bracelet, I need to control my emotions. Need to let the bracelet's emotions control me.

Now where did that thought come from?

I glare at the silver links surrounding my wrist. What does it think I am? If it controls me, I'm no better than the minion we chase.

"It doesn't control you. It guides you." Smythe

continues walking, speaking over his shoulder.

"How the hell did you know my thoughts?"

"You spoke that one out loud."

"Oh." Whew. For a minute there I thought he read minds.

"The trail leads into the cemetery." He points to the entrance, to the open iron gate, curved bars forming a sign over the entrance, proclaiming Pecan Grove Cemetery.

Dear God, not this cemetery. "I'll wait out here."

He stops, turns, one brow asking a question. I shrug.

"You're the one that has to find the minion."

"You're doing a good job. Go on now." I flick my fingers toward the gate, shooing him in. He cocks his head.

"Afraid of the ghosties?"

"Ghosts won't come out of their graves in broad daylight." They'll be happy to haunt your house anytime of the day, but walking in the sun is a whole other matter.

He blinks. "Study up on ghosts much?"

I shrug. "Everyone knows that." Especially if their brother has a ghost du jour keeping him company.

"Then what are you afraid of?"

Memories. None of which I'll tell him. I shrug again. It's been years since I walked through those gates, under the pecan tree guarding the entrance, clutching T's sweaty hand in a death grip. My eyes flick in the direction of the grave, return to Smythe's. A puff of breeze ruffles the hair on my nape, sending a shiver down my spine.

It doesn't help to note the minion trail leads toward

the grave I'm hell bent on avoiding.

"I'm not going in there. Feel free to chase out the minion, and I'll be happy to sword him, but I'm not going in there."

Clearly a mentee has never told Smythe no.

His eyes blink a slow open-close, his arms cross, biceps bunching under the cotton of his t-shirt. If possible, he seems to grow, expand, the silent challenge rolling off him like a wave of thunder, vibrating through my skin.

"If you are tracking a demon, you cannot stop for your sensibilities or fears. You must push through."

Yeah, sure, if my fears are the garden variety of death or pain. Past fears and hidden knowledge are way scarier.

All that aside, he has a point. I can't shake in fear from memories. I need to push past them, not let them control me.

Easier said than done.

"I'm here." His voice gentles, turns warm like melted chocolate. "If you run into trouble."

"That's not..." my voice trails off, refusing to speak of why I stand in front of the cemetery instead of marching inside it. Better he think me frightened of cemeteries. Some things are better left lying dead.

Literally.

I suck in air. Release it through my nose. I'm a big girl. I can walk through the gate. I can. Really.

Swallowing the nausea flooding my throat, I march toward the gate. One step. Two.

See? Nothing to it.

Inhale. Exhale. Remind myself that as an adult, I'm potty trained. I will not pee my pants.

Three steps. Four.

And I'm in.

Nothing happens. No loud trumpets. No shots fired. Just the stillness common to all graveyards coupled with singing cicadas. Heat presses sweat from my pores, dampness clogging my skin as if caught in a rainstorm.

I no longer see the minion trail. It's hidden by thorny emotions slipping past my control.

"You okay?" Smythe steps beside me, arms at his side, posture relaxed except for excitement shining in his gaze.

"Yeah. Where to?"

"It leads that way." He points to the right, to where...nope, not thinking about it.

"What do we do once we find the minion? Call the police?"

"Kill its ass."

"But..."

"No buts. That's what you do. You kill minions."

"What if it wants redemption?"

One brow skims upward. "They are beyond redemption. You touched one. You know what its thoughts were."

"Yeah, but are they all like that?"

He shrugs. "Does it matter?"

"Of course it matters! What if the minion didn't want to become a minion? What if it wants to rid itself of the demon?"

"Demons only choose those who have threads of evil to begin with. They don't possess those who have a good soul."

"Can they possess me?"

"Not to my knowledge. The *justitia* protects you."

I release a breath I didn't know I held. Nice to know I don't need to worry about being possessed while I'm killing the minion.

I nod.

"Why? You think you're evil or something?" Smythe speaks with a smile, curiosity bleeding out of his pores.

"Or something. Let's go get the bastard."

Doing something beats standing here lost in memories.

The minion trail leads past The Grave. I refuse to look, focusing on the colored ribbon as it makes a beeline to the east.

"Looks like it heads out of the graveyard. Right over the fence. How did he get over a six-foot iron fence?"

"Jumped, probably." Smythe's jaw tenses. "The fuckers get prolonged bursts of adrenaline. Kinda like certain drug users. Super-strength and such."

I stare at the ribbon, which does indeed hurdle the fence. "Do we hurdle the fence?"

"Do you want to?"

"Someone might spot us."

"Good thinking. We'll need to go around." Pivoting like a military cadet, he starts back the direction we came.

I still refuse to look in its direction. It is a hunk of stone buried in the ground. It cannot hurt me. Really. It. Cannot. Hurt. Me.

I'm such a good little liar.

Putting some speed in my stride, I pass Smythe, hurrying out of the graveyard, telling the memories to stay put. Not that they obey. Not that they ever did.

"You really don't like graveyards, do you?"

Only that one. "I have nothing against them. Just want to track the minion."

He makes a non-committal noise in the back of his throat, something between a grunt and a yeah-right. Whatever. As long as he doesn't fire up his computer and pry into my life.

Distraction is the key to forgetting.

We follow the iron fence around the periphery of the cemetery, picking up the colored strand on the east side, only to come to a stop. The strand crosses a busy street, forcing us to wait for the light. Unlike the minion, who from the look of things jaywalked, having the possibility of a car crashing into me did not sound like a good time.

Sweat beads along my hairline, little drops spiraling down my cheeks. My eyes squint against the sun. Note to self. Next time Smythe suggests hunting minions bring sunglasses and sunscreen.

"I'm going to burn."

"Walk." He gestures, striding in front to cross the six-lane street before the light turns green. As it gets me further away from my past, I choose not to complain.

A block from the intersection, the trail ends against the side of a house.

"This must be where the bloodhounds lost the scent." Smythe points at the house.

"Does that mean the minion is inside?"

"No. Look up."

I blink. "How did he get up there?" The trail jumped from the ground to the top of the two-story house. What was this minion? Spiderman?

"Remember how I said minions have super-strength and speed?" I nod. "He jumped."

Lucky for me, Smythe magnanimously decides our feet should remain on the ground. The minion jumped from rooftop to rooftop the entire length of the street. But instead of dropping to the ground, his trail vanishes.

"Do you see where it went?" As I can see the trail we followed, I assume the lack of continuation has nothing to do with my emotional instability and everything to do with the minion vanishing into nothing.

"Inside the last house."

"How do you know that?"

"Looks like the trail goes through a window upstairs." He points and then I see it. A colored ribbon of evil straight through a window.

Bingo.

"Do I need to climb through the window?" I point, letting the tone of my voice speak for my lack of joy at the prospect.

"I find the doorbell works well."

Whew. Scaling bricks is not my idea of a good time. Neither is walking around in this heat, but I won't complain about it. At least not now.

"What if he doesn't open?"

"We'll see when we get there."

Okay. It could be worse. I could be role-playing a spider and crawling up the waterspout. Maybe the guy won't answer the door, and we can go home.

And what are the chances of that happening?

Chapter 11

Smythe strides to the door, me following like a lost puppy anxious to get home. Rose bushes stand sentry on either side of the barely-room-for-two porch, their scent a sweet perfume in the humid heat. Bermuda grass grows in fits and starts, fighting a battle against crabgrass encroaching on its territory. The shade of the porch's meager overhang feels like an oasis in a desert.

I cram my body into the recesses of the shade as Smythe rings the doorbell and shift from one foot to the other, wondering how this is going to go down. Am I supposed to stab the guy as soon as he opens the door? Wait until he confesses? Force him to say why he did it?

Why did he do it? I got the impression from Smythe minions turned over their freewill when they became minions. Maybe he doesn't know what he did. Maybe he's as surprised by the crime as the city was.

Maybe he'll confess and ask for forgiveness.

It could happen.

Since the chances rank someplace between slim and not likely, I need to know how to get the sword to come out of the bracelet.

I could ask Smythe. But since he was ever so helpful with the colored ribbons, I decide not to bother.

How do I get the sword to appear?

Appear sword.

Nothing. Why am I not surprised.

Footsteps sound from inside the house, dull beats against wood. The door creaks open. A middle-aged man stands before us smoking a cigarette, dull brown hair plastered against his head as if he forgot the purpose of shampoo. Red-brown splotches stain his white tee-shirt in a splatter pattern which can come from exploding tomato sauce.

Or blood.

I swallow to keep from gagging.

His boxer shorts hang halfway down his thighs, exposing white hairy legs. Black tennis shoes and white socks complete his ensemble.

GQ he is not.

Yanking the cigarette out of his mouth, he narrows his eyes and a slide of unease prickles my skin.

"Whatcha want?"

Colored red-orange strands surround his body, ribbons indicating his minion status. It's so obvious now how to tell a minion from a normal person it makes me wonder why I didn't notice colored strands on the minion who broke into my house last evening.

Maybe because I didn't know how to use the bracelet then?

I swallow. What exactly am I supposed to do? Okay, I know I'm supposed to kill him, but the thought forms a cold ball of slithering snakes in my stomach. What if this guy wants a way out? What if he doesn't want to be controlled by the minion? What if Smythe is wrong?

Can I really kill another human just because he's covered in the colored strands of a minion?

The man drops his cigarette onto the wooden floor,

grinding it with his foot. "You gonna say something?" His fingers flex.

Whimpering sounds from inside the house, high-pitched and painful, the cry of a wounded animal.

"What's the matter with your pet?"

The man's gaze shifts from Smythe to me, and I swallow the lump of bile lodging in my throat. Flat brown eyes regard me with the same attention an exterminator pays to roaches.

My heartbeat echoes in my ears as I fight to get my rapid breathing under control. Freaking out before the minion is not an option.

"Don't know what you mean."

The crying continues, loud, insistent.

"What do you call that?" I point behind him, aiming for the noise.

He shrugs. "She wants out. You're prohibiting it. That's what she does."

Smythe glances at me. Thoughts move behind his eyes. A silent lesson in minion killing?

Since he leaves the next move up to me...

"I'd like to give you the chance to repent or whatever it is you need to do to get rid of the demon."

I'm not sure who's more surprised by my words, Smythe or the minion. Both wear identical popped-eyes, slack-jaw expressions. But the minion recovers first.

"What the fuck are you? Some sort of religious nut?"

"In a matter of speaking, yes. I'm here to save you or send you to your maker." Okay sword, anytime you wanted to make an appearance would be good.

The man laughs. Smythe's gaze focuses on a spot

behind the minion and his jaw tenses. A second later Smythe shoves his way inside the home. The man shoves back, but we're inside, being smothered by blessedly cool air tinged with the metallic scent of fresh blood.

"Gin!" Smythe screams my name as he wrestles with the minion. Above the noise of their scuffle cries the animal.

I hear a door slam and take a step forward only to come a complete stop as my gaze drops to the living room floor.

A medium-sized coal-black dog lies on the floor, covered in blood. My jaw locks.

"What did you do to your dog?" My yell freezes the fight, both sets of eyes turning to me.

"Fucking bitch." Does he mean me or the dog? "You don't know nothing. Nothing!" His yell snaps the hesitant part of me in half, freeing a healthy dose of anger.

It's like I'm possessed, as if the demon in the minion hopped into my body and filled me with its anger, its rage. I become aggravated as much as the next person, but this all-consuming rage startles me with its intensity.

A wordless yell barrels from my lips as I rush toward the minion. Midway through my punch aimed at the underside of his jaw, the bracelet transforms into the sword.

"No!" Smythe yells, but the momentum of my swing carries my fist forward. The sword stabs through the flesh under the minion's chin straight up into his brain.

Lights out, sucka.

I yank the sword out of his head, watching as he drops to the ground, dead.

"Damn it, Gin. That was the wrong minion. You let the other one get away." Smythe's eyes flash a disturbing snap of ice.

Wrong minion? Anger pulses through my veins, followed by surprise. "There was more than one?"

"I tried to tell you." His jaw tenses. "Didn't you hear him run out the back door?"

Yeah, sure, but rage at seeing the poor dog consumed me, and all thoughts focused on killing the one responsible. It seemed like a good plan at the time.

My breathing hiccups, small bursts of panic, as my gaze fastens on the dead minion.

I killed the wrong person.

As soon as the sword disappears, I drop to my hands and knees, retching.

The rush of anger dissipates as I empty my stomach onto the wood floor. How could I be so angry that I killed a man without checking it was the correct one? That my body acted without my mind weighing in?

Smythe rests his hand on my back. "Gin?"

Dry heaves shudder through my stomach, the scent of blood and death and puke mix with the pain-filled cries of the dog, and I can't stop retching.

Tremors shake my body, the scene replaying in my mind. I'm no better than the minion. A demon might not control me, at least not one who preys on innocents, but I'm controlled by a power not my own.

I don't like it.

I still crave it.

"Gin! Look at me!"

Smythe's command snaps my head up. I put a hand across my mouth. I will not puke on my mentor. I will not. I swallow.

He kneels beside me, avoiding the messes staining the floor. "It's okay. We'll chase the escaped minion later. We need to call in the cleanup crew."

"The dog?"

"We'll take it to the vet."

I nod, making sure my gaze stays trained on him and not the minion. Holding my gaze, he pulls out his cell and makes the call for the cleanup crew to come. After pocketing his phone, he grabs my arm and gives it a little shake.

"How do you treat the dog?"

Why does he expect me to know? I'm a nurse, not a vet. Then I realize he's trying to force me to think of something besides blood and puke and minions.

Wrap an injured animal in a blanket to prevent it from biting you. Right? "Maybe a blanket? So it won't bite you?"

He nods. Go me. I gave the correct answer. His gaze pulls me in, focuses me on him and him alone. The whimpering of the dog fades into the background hum of air conditioning, the scents of vomit and blood disappear. Nothing matters. Nothing but him and me and the blue depths of his gaze.

A piece of me screams he's casting a spell. Screams to look away, to forget about the enthralling blue of irises flicked with yellow, the way his pupils dilate as they stare at me.

Warm air blows against my arm, unnatural, lights dance in my periphery. Portal. I should turn to see who is on the cleanup crew, but Smythe's eyes beckon and my gaze remains fastened on his.

I'm floating in a blue-green sea, drifting in calm, my subconscious flat-lining in bliss. I hear noises, but not the rush of the ocean, the crash of waves over sand. No, these sounds fail to keep me in my calm bliss, instead, they remind me of fear, of pain, of powerlessness.

"She's coming out of it, Aiden."

"Fuck." This voice I recognize. This voice is the reason for the fear. Along with the calming bliss.

A gentle touch against my cheek and I'm drifting in my sea of peace. Voices and noises don't belong here. Wherever here is.

They fade. It's only me and the ocean and the waves.

And the cold.

Cold?

The bliss of the ocean disappears as my conscious snaps back to reality. I'm in Smythe's arms, held against his chest, and we've just come out of a death-cold portal.

I blink and look around. My living room stares back at me. "Put me down!" I smack his chest, but the effort is feeble, weak.

"Not yet." He walks to my couch and lays me down, placing a hand over my chest when I try to rise. "Stay still. I had to put you in a trance and you'll be a little groggy."

Do I say thanks? Do I curse him? Do I care? "A trance?"

"You freaked out. Why?" Obviously content I'll stay put, he picks up my legs, sits, and rests them in his lap. Aw, how sweet.

I want to bitch-slap him. Now, not only do I feel groggy, nauseous and disgusted, but since one of my body parts touches one of his, I'm horny.

Dammit.

"I killed the wrong person."

"Any minion kill is a good kill." He pats one of my legs. "We just needed to interrogate that one. Find out where the other one went."

"How do you know it's the wrong one?"

"The colors were different. Didn't you notice?"

"Not by much, they weren't. Red and red-orange? Good thing I'm not colorblind."

"Most women aren't."

"Yeehaw."

He huffs. "We still don't know where the other minion is. Or what he looks like. Security camera caught him, but his face was mostly hidden."

"So, go back to the house and look at the pictures. Maybe he's in one of them."

"Hey, that's a good idea. Let's go." He picks up my legs and rises.

I remain in my comfy place. "Have at it. I'm not so sure I can go back over there."

An urge to fight, to conquer, slams through me, the bracelet's attempt to tell me to get the lead out. This time it doesn't control me. I control it.

I think.

"It wasn't the blood and death was it?" He squats next to me, forearms resting on his knees.

I close my eyes, see the scene again in my mind and pop the suckers open. Smythe's blue irises hold more appeal than my minion killing. And more insight. He sees me. Into me. And understands.

Freaking scary.

"No."

Nothing moves but the tick of the kitchen clock, a steady beat counting away seconds of my life. Smythe waits on my answer, close enough for his breath to caress the hairs on my arm. Close enough for the heat of his body to warm my skin. I should tell him what went wrong.

It's doubtful he'll move until I do.

"The bracelet controlled me. I couldn't stop the anger inside when I saw the dog. I just wanted to kill the one who did that to her." My voice drops to a whisper as I stare at his lips. "I didn't think."

"And not being in control scared you."

My gaze snaps back to his, tethered to his insight. "If it controls me, then I'm no better than the minion. I'm possessed, too."

"No, you're not. The *justitia* can amplify your emotions. It can give you suggestions. But it cannot control you."

"Then why did I become so overwhelmed with anger that I couldn't stop myself even when you yelled at me?"

"For one, it's harder to pull back a strike than movies make it. And two, you were angry and wanted to kill the guy. The *justitia* merely amplified that feeling."

"Are you sure? It felt like a possession."

"Anger can do that sometimes. Control the person." His gaze cuts away, as he stares at some point over my head. Remembering.

I don't need to touch him to know what that far away look in his eyes means.

Someone else has an anger issue.

He clears his throat. "You can't let it control you." Who's he talking to now? Me or himself? "So, you up for going back over there?"

The bracelet fires a yes through my veins, its excitement a palpable throb. I'm not so sure. But I'm also the one who fastened the bracelet around her wrist. Who didn't wait to see what the damn thing was before clasping it on and letting it take over.

Guess that means I'm going back.

"You gonna spell me again?"

"You gonna freak out again?"

Was that a smile curving my lips? "I'll try not to."

"Still feel groggy?"

I try vertical while he watches my attempt. Instead of a crazed rave dance, the room remains still. Nausea no longer presses against the back of my throat. Both signs I interpret as a lack of grogginess. Go me. "Nope."

"Good." He holds out a hand and I grasp it, the warmth of his palm sinking into my soul.

You can say a lot of things about Smythe.

Unexciting was not one of them.

The portal belches us out in the living room of the minion house, smack in the middle of a "cleaning." Interpretation: staging a scene.

"Don't touch anything!" A white coated man yells, eyes wide, hands shaking a negative. I freeze, surprise grounding my feet to the floor. The last thing I ever thought to be involved in was staging another crime scene.

Where's a portal when I need one?

The dog no longer lies in the living room, which I

assume means someone took her to the vet. Although how they would explain her injuries to the veterinary staff boggles my mind.

"This way." Smythe obviously has his minion-vision running as he leads the way into the kitchen, which is separated from the living room by a wall with a cutout over the sink.

"How do you explain the dog to the vet?"

"It was hurt, and they found it."

"Then what?"

"They'll pay the bill and leave it with the vet."

"So who picks her up?"

He stops and stares at me. "You're really caught up on this dog."

"I'm an animal lover. Who picks her up?"

"It's up to the vet to find a shelter."

"Which vet?"

"Pecan Grove Animal Hospital."

I make a mental note and nod. "Okay. Lead on oh fearless one."

He cocks a brow and continues into the laundry room off the kitchen. Dingy brown and yellow linoleum, fashionable in the 70s, downright scary now, hugs the floor. An ancient avocado green washer and dryer set rests against one wall. Haven't the owners heard of energy efficient appliances?

Apparently minions take going green to a whole new level.

"What do you see?" Smythe asks.

"A bunch of bad fashion."

"No. Over here." I turn. Smythe points toward the doorknob as if it holds a secret treasure and it's my job to find it.

"A doorknob."

He huffs. "Quit being a smartass."

"Fine. I'm assuming the door leads to the garage?"

"Yep."

I open the door and peek inside. A whole lot of muggy Texas heat slaps me upside the head. An oil stain bleeds into the concrete floor, the space around it free with room to park a car. Shelves filled with decaying cardboard boxes line the walls. Various pieces of lawn equipment and a table holding an assortment of tools invades the other side of the garage.

"Unless he's hiding out there," I jump as Smythe's voice brushes like chocolate syrup across my skin, "which the team's already looked and he's not, he jumped in a car and got away. They're next to impossible to track in a car."

"Okay." I shut the door and face him. "So now what?"

The turn of his lips reminds me of a psychopath proud of his kill. "I work a spell to track him."

"You can use a spell to track him?"

"Yep."

"So if you can track him this way, why didn't we just do that from the start?" I throw up my hands. "Why follow colored strands around in the heat?"

"It uses a bunch of energy. Why waste energy when you can use the easy way of following the minion's trail instead?"

Why indeed. Let's see. Sunscreen and hotter than hell heat come to mind.

Smythe ignores my get-real glare. "And you needed to learn how to use your *justitia* since you can't work spells. Following the minion strands is how you track."

I suck in a breath. Close my eyes. Exhale on a sigh. Okay. Smythe makes sense. If I'm to kill minions, I need to know how to find the suckers.

"Step back, Gin. I need to cast the spell, and it will take a minute."

Swallowing my last remnants of heat-induced irritation, I step to the side while he reaches around me to open the door. So much for staying inside the air conditioning. But like a mirage over asphalt, the thought vanishes when Smythe uses a finger to draw a circle about three feet across on the concrete garage floor. Curious, I lean against the doorframe, watching as he draws the circle around where he squats. He sits cross-legged in the middle of the invisible circle, hands resting palms up on his knees, eyes closed.

Focusing on seeing the minion lines, I bring into view the red ribbon of evil. The strand runs through Smythe's circle, through Smythe, to a spot a couple of feet back from the oil stain. Right where a car door would be if the car was still parked in the garage. No lines run out the garage door, and a quick peek around the garage shows Smythe's cleanup crew spoke true. No minion in the garage.

Smythe mutters words under his breath, each syllable strengthening a glowing green/gold aura around his upper body. The glow overlays the minion trail, fusing the colors together, absorbing the red ribbon into itself. He jerks like a body does when drifting off to sleep.

But unless he's mastered the art of sleeping while spell-casting, I doubt he's dozing.

One hand sweeps across the floor next to his leg,

crossing the invisible line of his circle, then lifts toward me.

"Come, Gin."

Swallowing, I take his offered hand, allowing him to pull me down into his lap. His eyes remain closed, but a bead of sweat bands across his forehead. A reaction to the heat or the spell?

I'm happy to note my lack of sexual tension despite the large quantity of his body touching mine. Thank god for small miracles.

"Hold on. No matter what, don't let go."

Now don't those words give a girl confidence?

Uh-huh, right.

I wrap one arm under his, the other arm around his shoulders, my hands clasping the opposite wrists, my chest flush against his. One of his arms snugs around my waist, locking me against him tight enough for his bicep to tremor from the tension. He holds his other arm bent at the elbow, palm facing out. Like he's going to form a portal.

But he's never gripped me this tight to go through a portal. And don't we have to walk through one?

Apparently not.

A rush of warmth surrounds me as a portal opens. I tilt my head back to stare into the sickening entrance of the in-between. The thing's not beside us, in front of us or behind us. Damn portal has formed on top of us. On. Top. Of. Us.

What the hell?

My eyes expand hard enough to hurt and before I can snap them closed, the portal swallows us into its frigid depths. Kaleidoscopes of color swirl around, nauseating, blinding.

Unlike our usual trips—if one can call using portals usual—winds buffet our bodies, gusts of ice-shards scraping across our skin like talons. No wonder Smythe clutches me to him like diamonds in a heist. What happens if we blow away in here?

Whoever said, there is nothing to fear but fear itself, had clearly never traveled through a portal.

A brush of warmth caresses my arm. The other side of the wormhole.

And where we arrive makes me wish we'd stayed in the portal.

Chapter 12

The roar of an engine growls into the frigid light show, my first warning of trouble. Air gusts against my arm, a blast of what should be cold appears warm after the colder than outer space of the portal. My vision kicks in at the same moment the portal dissipates.

Shit, shit, shit, shit, shit.

My muscles tense from fear or adrenaline, I'm not sure which. Smythe has lost his ever-lovin' mind.

I notice the minion the same time he notices us.

"Fucking hell!" he screeches, swerving the car to the left, as if to get away from his newest passengers. The left tires bounce across the shoulder, skid on the grass of the median.

Yep. We've materialized inside the minion's car, Smythe sitting on the front seat, me sideways in his lap facing the driving evil. Good thing Smythe still has a death-grip on me as the next yank the minion gives the steering wheel propels the wheels back onto what looks like 75 North, halfway to Oklahoma. But instead of evening out, we cross the two lanes of highway to veer onto the shoulder.

Holy shit.

Smythe releases me with a push. "Wheel!"

Time slows as small details come into focus. We're in a 70s muscle car. 70s muscle cars don't have airbags. If the minion slams on the brakes, my ass will be splattered on the highway in a nice shatter of windshield glass.

The minion's eyes narrow. His leg twitches as if he read my mind.

All that happens in a blink of an eye.

And then I move, grabbing the steering wheel, jerking us back onto the lightly-trafficked highway. The minion elbows me, but I hang on to the wheel. I need to get the car to stop, but the nasty minion stomps on the accelerator. Using the wheel as leverage, I shift and throw my left leg across the console, shoe reaching toward the brake.

The minion releases the gas pedal, slamming his jean-clad knee upward, trapping my bare shin between minion leg and the dashboard. Ouch, ouch, ouch! I glare at the minion. His shit-eating grin causes the spit to dry in my mouth. I read my death in his eyes, and shivers cascade down my spine like a waterfall of ice.

A flash of skin to my left, and Smythe's fist slams into the minion's head, rocking it against the driver's side window, hard enough to break the glass. Anyone else would be unconscious. The minion just shakes his head.

Shit.

Lucky for me, Smythe's hit distracts him so he no longer focuses on me. Instead, he unfastens his seat belt, lunges across the seat and slams his fist into Smythe's face.

Somehow I manage to swing my right leg over the console, but before I can put my foot on the brake, the minion kicks me in the arm and ribs. The air explodes from my lungs. Pain bursts red-hot. He does it again, one foot in my aching ribs, one against my head right over my temple.

Black spots dart across my vision.

Movement seems sluggish.

Shallow breaths hurt.

I stomp on the brake too hard and bump against the steering wheel. We're on the shoulder, but I have no memory of driving us there. I need to help Smythe, but the inside of the car spins, flickering dots flooding my vision.

"Gin!" Smythe's yell startles me, I need to...

Do what?

I can't think straight.

I need to...

What?

Fight! The silent yell screams through my veins, driving away the black spots of my vision, filling me with a healthy dose of anger.

Adrenaline spikes through my system, making me forget about my bruised ribs, my flickering vision, allowing me to focus on the fight next to me.

Smythe has one arm around the minion's neck, another around his chest, both legs pinning the minion's against the seat and console. Eyes wide, the minion faces me, staring at my right hand. No, he stares at the sword jutting from the bracelet, the silver gleaming in the glare of sunlight. A snarl splits his lips. Laughter, interspersed with garbled words, bubbles out his mouth.

"The thirteenth! I'll be damned. You have no idea what they want. No idea."

"Who's they?" And what do they want with me?

"Gin." Smythe growls my name, the urgency in his tone vibrating my hair follicles to attention.

Or maybe those prickles were from the maniacal

laughter of the minion.

The noise fills the car, turning the bright space chill with malice. He's still laughing when I slam the sword under his ribs, into his heart. His eyes widen as the sword strikes home, the snarl permanently etched on his lips. A gray mist floats out of the wound, hissing into steam where it touches the sword. Smythe relaxes his hold, shoving the body onto the floorboard.

The sword disappears, reforming into the bracelet, taking with it the anger flooding my veins. And my vision.

"Oh, shit," Smythe reaches for me, but unconsciousness embraces me first, and I fall headfirst into its soft depths.

****

Warmth surrounds me, comforting, healing. Beckoning me to wake. Pulling me from the darkness. My eyes open and I suck in air, trying to calm my heartbeat's pounding dance.

Red eyes, surrounded by gold frames, peer down at me, unfocused, the sightless stare of the blind. White-blonde bangs brush the thin eyebrows of a pale face. A light touch brushes against my hair on both sides of my head where her hands hover above my skin. Pulses of healing energy spread down my body. Relaxing. Soothing.

"She's awake, Aidan." Her voice reminds me of a child, high-pitched and vulnerable.

She shifts to the side, keeping her hands in place, and Smythe's head appears beside hers. I lay in the backseat of the minion's car, staring at the ceiling, head by the open door, while the woman and Smythe squat outside. His hand touches my shoulder, squeezes.

"How you feel, Gin?"

"Pretty relaxed, all things considered." The woman's lips turn for a second, her eyes crinkle at the corners. "Who's your friend?"

"This is Eloise, one of the Agency's healers. You were hurt."

Really? Never knew cracked ribs and a head shot caused injury.

But as he noticed and did something about it, I need to be polite. "Thank you."

"Eloise came with the cleanup crew."

Why did it take me until now to notice the stench of the minion's car? It smells like dried blood and baked death despite the car door standing open. I swallow.

I will not puke. I will not puke. I will not puke.

"You did really good today, Gin. Two minions. And on your first day, too." His tone implies enthusiasm for a job well done.

So why did he look so nervous?

His hand squeezes my shoulder before he steps out of my line of vision.

"I'm almost done," Eloise says, "and then you can try to stand. Okay?"

"Sure."

I close my eyes and try not to breath. Less chance of puking that way. I hope.

Despite the violence, the injuries and the scent of death, I like this new venture. Not many of us can rid the world of evil doers and knowing I'm helping to make the world a better place gives me a shot of pride. I'm still not down with killing minions. Yes, I understand it must be done. Evil must be fought. But after having some violence done to me in my younger years, I'm not so eager to turn around and perpetrate the pattern.

"There you go." Eloise slides her hands to the edge of the seat. "Your head is healed. Nasty concussion. Ribs are mostly healed and will be sore until tomorrow. Aidan says you heal quickly."

"Thank you. Do I need to go to the hospital?" Because nothing says emergency care like a set of cracked ribs.

Her lips flatten. Oops. I think I've insulted her. "I'm a healer. Who needs a hospital?"

"I'm sorry." I sit up, thankful my vision stays steady and my ribs barely hurt. Eloise is better than a shot of morphine. "I didn't mean to insult you. I'm new at this."

Her hand touches my arm with a pat, and I'm sucked into her emotions, her thoughts.

Blurry shapes form a landscape devoid of color. I've never peeked into a blind person's mind before and the lack of visual shocks.

Her hand jerks away and she wipes it on her thigh as if it's dirty. "You're an empath."

"How did you know that?" No one has ever known without me telling them.

Except for Smythe.

One hand waves in the air between us. "Never mind." She squints her eyes, sucks in her bottom lip. "Does Aidan know?"

"You mean Smythe?"

One sculpted white brow rises. "He has not told you to address him by his first name?"

"Should he?"

"Hmm. Interesting. Does he know?"

"About the empathetic abilities? Yes." About other things? Hopefully not.

"Very interesting."

"You mentioned that."

"It's been a long time since a *justitia*n has been an empath. Not in my lifetime."

As she appears to be the same age as me, I'm not sure what to make of her statement. "Oh?"

"Come along now. The crew needs to work their magic on this vehicle." She stands, a willowy figure dressed in a gossamer blue flowing dress.

I climb out of the backseat, onto long brown grass waving beside the highway. Sure enough, another Agency cleanup crew mills around the car. Four men talk in hushed tones a few feet from us, two women stand at the hood and trunk, hands turned palms up. Traffic speeds by on 75, not paying attention to the group clustered around the car.

As if they didn't see us.

It dawns on me the two women cast a spell to prevent prying eyes from observing the cleanup crew tampering with a crime scene.

As my DNA litters the crime scene, more power to the two women. Magic on.

"You no longer require my assistance?"

At the sound of Eloise's voice, I turn to see her standing by Smythe. He shakes his head.

"No. Thank you for coming."

"Any time. Good-bye, Gin."

"Thank you."

A smile crosses her lips as she bows her head. One hand faces up, makes a circle in the air chest high. I barely make out a portal before it swallows her and disappears.

I blink a couple of times for good measure, but she doesn't reappear. Smythe takes one look at my face, and his eyes start twinkling.

"She's more advanced at portal forming than I am."

You don't say. "Was she the better student or something? She looks about our age."

"Remember, in my...I mean our line of work, looks can be deceiving."

I swallow. "So how old is she?"

"Let's get you home. It's been a rough day for you."

So much for learning Eloise's age. "Understate things much, Smythe?"

He forms a portal in front of us, a riot of colors exploding in the deceptively warm breeze. His hand closes around mine, tightens. "Nah. Not me." With a grin, he leads me into the portal.

I think he just showed a sense of humor, while simultaneously avoiding the question of Eloise's age. Impossible. Men can't multi-task.

And then the coldness of the portal sweeps away all thoughts not pertaining to survival.

Chapter 13

When we arrive in my living room, my hands are blanched, aching like I stuck them in snow. Hopping distances in the portal rocks, but the chill of the experience makes it difficult to get on board with the new mode of travel. How long does it take to get used to traveling in the equivalent of a deep freeze?

Smythe strides into the kitchen as if the cold doesn't bother him. As if he likes freezing almost to death.

Maybe he does.

Rubbing my crossed arms, I follow. By the time he pops open his laptop and drops into the table chair, the portal's lingering effect on my hands disappears.

"Whatcha looking for?" I stand behind him, peering over his shoulder. It's not Google dancing across the screen. I shift to see better and he moves with me, blocking the screen from view.

"Don't you need to go grocery shop?"

"Don't you need to tell me what you're doing and how old Eloise is?"

His shoulders raise then lower as he sucks in a deep breath and releases it with a noisy puff of air. "Healers age slowly," he tells the computer screen, "so she's older than she looks. And something's off. That's what I'm looking up."

"Off?" Lots of things are off in my life. Which one

is he referring to? Healers aging slowly? Demons inhabiting humans, turning them into minions? Bracelets turning into swords? Plenty of weird and wacky things to choose from, yet I'm sure he'll answer with none of the above.

And he fails to disappoint.

"Don't take this the wrong way," Smythe turns in the chair so he faces me, "I'm proud of your kills today, but minions don't normally congregate in one house. And two kills in one day by a newbie is unheard of. Something's off." He glances at the computer screen, taps it, meets my gaze. "I'm going to find what it is."

"Well, before you do, think you can answer a question?" One of many, but one I've been meaning to ask and keep forgetting in the rush of learning the new job.

His raised brow subs for a response.

"What's the gray mist coming out of the minion when I stab them?"

"You haven't figured that out yet?"

"If I had, you think I'd be asking?"

A corner of his mouth twitches. "It's the part of the demon that animates the minion. When you stab the minion, the demon's spirit tries to return to its host, but the sword damages it, which causes injury to the demon. Enough damage and the thing dies. That's why you only want to kill a minion with a *justitia*."

"Oh." Interesting. That explains why the Agency has a team of *justitians* to hunt minions instead of giving the job to their guardians.

"Any more questions?"

I shake my head, and he swings back around, fingers flying across the keyboard. Good luck to him. I have better things to do. Like change clothes and grocery shop. Eloise's healing took care of my bruises and the beginnings of a sunburn, but did nothing for minion blood splattered on my clothes.

I need another shower.

Smythe still sits in front of the computer when I finish dressing and return to the kitchen. A quick glance at the clock shows three thirty. I should be hungry. Instead, I'm hyped with energy.

And curiosity.

"I'm going to the store. Are you staying here? How does that work?"

"Going to the store?" He turns, one arm draped over the back of the chair, face a mask of seriousness. "You get in the car—"

"Now who's the smartass?" His lips turn, eyes crinkle, as I cross my arms. "No, silly, since you're my guardian, are you with me twenty-four-seven?"

Smythe in possession of a smile is a sight to behold. Aaannnddd, there went the libido, all fired up and ready for some horizontal action.

As if that will happen.

You'd think it would've given up by now.

"Why? Do you want me to be?"

I give him a glare and hope to god he can't read my hormonally-induced fantasies of us getting down and dirty.

"Okay, okay." Why do I get the feeling he read my mind and finds humor in it? "I have an apartment. I'll stay there, you stay here. But when demons or minions strike, we'll need to work together to defeat them."

"Okay. How often is that?" How disrupting is this new gig going to be to my life?

"It depends. Lately there've been a bunch of outbreaks and the *justitians* have been busy. In general though, maybe about once a week."

"And my job?"

"What about it?"

"If I'm at work, I can't just up and leave."

"Most *justitians* don't have jobs."

"Yeah, and I bet they're all independently wealthy, too. Some of us have to work to live, you know. Unless this gig pays?"

"It's not a gig. And it doesn't pay."

I shrug. "No problem. Until it pays, I work my job. Which means if you have a demon or minion outbreak while I'm at work, you can find someone else." The words barely leave my mouth before my *justitia* reacts. Emotions ping through my system, distress racing a sprint through my veins. It does not like my decision. It thinks I should stay home and only hunt minions.

It needs to get over itself.

"You'd rather work a job than fight evil?" Of course Smythe agrees with the *justitia*.

"I didn't say I wouldn't fight minions. What I meant was some of us plebeians have to work for a living. I can't fight evil and expect to pay the bills."

A hint of red stains his cheeks. "Ah. We'll see what we can do."

"You do that." My job is my identity. I worked hard to get into nursing school, to graduate, to overcome enough shit to give a therapist nightmares. I'm proud of what I do, how I help people. I'm sure I'll be proud of conquering minions and taking down demons too, but until it pays, you can find my happy ass in the ER.

"Give us time. It's new for us, too. We've never had a *justitia* go missing and then appear on someone else's wrist. Which makes you a learning curve."

I nod. Makes sense. Maybe they will pay me, eventually. Even if they do fork over the money, do I really want to quit my job? "I'm going shopping." Because I need time to think, to process too many things thrown at me at once.

"I'll be here."

The ol' hormones leap with happiness at that announcement. Down, girls, down. Is there such a thing as a hormone-ectomy?

I shut the back door behind me, take a step to the right on the back porch, and open the garage door. Three stairs down and I'm beside my car.

My butt no sooner hits the seat of my car than Will's face flashes into my mind, bringing with it a healthy dose of guilt. Some friend and co-worker I am. Had I even spared him a thought today?

Picking up my phone, I make a quick call to the ER and speak with Sally Ann. No changes. But he was still alive, which was pretty amazing considering the number of bullets he took to the chest.

Guilt assuaged, I drive to the grocery store, buy groceries, and return home. The trip was supposed to help me think and process my getting-crazier-by-the-day life. Instead I spent all my time driving the cart up and down the aisles looking for deals. Deals I found. Thinking and processing? Not so much.

I lug my deals and groceries into the kitchen. Smythe remains parked in front of his laptop, jaw tense enough to crack nuts. Guess he didn't find what he wanted.

And where was he looking anyway? Minions for Dummies? Website of the Walking Evil? Minions-R-Us?

"Un-fucking-believable. There is nothing on here. Nothing!"

Fists slap against the table and I freeze mid-reach into the pantry. Taking a deep breath, I put the mac & cheese on the shelf and shut the pantry door. "Maybe you're looking in the wrong place?"

His glare ices my skin and I squeeze my hands until they blanch. But manage a grin. He's frustrated, not crazy angry. I've dealt with worse.

"Huh. I don't look in wrong places." The fingers of one hand drum a beat against his laptop. "I'm missing something."

I continue to put away the groceries. Milk on the top shelf of the fridge. Apples in the crisper. Tension dissolves from my neck as I work. You'd think after all this time, I'd stop reacting to certain sounds.

Facing him, I lean against the pantry door, trying to appear nonchalant. "Maybe you need some rest."

One blink. Two. "Yeah. Maybe."

I cross my arms, willing myself to come across as his equal, not some simpering mass of irrational fear.

"Yeah." His eyes take in my posture, narrow. "Well, then. I'll stop by tomorrow."

"I'll be at work. Make it around eight in the evening. After I get off."

"Okay." He snaps the laptop closed, drums his fingers on top of the case. His mouth opens, closes, eyes focus on me as if they see through my skin into my psyche. Maybe he does.

Scary thought.

A grin turns his lips as he opens a portal against the wall behind the table. "Good night."

"See ya."

He steps into the opening, laptop clutched under his arm. Warm air gushes out like a wave, before the portal sucks it back like an uber-vacuum. A small pop later and I'm alone in the kitchen.

Nothing but me and my thoughts.

Great.

Might as well get dinner started. Comfort food coming up. Putting a pot of water on to boil, I begin the prep for chicken and spinach lasagna. Homemade. Lasagna might not be the healthiest thing, but neither is minion killing. Healthy no longer seems to fit in the playbook.

I'm putting the lasagna in the oven when I see T drive up, parking in the driveway. He pulls out two plastic bags and heads toward the front door. I set the oven for an hour and begin to rinse the dishes, which is where T finds me, dish mid-way between the sink and dishwasher. He gives me a noogie as he talks.

"How's my favorite sister doing? Is that asshole still around?"

"I'm fine." I put the dish in the rack and give him a hug. "It's Smythe, and he's gone home for the day."

"Don't think I like him much." One finger tilts my chin back, turning my head from side to side. "That bruise is gone. Cover-up?"

"Nope." I hold up my wrist. "The bracelet makes me heal fast."

"Impossible."

"Believe it."

"Humph. Your day good?" He speaks into the open

fridge as he pulls out a beer.

I turn back to my dish clean-up, wondering where he put the bags. Definitely not in the kitchen. "Yep." What do I say? Killed a couple of nasty minions today and oh, by the way, saw the old house and graveyard. Remember that one?

Yeah, right.

I snap my mental shields in place on the off chance he gets a notion to snoop around in my head. "You?"

He shrugs. "When's dinner gonna be ready?"

"An hour. Where's Jackie?"

"Home."

"Then why are you here?"

"What? A brother can't stop in and check on his hurt sister who harbored a grade A asshole on the couch?"

"Course he can." I grin. "Whatcha got in the bags?"

"A bit of this and that for a project. Unless you need help, I'm going to go watch the Rangers and work on the project."

"What project?"

"You'll see." He tweaks my nose as he saunters into the living room. A moment later the sound of the Rangers' ballgame fills the kitchen.

Project? I hear plastic rustle over the roar of cheering fans. Leaning back, so I have a clear visual shot into the living room, I see T by the window, something in his hand. I squint, trying to see what he's holding, what he's doing.

Then my cell rings, snapping me out of spy duty. I scramble across the kitchen, hands dripping water, trying to find the thing on the table. The screen flashes

Blake's picture as I swipe my finger across the talk symbol.

"Hey, babe!"

"Hey yourself." Blake's rich chocolate baritone reaches across the airwaves, soothing, relaxing. "Whatcha doing?"

"Cooking dinner."

"Which is?"

"Chicken and spinach lasagna."

"Mind if I stop by?"

"Of course not! T's here for dinner, too."

A long pause. "All right. I'll be there in thirty depending on traffic."

"Where's Jordan?"

"Does it matter?"

I should feel guilty about being the other woman. About wanting more out of our relationship than the occasional sleep over. But I don't. "I guess not."

"See you in thirty."

He hangs up before I respond. Now that was interesting. Blake doesn't usually offer to drop by when he's dating someone. It might make me a bad person, but I don't care. His relationships are his own problem.

I return to rinsing the dishes, then move on to buttering the loaf of French bread and making a salad. Got to have those greens for health.

Or so they say.

Mid-way through the salad prep, T walks into the kitchen and opens the door under the sink, pitching two salt containers into the trash.

I place the knife on the cutting board, turn to face him. "Salt?"

He shrugs, closes the cabinet door. "Bad ghost last

night. Thought salt and iron around the windows would help."

"Oh. Thanks." You know you live a bizarre life when you don't bat an eye at a comment like that. "You didn't do the windows in here."

"Not finished yet."

"You think it's coming back?"

He shrugs. "No idea. Figured it's better safe than sorry."

"Good thinking. By the way, Blake's stopping by. Going to join us for dinner."

Emotions play across his face, flit then fade, too quick to identify. A soft touch brushes against my mind, a whisper of a thought. Blake doesn't bother him like Smythe does, but he'd prefer me not to get involved with either of them.

Fat chance.

Another shrug, shoulders rolling as if he doesn't care. Name me a person who likes their sibling's significant other on first sight and I'll show you a Blue Shores client. T thinks Blake jerks me around, promises me forever and then leaves me high and dry. I think Jackie's too dumb to live.

As long as we keep our mouths shut, we all get along fine.

"Okay. I need to finish up the window in here."

"Have at." I wave my hand toward the window and turn back to the cutting board. Sliced tomatoes coming up.

T finishes coating the windowsill with salt the same time I finish the salad. No Blake and the lasagna still has another ten minutes. Our gazes meet, my thoughts reflecting in his eyes. Beer, couch, game. The comfort of the others' touch.

I put the bread in the oven, the salad in the fridge, grab two bottles and follow him into the living room.

Chapter 14

Ding-dong! The peal of the doorbell yanks me from where my imagination floats on a peaceful sea, depositing me into reality. My beer sits untouched on the coffee table, sweat beading off the bottle, rolling down to sink into the thirsty-stone coaster. I blink a couple of times for good measure before releasing my hand from T's.

The loss of his grip disorients me, shakes me free of that sense of grounding which binds us together in our own private universe. Reality slaps me in the face, nauseating, prickling my awareness with an overwhelming sense of unease. Unease at leaving his side, at venturing out on my own. Touching the other brings us a sense of calm, of peace, a bliss missing in our daily lives. Especially when one or both of us has had a lousy day. Killing minions might be part of my new job duties, but seeing them dead qualifies as pretty damn lousy.

Ding-dong!

"Coming!" I yell, ignoring T, who rubs his ear like my scream damaged his hearing.

My feet hit the ground, and I grab onto the arm of the couch for balance. Withdrawal from bliss-land is a bitch. Dizziness crashes over me, drenching my sense of balance. But like a receding tide, the feeling of vertigo slips away, giving me a temporary reprieve from uneasiness.

It will return. It always does.

The oven buzzer sounds right when I grab the doorknob. Cacophony in House Crawford.

"I'll get it," T mutters, drawing a hand over his head, rubbing the millimeter long hair strands as if they bring good luck. He staggers into the kitchen holding our beers as I twist the knob.

Then release it as a shot of adrenaline races across shattered nerves. Ohgodohgodohgod what if it's another minion come to kill me? Opening the door lets in evil guys on a vengeance mission. WhatdoIdowhatdoIdowhatdoIdo?

Get a fucking grip, Gin. You've killed every minion you've come up against, what's another one? But the fear mind-fucks my nervous system, overriding my common sense. My hands shake, palsied flesh covering fragile bones. *Get a grip, Gin.* Deep breaths. In and out, in and out.

Ding-dong!

"Gin?" T stands in the doorway between the living room and the kitchen, brows furrowed, concern stamped on his face like a tattoo. T's in the room. T won't let the evil minion get me.

T being in the room knocks the panic back a notch, allowing me to think. Stupid panic attack. I know better. There's not a minion on the front porch. And even if there is, I wear the *justitia*. No reason to panic.

But just to be sure it's not Evil Guy Part Two, I put my eye to the peephole and spy Blake loosening his tie, pulling the knot away from his neck. Sweat beads on his forehead, a side effect of standing in the hot Texas sun.

See, Gin? All that panic for nothing.

The rapid fluttering of an over-excited heart smoothes into a more normal rhythm. Hard to believe I killed two minions today and one last night, and yet I allow a panic attack to overwhelm me.

Some demon slayer I am.

I yank open the door, plastering a grin on my lips, hoping it masks the last remnants of fear.

Blake stands on the porch, looking spiffy—albeit a touch overheated—in a charcoal gray suit. A red and white striped tie hangs in a loose knot over a white shirt, top button undone. Oh, yeah. Mister Sexy has arrived.

And all traces of the panic attack disappear.

Score one for the lawyer.

"Hi, lover. It took you long enough." He bends, gives me a kiss, his tongue slipping past my lips.

Gotta love a man who isn't afraid to show passion in public. Not that I saw any neighbors on the street, but still, it's the action that counts.

"Sorry." I mutter as my arms wrap around his neck and I take a step backward, silently encouraging him to follow me into the house. His arms snug around my waist, tighten, lift. I break the kiss, let out a small screech as my feet leave the ground. His dark chuckle ripples like chocolate waves across my skin, delicious and sinful. Very sinful.

"Blake!" My voice trails off on a giggle.

His lips find mine as his foot kicks the door shut.

"Dinner's ready."

Blake and I startle, take a step away from each other as T's words pierce our greeting. I swear my brother spoke on purpose, interrupting our passion for his own personal glee.

Not that I've ever done anything like that to him. Nope. Not me.

"Heya, T." Blake holds out his hand, acts like nothing happened, like slipping me the tongue at the door was an every day occurrence.

T plays nice, shakes Blake's hand, manages to glare without looking too threatening.

"Let me get the table set. Dinner'll be ready in a minute." On my way to the kitchen, I grab T's arm, tug. No sense leaving him alone with Blake. God only knows what will happen.

You can do better than him.

He's my friend. And the sex is good.

Dark thoughts move in T's mind, thoughts I understand and sometimes share. For now, I ignore them, ignore the implication.

"Here." I shove three plates into T's chest, holding on until he grabs them. "Set the table. Please."

The lasagna sits on the stove, steam rising, circling a dance before it dissipates into the air. I cut it into squares, lay a spatula on top, put on mitts and carry the dish to the table. Without being asked, T placed a trivet in the middle of the table, and I set the casserole dish on top of it. No sense burning the table. It might be cheap, but so far it still looks nice.

Blake strides into the kitchen, sans jacket and tie, grabs a beer from the fridge and sits in the chair closest to the back door. I place the salad on the table and wave my hand over the food.

"Dinner is served."

It doesn't take long for the men to consume half the lasagna, three-fourths of the bread and the entire salad with only mild complaints. Yes, chicken and spinach are better for you than sausage and ground meat. No, you may not complain and expect to be served again tomorrow.

Want a man to stop complaining? Deny him food.

Works every time with these two.

After dinner T leaves to hook up with Jackie, stating he'll return later to salt the doors. Apparently doors require him to remove the threshold and pour salt underneath. Then he has to replace the threshold and poof, no more ghosts.

Not that I'm having a problem with the invisible buggers, but pouring salt seems to make him happy and who am I to complain about his happiness.

The door clicks shut behind him, leaving Blake and me alone. Yeehaw. Ride 'em cowboy.

Although the practical, neat side of me screams to clean the kitchen first.

Damn practical voice.

"So, what's going on with you?" Blake pushes his chair back, hands cradling his beer, fingers slick with the bottle's sweat.

Where to start? With the obvious or a lie?

Since when do I lie to Blake?

"You won't believe me."

"You said that last night." He waits, twisting the bottle in his hands.

I lick my lips, swallow. Grab the plate, the ceramic cool against the pads of my fingers, and shove my chair back. "It's rather hard to believe."

"Worse than empathic abilities?"

I turn on the water, let it wash over my plate, food particles swirling down the drain. Like my life, the nicely built lie swirling away in a rush of discoveries.

"It's a long story. And confusing."

"Hey, I'm a lawyer, remember? I specialize in confusing." He smiles, his eyes getting in on the happy action, his demeanor willing me to confide.

What's the harm? While I wouldn't tell just anyone about my new bracelet and the powers joined to it, Blake was my friend, my lover.

Sharing went with the territory.

"It's weird."

"You've said that."

"Fine." And I tell him, turning to face him, watching the emotions, the surprise, play across his features as he struggles to grasp the idea of evil walking among us.

He's silent as I grab the lasagna, cover it with foil and stick it into the fridge. Maybe he doesn't believe me. Maybe he thinks I've finally slipped into la—la land.

Maybe he's reciting poetry in his head.

"I don't know what to say."

"I gathered that."

A swig from his bottle, his Adam's apple bobbing in desperation. I continue to clean up, letting him stew over his words, his emotions. Learning evil exists and walks among us, that women wear bracelets which turn into swords to fight minions, that a war is being fought—and lost—daily, takes awhile to grasp.

If ever.

"You kill these, um, minions, was it?" He looks a little pale.

"They're evil cloaked in a human's skin."

"How do they get in there?"

"I think some humans are more susceptible than others."

He swallows. "What's it like to kill one?"

The *justitia* comes to life, filling me with pleasure, with pride. It likes killing, enjoys the hunt, longs to rid the world of evil.

"I dunno," liar, liar, "I just do it." As if I'm the poster child for a pair of running shoes.

"What happens to the bodies?"

I explain the cleanup crew. Should I even explain these things to a lawyer? Even if he doesn't do criminal cases?

My fingers itch to touch him. Itch to see if he really believes me or if he's planning a way to get me admitted to Blue Shores.

His lips twist, eyes blink. "You're telling me, some crew comes along and makes it look like something besides that thing's—" one finger points at my bracelet "—sword killed the guy?"

"Yep."

"Damn. Imagine the crimes you could commit with a crew like that."

"What? Are you some sort of psycho killer now?" I lean against the counter, arms crossed, offering him a grin.

He laughs. "Nah. You're right, that's pretty unbelievable."

"But you believe me, right?" *You don't think I should spend the rest of my life at Blue Shores?*

He upends the bottle, swallows several times. "Love, I believe whatever story you say." He sets the bottle on the table, focuses on my eyes. "Tell me you want me to stay the night, and I'll believe that, too."

I catch his gaze, my grin disappearing under a layer of seriousness. "It's easy to believe things you already know for truth."

His lips twitch. "Yeah, well, what can I say?"

"Are you sure? What about Jordan?"

"Eh." His hand gives a dismissive flip. "She probably won't notice."

"Bad times at the Okay Corral?"

"It's about time to end it. Besides, I think she's found someone else."

"I'm sorry."

"I'm not." He gets up, leaving the bottle on the table, and walks toward me. Gathers me into his arms. "I have more believable things planned."

"Oh? Do tell."

"Why don't I show instead?"

A man of action. What more could a woman want?

Chapter 15

I drive into my driveway a bit before eight at night. I half expect to see Blake's car in front, parked like a diamond on a hooker's finger, but the road in front of my house sits empty.

Guess he's not stopping by tonight.

A seed of disappointment roots in my chest, spreads outward. I shake it off. He promised last night to stop by and stay over, but men will promise most anything in the middle of doing the dirty, so I shouldn't have taken him seriously.

But I did. And now I'm disappointed.

Boo-hoo. Ah, well, several more hours remain before I need to go to sleep. Blake still has time to get his fine ass over here and sex me up.

Oh, crap. Smythe was due over, too. And not in the three's company type of way either.

Great. Just great. After the day I had, the last thing I need is a lesson in demon killing and *justitia* powers.

Flipping down the visor, I punch the garage door opener, waiting not so patiently for the door to rise. I need to eat, but all I want to do is prop my aching feet up. Preferably around Blake's waist, but I'll take sitting on the couch with the feet on the coffee table.

Thinking about sex with Blake puts me in my happy place. Although, after the news we received today, I'm pretty much already Miss Happy-happy-joy-

joy.

Will stabilized, amazing the ICU doctors.

And the entire ER staff. None of us thought he'd live. Although we're still holding our collective breaths on the matter. A lot could go wrong between now and full recovery.

The open garage beckons, and I ease my foot off the brake. A rope with a STOP HERE sign attached to it hangs from the ceiling, letting me know how far to pull my car forward. Tonight the hanging rope reminds me of a patient, and I chuckle as I hit the button to close the garage door.

The rope looks like a vine. And why is that funny? I get out of the car, grab my purse, slam the door shut, all the while thinking about that ER patient. The woman walked stiff-legged into the ER, the gait of a newly broke-in cowboy or someone with a stick up their ass. When I went into her exam room to ask what problem brings her in, I'm informed her jojo has vines growing out of it.

After seeing the blank look on my face, she gestured toward her crotch and yanked down her pants and panties. Yep, definitely vines growing where no vines should grow.

My lips twitch as I reach into my purse, grab out the keys to the back door, remembering Dr. Patterson's face as he saw the vines in the patient's "jojo". Someone had informed our patient potatoes worked as a type of birth control. Insert one in and they stop sperm from fertilizing an egg.

Unfortunately they forgot to tell her to remove the potato after use.

Chuckling, I stick the key into the lock on the back

door, twist then turn the knob. Throwing the deadbolt with one hand, I flip the light switch with the other, bathing the kitchen in a nice glow. When I turn, the laughter dies in my throat as it's a bit hard to laugh while sucking in a gasp.

The cold shot of fear drenching my system turns into anger bathed in wariness.

"What are you doing in my house, Samantha?"

She leans against the sink, arms crossed, back to the window, the dying sunlight a dull gleam on her bleached locks. Her eyes narrow into small slits of ire. "You're late."

Oh? Since when am I on her schedule? Since when is she supposed to have anything to do with me? Clearly interacting with the new white trash *justitian* is not her idea of a fun time.

"Excuse me? I didn't hear your answer. Why are you in my house?"

A blast of hatred coats me, tendrils threatening suffocation. My memory jumps back to when I touched her arm and saw her inner essence. Not evil in the sense of a minion's vileness, more like bitterness and disgust weaving a tangled mess through her soul.

Bitterness and disgust now directed at me.

Pushing off from the counter, away from the gasping rays of sunlight, her arms drop to her sides, her combat boots thunking against tile. The door hits my butt as I reach behind, fumbling for the doorknob, my damp palm slipping off the metal.

I should not fear her. I wear the *justitia*. I fight and kill minions. A bleached blonde bitch should not make me afraid. And yet as I watch her come closer, drawing out her steps as if she enjoys seeing the fear spreading through me, none of those thoughts stop an irrational jolt of full-body shivers from coursing through my veins.

Damn shame the sword only appears around minions. Whatever else Samantha was, a minion was not it.

She stops an arm's reach from me. "You're needed. There's been a minion outbreak in San Antonio. A big one. We're taking all the *justitians* in the States to fight."

"Why didn't Smythe come?"

"He's busy. And you're later than I thought you'd be. We need to get going now."

"Can I change?"

"Are you kidding? Put your purse down and get your *justitia* ready."

"How do I get it ready?" I put the purse on the table, face the bleached blonde bitch.

One fine brown brow rises. "Damn. You are so freaking new. I'll need to talk to Smythe about his training. Again."

She sticks her hand out, palm facing the door. Before I can blink, a portal forms, a rush of air beckoning, deceptive in its warmth.

"Come on." Grabbing my upper arm so her palm rests against my scrub top sleeve, she yanks me into the portal.

It happens so fast I fail to react, fail to resist, fail to do anything but follow. The ice chill of the wormhole sucks my breath away, a plunge into the North Sea would be warmer. The trip seems longer than normal. Due to distance? Or Samantha's portal forming skill?

And then I'm stumbling onto solid ground, tripping

over grass strands as my body tries to adapt to re-entrance into reality. Stillness surrounds us, not the sounds of chaos I expect, but the quietness of an evening stroll along a tree-covered trail. Insects chirp their twilight sounds as pinks and oranges splash across leaves and grass, bathing the park in peace.

A park? What the hell? Where's the fight?

"Told you she'd come. Don't forget our deal." Samantha's voice carries over the insects, quieting their chatter.

A man steps out from the trees, only a man, but the *justitia* reacts. Fire shoots along my nerves, sending my body into fight mode. My bad. Not a man. A minion. Dead ahead. And about to just be dead.

And then another minion joins him. Followed by another and another and another until the park resembles an overcrowded stadium waiting for a sporting event.

Or a set up.

I knew I shouldn't have trusted that bitch. What had I been thinking?

Hoping to get an emotion hit from touching Samantha, I whip around, reaching for her arm. But the bitch evades my grasp, jumps into another portal without even a fare-thee-well. I leap, but the damn thing shuts before I make it, and I crash into the ground, skinning my palms. Jiminy Christmas that hurt.

"Little *Justitian*." Minion Number One's voice scrapes across my skin like a dull razor, tearing goosebumps into my flesh. "Where's your guardian?" He walks toward me, each step sending a jolt of panic through my system not even the *justitia's* joy can erase.

I stand as the others fall in behind him, a vee of

death directed my way.

Shit, shit, shit. Why did I believe Samantha? Because I didn't think she'd plan for my death. Hate me, yeah. But kill me?

Now I knew better.

The *justitia* springs to life, the sword shooting outward like flames from a blowtorch. The first minion reaches over his shoulder, pulls a sword from a hidden back sheath, twisting it so the remaining sunlight reflects in flashes which dance around the park. If he thinks one of those light flashes is going to blind me, he has another thing coming.

I jump to the left, out of the way of light flashing off his sword. A glance shows the other minions standing back, unarmed, a waiting mass of evil. Maybe they decided to be sporting and only take me on one at a time.

Even so, twenty or so to one was not sporting at all.

If I get out of this—*when I get out of this*—Samantha is dead.

Minion Number One rushes me, sword swinging. Despite my lack of training, my arm counters his swing, metal screeching against metal. He disengages, kicks out, but I sidestep the blow, my body's movements not my own. Under normal circumstances knowing I'm controlled by an entity fused to my nervous system would bother me.

But these circumstances were far from normal.

Control away bracelet.

Number One steps back, gesturing for another minion to take his place. The next one obeys, pulling his sword from another back sheath. Really? Some outfitting store must have made a fortune off these guys.

I don't have time for thoughts, they fade away under the onslaught of blows. Blows which I block. Block. Parry. Thrust. The minion grabs his stomach, drops his sword, falls in slow-mo to the ground.

One down. The rush of adrenaline spikes through my blood, giving me an expectation of survival. I will win.

No other choice exists. My vow to see Samantha dead remains a strong motivation to live.

Following some minion attack rule, they engage me one at a time and one at a time they die. It's as if adrenaline supercharges my body, hyping it into a killing machine. Invincible. Unstoppable.

And then one of them gets a slice in, their sword cutting through the muscle in my thigh. Pain explodes along sensitive nerves, stiffening my breath, quickening my heart rate.

I stumble, almost fall. Blood runs down my leg, into my sneaker, bringing with it a good dose of nausea. Yep, I can assist in emergency operations, stabilize mangled bodies, but the sight of my own blood makes me gag.

The thought no sooner arises than the bracelet squelches it, overrides the nausea and pain, forcing both to recede.

Bitchin'.

Score one for the *justitia*.

It might stop the nausea and pain, but can do nothing for the leak. The cut missed an artery, but still manages to soak my scrub bottoms.

I'm so busy looking at the slice in my leg, that I miss the minion's uppercut until I'm flat on my back, staring at a darkening sky. Another round of pain rushes in, dances a jig on my jaw, my head. My eyes close and when I force them open, the minion stands over me.

His sword raises, descends. I roll, then jump to my feet, stumbling as weight lands on my injured leg. A quick adjust to my posture. A swing of my sword. The sharp metal blade slices through his neck easy as cutting through chocolate pudding. Body and head drop in two different directions.

Gross.

"You think you're so smart, don't you?" Minion Number One's voice snaps through my conscious, pulling me into better off forgotten memories. That voice. The tone. Those words.

I shake my head. It's nonsense. Just my imagination playing tricks.

Dropping into a fighting stance—one foot back, knees loose—I raise my sword, facing the nearest minion.

"You're nothing but a whore. A split-tailed whore!"

Number One might be standing on the edge of the fight, but his voice slams into me with the force of a tornado and I stumble. Buried memories burst free of their confines, swamping me in a rush of emotion, a thick terrifying fear.

A fear even the *justitia* can't control. A fear of a ghost, of an evil killed well over a decade ago. It should not control me.

And yet it does.

Memories surround me. Pain. Terror. Sounds of flesh smacking flesh. Blood, a coppery taste filling my mouth, clogging my nostrils.

"You'll never be worth nothing. You're a wasted piece of human flesh!" Whose voice? Past or present? Dead or alive?

Maybe the voice is right. Maybe I am worth nothing.

Gin! T's voice screams through my mind, painful enough to stop the wisps of memories from congealing into reality.

I shake my head, trying to clear the memories from my vision. *T! Get me out of here!*

My head snaps back, the force of the minion's punch sailing me around.

Where are you?

The ground rises to meet me. I smack it hard, but manage to roll. The minion's foot stomps where my body was.

I don't know. Some park. Get Smythe.

Nausea sneaks in, a sucker punch to the stomach. Apparently the bracelet has no way of counteracting memories and any feelings those memories might cause. I risk a glance at Minion Number One.

Where the fuck is Smythe?

My house. I close my connection to T. Talking creates too much of a distraction. Not as much of a distraction as the minion's words—holy shit, how did he know to say those words—but an unneeded distraction nonetheless.

A shit-eating grin plasters across Number One's face, widening into a showing of teeth that foretells my death. The hairs on my nape stand at attention as despite my best intentions, memories creep across the edges of my vision.

A kick to my leg snaps my attention to the fight. A

fight I'm going to lose if I don't get my mind in the game. My thigh turns into a screaming ball of agony, throbbing with each heartbeat.

"Worthless tramp! You are nothing! Nothing!"

I feel my body shut down like it had all those years ago. Before I learned to fight, to overcome.

But I learned, hadn't I?

My attention snaps back to the present. I focus on the pain beating through my body, focus on each agonizing breath I take. Allow it to drive me back into the fight.

And once I return to the present, the *justitia* overrides screeching nerve endings, shutting down the pain better than a dose of morphine. Go team Gin.

Striking out with my legs, I catch the kicking minion's feet and twist. The bastard lands on his back, an overturned turtle. Then I'm on top, stabbing into his chest, into the heart.

Another one bites the dust. Only to be replaced by his comrade.

I kill it, but not before it slices a thin gash in my left arm. More blood. More nausea shut down by the bracelet. My breath comes in shallow pants. Spots dance along the edge of my vision. It hurts to stand. Hurts to move my arm. Hurts to move my jaw, my head.

Yet another one engages me.

I fight. I always fight. It's part of my core strength to never give up. Never. Not since that day...

"You are nothing!"

Bam! Another minion's fist slams into my already bruised jaw, and I feel something crack. My vision grays, black spots appearing at the edges, insects swarming carrion. The ground slaps against my back, my mind screams to move, the *justitia* joining its cry, my body unable to obey.

A brush of warm air caresses my going-numb arm, driving away the chill creeping through my veins, the knowledge of imminent death. The swarming black dots overtaking my vision recede as the bracelet tries to get me to move, to fight. I lay staring up, one eye swelling shut, one open wide, so I see the minion, sword raised, when he aims the weapon straight at my heart.

Roll! My body refuses to obey my mind's command.

Death descends, and I can do nothing but watch.

Chapter 16

Before the sword makes contact, the minion flies backward, a possessed human bowling ball as it topples several of its buddies like pins on a lane. My breath freezes in my throat then rushes out in an expression of relief. No judgment day for me.

At least not today.

A cry of an enraged animal slams through the park, coating the trees with its anger until leaves drip with its agony, until the ground vibrates under its wrath. The scream condenses into one word, gaining in intensity, distorted until almost unintelligible. "Noooooo!"

It hurts to move. Hurts to turn my head and see who yells, whose rage blankets the park with a sulfuric stench. And then it hurts to see as the mass of minions explode into flames. Fire consumes their bodies, the screams of death and the stench of burning flesh filling the clearing, eradicating the sulfur stench of rage. I roll onto my side and retch, gagging on bile, my stomach empty of all but the knowledge I'm saved.

"You fucking son of a bitch!" Smythe, my hero, my savior, moves into my line of vision, a sword at the ready, engaging Minion Number One in a dance to the death. Since when does he carry a sword?

And damn me for a fool, but can the man move. The minion is no match for him. None. It's like watching Ray Park fight Liam Neeson in *The Phantom*

Menace. In the end, the minion's head flies in one direction, his body in the other.

Smythe stumbles to me, drops to his knees, his face a mask of grief overlaid with rage. Shadows from the now-dying minion bonfire dance across his skin, his clothes, dance but come no closer. One hand reaches toward my face, draws back. "Oh, Gin."

I blink, or try to, the swelling in my left eye—the eye on top—prohibits much movement. But he notices. Grief vanishes in a rush of anger.

"What the fuck did you think you were doing? Taking on a troop of fucking minions by yourself? Goddamn it, Gin!"

Hey, it wasn't my idea. But I can't form the words. My only movement the open and close of my right eye, the flicker of my left. I want to thank him, but my mouth is full of blood, of pain, my tongue thick against my teeth. My lips fail to work right, moving with the motions of a grounded fish. I reach a hand toward him, fingers brushing against the denim of his jeans.

"You were supposed to be at home." The words hiss as he pulls a knife from somewhere behind him. Light flashes on metal, bathing the blade orange, as he cuts off two strips of material from my scrub bottoms. His hand holding the knife reaches behind him—maybe he re-sheaths it, maybe he drops it on the ground, I can't see what happens to it—he then grabs a strip of fabric and wraps it around the cut in my arm. The other strip he wraps around my leg.

He's shaking as he ties the knots, as he lifts me into his arms.

I cry out at the movement, then force my lips together and my eyes shut. I will not act like a baby. I will not. But I want to cry, to shake, to wail with agony. Whatever the bracelet does no longer works. and my body throbs in time to each heartbeat.

A moment of warmth followed by the frosty air of the portal, the cold freezing my blood like an ice pack on a bruise. For once it feels good, being inside the cold agony as it eases my pain, but all too soon we arrive in my living room.

Smythe lays me on the couch. Darkness shrouds the room, the hum of the overworked air conditioning a relief. I'm home. I'm alive. I'm going to kill that blonde bitch.

Provided someone can stop the leak in my leg. Judging from the way I feel lightheaded lying down, that someone is not me.

"Gin! What the hell happened?" T storms in from the kitchen, shoes thudding against wood.

My lips refuse to move. Not a problem. Telepathy to the rescue. *Samantha set me up.*

The overhead light flips on as Smythe finds the switch. I squint in the sudden brightness, head throbbing. Being hurt sucks.

Who's Samantha?

Some guardian bitch.

The floor squeaks as Smythe walks back into my line of vision. You know there's a problem when the two stand beside each other without puffing up on aggression.

I must look worse than I feel.

"Who the hell," T grabs Smythe's shoulder, "is Samantha, and why did you leave her alone with my sister?"

Oops. I spoke too soon.

Men. I swear. It's a wonder they survived evolution.

Smythe shrugs out of T's grasp, the air around him vibrating his rage. He sucks down a breath, then another one, tension melting down his frame.

"Do. Not. Touch. Me. Again."

T, leave him alone! He just fried a dozen minions with a word! The last thing I need is for my twin to become a testosterone-fueled shish kabob. For a second I thought T would take a swing, but he raises both hands, takes a step back.

"Sorry. She said Samantha set her up."

"What?" Smythe turns to me, all surprise-surprise until his gaze fastens on my face. "Oh, shit. Don't move." One finger points at T as he reaches into his pocket with his other hand, drawing out his cell phone. Fingers flash and then he slams the thing against his ear. "Eloise, I need your help. Gin's injured. Yeah. Please," his voice breaks, he clears it, "if you don't mind. Okay."

The phone remains next to his ear, but I see the portal form next to him, feel the dash of warmth followed by the appearance of Eloise, hear T's indrawn breath. Smythe turns to her, pockets his phone.

"She's hurt. Took on a whole contingent of minions by herself."

"Show me."

Oh yeah. Blind. Smythe takes her hand, leads her to the couch where he shoves the coffee table out of the way.

"Here." He reaches her hand toward me, pressing down until she squats beside me.

T kneels by my shoes, one hand touching my lower

leg. I'm hurt so bad the usual comfort his touch brings remains elusive.

Eloise's hands touch my face, cool, impartial, no emotions running into me this time. Fingers probe my swollen eye, jaw, run across my arms, down my thighs.

"Hmm. Shallow cut on the arm. Stings more than anything. The left leg's slice is worse. Right leg has massive bruising. Blood loss. Broken nose and maxilla. Not sure about loose teeth. Why weren't you with her?"

"I show up here for training and she's gone. Her brother here—" he gestures toward T as if Eloise sees his hand move "—states she's in the middle of a fight and I need to find her." Surprise, surprise, words really can come from a jaw clenched tighter than a death grasp. "Lucky for her I can track the *justitia*."

He can?

"You can?" Eloise's hands rest on my upper arm, head cocked to the side. Her brow furrows then smoothes.

Smythe shrugs, but she doesn't see it. "Will you heal her?"

"Of course. But her brother needs to remove his hand. Other energy fields interfere with the healing." She looks at T who stares at her with a mixture of an ogle, awe and wariness. But he does as she asks, stepping backward until she motions him to stop.

If I'm not mistaken, my twin is smitten by the healer.

Once T steps far enough away from me, Eloise moves to kneel behind my head, placing her hands over my forehead. "Close your eyes, Gin. Just relax."

A rush of warmth flows over me, across my chest, down my legs, taking with it my pain. And then I'm floating in a sea of bliss, where nothing exists except fluffy clouds and turquoise waves. Time is meaningless here, a minute is like an hour, an hour like a minute. I float. Water befriends me, keeps me adrift, alive. Waves break over sand somewhere close, the in and out of the tide comforting to hear.

I drift.

The tide grabs me, pulling me into the shore, away from the bliss. I fight it. I want to float. To drift.

I have no choice. Clouds crumble, falling like thrown sand into the waves. Even those disappear. Instead of a blue sky, I'm staring at my living room's ceiling, remnants of peace clinging to my skin, a spiritual surgical strip.

I flex my jaw, wiggle my toes. All pain free. And I'm looking out of both eyes.

Eloise rocks.

"Thank you." I tilt my head back, locking gazes with her. Her eyes are unfocused, unseeing, but I get the impression she sees more than she lets on. "I feel much better."

"You're welcome." A tight smile pulls her lips. "You need to be more careful. I cannot heal you every time."

"Thank you." Once I roll to a sit I realize her words aren't just meant for me. She's looking at Smythe.

"Glad to see you up." Relief saturates Smythe's expression, crinkling his eyes, twitching his lips upward.

"It's all Eloise's doing."

"How did you do that?" Awe saturates T's voice, flows into his wide-eyed pole-axed-bull expression.

Eloise rises from her crouch, faces T. "I am a

healer with the Agency. This is what I've been trained to do."

"Thank you for making her better."

She takes several steps toward him, placing her hand on his arm. For a blind woman she navigates well. Perhaps she sees shadows. Because I get the distinct impression she's returning T's ogling with a bit of her own.

Her expression remains peaceful with a hint of a smile, but tension flows around her and T and not the aggressive kind either.

Interesting.

She turns to Smythe, breaking contact with T. Who still looks like a pole-axed bull. Or maybe a love-sick fool?

"He's valuable. Untrained though. Have you done more research on their linage?"

"Valuable?" T blinks and I get a peek inside his thoughts.

And fight to keep my lips from twitching.

His idea of valuable and hers are undoubtedly different. I sincerely doubt she wants to use him as her own personal stud.

She might. And stay out of my head.

A chuckle bursts free, turning all gazes on me.

"Sorry, nothing." I give a dismissive flip of my hand.

Smythe cocks a brow, lowers it as he speaks to Eloise. "Haven't been able to turn up anything. But I will. How valuable?"

"He's a ghost talker."

"I am not. I don't talk to those things." The tan slides off T's face, leaving behind a sickly gray.

I know why he no longer speaks to them. Know what memory he fears and why that fear controls his actions.

With that thought, I'm pulled back into the minion fight, into the memories bursting free from Number One's words.

Maybe the minion's right. Maybe I'm not good enough. I sure couldn't stop the memories from overwhelming me. From causing mistakes that lost me the fight. Maybe I need to stay home and train more.

Or stop hunting minions altogether.

The *justitia* howls, a sound for my ears only. Giving up is not in its vocabulary. But how can I fight when I'm so easily distracted by memories?

Why do I want to fight? Because the bracelet tells me I do? What do I want in this?

"You are?" Smythe's words return me from the land of Gin's head.

"I see them. I don't talk to the fuckers." T's head shakes in negation.

"Why do you care if he speaks to ghosts?" I ask, trying to draw the attention off my twin.

"It's a rare talent," Eloise says. "Plenty of people can see them, but the number of those who can speak to them drops off significantly."

"No. You are not getting your claws in me like you have my sister."

Eloise inclines her head. "Very well. We cannot make you do what you don't want to do. But if you ever change your mind, we are very interested in your talent."

"It's not a talent, it's a curse." His biceps bunch as he crosses his arms, but the aggressive stance falls flat in the wake of his pale face.

Eloise makes a non-committal noise. "Well, then, it was nice meeting you. Gin, endeavor not to be on the losing end of a fight again. Aidan, I'll see you soon."

Smythe touches her arm, shows her an area to form a portal. She raises her hand, but before she forms the portal, I move to stand beside her.

"Thank you. I don't know what I'd do without you."

She tilts her head toward me. "I find I do not mind healing you. Call me anytime." With a wave of her hand, she forms a portal and steps into it, vanishing from view.

T gasps. "That is one freaky-ass way of traveling."

I place a hand on Smythe's arm. "Thank you."

His jaw moves, tension lacing the muscle as if he wants to speak but thinks better of it.

For all of two seconds.

"What were you doing in the park, Gin?" His voice takes on the tone of baker's chocolate, deep, dark and bitter.

"I told you, Samantha set her up." T glares at Smythe, pale face gone in a rush of anger.

"I heard you the first time. I'm asking Gin."

"He's right. She set me up. Came over here, all I-need-help like and took my ass to that park. Where she promptly left. After reminding the minion of their deal."

"What deal?" Smythe's eyes narrow.

"I don't know."

"I'm not saying I don't believe you, but I can't picture Samantha setting you up like that. She's a guardian. And a damn good one."

"She's a bitch. Who hates my guts."

"That's only because—" his voice trails off into silence, a splash of red dotting his cheeks.

"Because?" T asks.

"No offense, Gin, but she's a purist. She doesn't think you should wear the *justitia*. Which doesn't mean she wants you dead."

"I beg to differ. She clearly wants me dead. You think I get my jollies having the shit beat out of me?"

A tic starts in the muscle of Smythe's jaw. "You think I get my jollies seeing you with the shit beat out of you? You. Could. Have. Died!" For a second I thought he might help me out in that regard. His fingers clench into fists, rage pours off him like a wave, hitting me with a tangible force. No, not rage. Fear.

Seeing me hurt scared the shit out of Smythe.

And my damn traitorous body fires off tingles of glee at the realization he cares. Stupid tingles. Of course he cares. I'm his freakin' mentee.

"You think I don't know that? That bitch set me up. I need to even the score." My hands slam against my hips as I let anger sweep away desire.

Smythe glares, nostrils flaring as he practices deep breathing exercises, clearly trying to get control of his emotions. A couple of breaths later he runs a hand through his hair. "Let's go see."

"Go see what? Samantha? Because I need to get my gun if that's the case."

He glares at me. "No gun. But we will talk to her at the Agency."

"I'm coming with you," T says.

"No." Smythe and I speak simultaneously. Under any other circumstance it would be funny.

"Blake's supposed to come over." Although by this time, he's probably not, but still. He might. "You can tell him I'll be back."

"Babe—" T gives me a surely-you-didn't-fall-for-that-line look "—he's not coming over."

"He might." I cross my arms.

"He's just using you."

"Is not. He's my friend."

"Is too. He's a guy."

"Okay, okay." Smythe interjects. "Let's go."

"I'm not going anywhere until I change clothes." I've already been to the Agency once dressed like a hooker. The last thing I need to do is show up looking like I've been on the losing end of fight.

Even if it is the truth.

"Make it snappy." To illustrate, Smythe snaps his fingers.

"Quit being a smartass." But I can't stop the grin from turning my lip.

"Quit stalling."

Flipping him the bird, I walk down the hall to my bedroom, leaving Smythe and T alone in the same room. Hopefully they'd both still be alive when I finish changing.

The scrub pants are ruined. I pitch them into the trash. The top can be salvaged so it gets pitched into the laundry hamper. Beneath the clothing my skin is smooth, unblemished. Healed.

Not a scratch on me. At least not on the outside.

Blood cakes my left leg. Dried blood on my sock and shoe. I carry the sock into the bathroom, put it into the sink, and cover it with water. Grabbing a washcloth, I rinse the blood off my leg, the thin stripe on my arm.

A pair of jeans, black T-shirt, and a quick swipe of the hairbrush and I'm ready to go. Sticking my feet into flip-flops, I march back into the living room.

Which is still in one piece.

T and Smythe sit on either end of the couch, mirror images with arms crossed, legs apart, staring at the blank TV screen. Neither looks happy.

Oh well. At least they weren't fighting.

"It took you long enough." Smythe looks me over from head to toe and back.

I shrug. He likes what he sees. His words don't matter.

Gah! What am I thinking?

"I should come with you." T glares. It dawns on me his protectiveness stems from fear of losing me. Am I stupid or what? You'd think I would've picked up on this earlier.

Say about thirty-two years ago.

I walk to my twin, bend over, wrap my arms around his neck. A pause, and then he grasps me around my waist, holding me like I was a saving rope to a drowning man.

Which I am. But only to him.

I'll be fine. Smythe's with me.

Not sure I trust him.

He saved me. He'll do it again if necessary. Besides I need to kick that blonde bitch's ass.

You sure you don't want me to help?

Doesn't that break your vow not to hit a woman?

A long pause. *She lost her woman status when she set you up to be killed.*

"We don't have all day. Or night as the case may be. Come on, Gin. Let's go." Smythe holds one hand toward me, palm up.

T's arms tighten, release and I straighten. "Keep my sister safe."

Smythe nods, keeps his mouth closed. But his gaze hops between T and me, eyes narrowing. I can almost see his brain turning things over, puzzle pieces falling into place, deducing things he shouldn't.

"Let's go get that bitch." I grab his outstretched hand.

Smythe sighs, stands. Mutters words under his breath until a portal gapes in front of the TV. Tightening his grip on my hand, he steps into the wormhole. I glance over my shoulder, offer T a grin and a wave before the portal sucks me into its depths.

Chapter 17

We arrive in the white room of the Agency, freezing cold and not likely to warm up in this white icebox they call a computer room. Only a row of pubescent teenagers manning computers greets us, their gazes giving us the once over before focusing on their screens. No one speaks.

The scent of lavender hangs in the air in sneeze-inducing quantities. I press my tongue against the roof of my mouth and hope the pressure wards off the sneeze. What's wrong with pumpkin spice or apple cinnamon air freshener?

At least I'm not allergic to those scents.

Still holding my hand, Smythe gives a brief hi-how-are-ya wave to the row of teenagers and heads for the door on the opposite side of the room. He pulls it open, steps through and drags my gaping body into a hallway.

Where I promptly forget to keep my tongue against the roof of my mouth. Applying pressure when one's mouth resembles a newly formed sinkhole is a little hard to do.

We stand in what looks like the hallway of an office building crossed with Trump's apartment, minus suite numbers beside the doors. Gold knobs decorate the doors and instead of the standard office building overhead florescent lights, gold chandeliers with dangling crystal beads dot the ceiling, giving off a soft glow.

"Wow!" I can't help it. I've never seen such opulence in an office before. They sure don't decorate this way at the hospital.

"These are the offices." Pride laces his voice. "Nice, eh? I doubt Dad's here, so we'll probably have to go to his apartment."

I meet his gaze. The same blue gaze David possesses. A gaze easy to get lost in, easy to be controlled by. "Your Dad's David, right?"

"Yeah."

"So why didn't you just portal to his apartment instead of the white room?"

"The white room?" His lips twist with obvious mirth as he gestures over his shoulder at the now-closed door. At my nod, he sets the grin free. "That's the landing room. Wards around the building ensure you only portal into and out of that room. Only one entry point ensures security can monitor who comes and goes."

"Security? Those teenagers are security?" He nods. "So what do they do if an intruder arrives? Pop a zit on them?"

A laugh barks out of his lips as his eyes twinkle. "Pop a zit? Gin, Gin, Gin. Those are guardians in training. At the least they can form a containment field around a demon until help arrives. Trust me, they aren't as weak as they look. Now, come on and let's find Dad."

He continues to hold my hand, but it's probably more to keep me from running off than because he enjoys it. I'm so busy gawking at how rich people live I can't think of anything else. Including the evening's events and the emotions the minion's words released.

Some things are better off buried and left alone.

We stop in front of a door, indistinguishable from the others lining the hallway and Smythe raps three times on its wooden paneling. Maybe three is the secret passcode around here.

No one answers.

The plush carpeting muffles all sounds except for a low buzzing, like a radio in-between stations. So this is what white noise sounds like. Guess that means we really are in spy central.

"He's not here. We'll need to go to his apartment."

"Where's that?"

"On the top floor. He has the penthouse suite."

Oo-la-la. Smythe's daddy is ri-ii-ich.

"Do you live here, too?"

"Yeah. Most guardians do."

"Do you share the penthouse suite with your dad?"

"Not anymore. Apartment locations are dealt out by seniority."

"So that means you live..." I make a circling motion with my hand.

"Third floor."

Hmm. Looks like my mentor fell off the turnip truck yesterday. Not sure what that says about me. "Where's Samantha? Will she be there with David?"

"Doubtful. She and her ward share an apartment so she's only here when called."

Drat. Guess I won't be getting my revenge tonight. "Didn't realize she swung that way."

"She doesn't. Trust me." He turns, heads back the way we came, stopping in front of a bank of elevators and hits the UP button.

"Oh?"

He shrugs, drops my hand, passes his over his head.

I grin. "Why, Smythe. I think you have the hots for my would-be killer."

"It's not the hots. We go, um, back a ways."

"Uh-huh. Whose back? Yours or hers?"

The elevator chose that moment to arrive, its barely audible ding a prelude to the doors opening. Smythe ignores my verbal jab, gesturing for me to step into the elevator in front of him.

What a gent.

Who used to screw that blonde bitch I want to strangle.

Wonder if he's any good in the sack?

Geez, Louise, Gin. Pull your out-of-control sex drive back to normal. Who cares? It's not like I'll be finding out the answer to that question anytime soon.

Or ever.

Smythe pushes a button for the 15th floor. After a pause, the doors close and the elevator whooshes upward.

"Where are we? City-wise, I mean." I face him, rubbing my hands up and down my arms. Has anyone in this building ever heard of setting the thermostat to conserve energy?

"Boston."

"For real? I've never been to Boston." At least not when I knew where I was. Being in the white room a couple of nights ago might legally count as being to Boston, but not to my way of thinking.

"It's nice."

"Did you grow up here?"

His gaze meets mine, one brow raises as if in question. What? It was a perfectly logical question.

Ding! The elevator sounds a warning we've arrived before sliding open the doors. We step into a small entrance room decked out in marble flooring with gold trim on the wainscoting. A small sconce with gas flames flickers the only light in the room. Hello, don't these people know not to leave a fire unattended?

Smythe steps the two feet to the door and knocks as the elevator doors slide closed. "Dad?" Another three knocks and he sticks his hand on the hand reader next to the doorframe. A click sounds and he turns the knob, cracking the door an inch.

"Dad? It's me. We need to talk." He pushes the door open, motions me to follow.

A breathtaking expanse of wall to ceiling windows opposite from where we stand captures my attention. David's apartment overlooks the city and tall towers decorated in lights dot the night view. Shadows coat the room in dark imagination, the light flowing over furniture from the left side of the room. I take a step forward, squelching a scream when the door snaps shut behind us.

My hand flutters over my chest in a futile attempt to calm my trying-to-run-a-marathon heartbeat. Smythe glances over his shoulder at my squeak with another one of those brow-cocking things he excels at.

Voices sound from the left, toward the light, their hushed tones reminding me of children whispering as they try to avoid their parents' notice.

But unlike normal children's, these voices creep across nerve endings and make me check the shadows for hidden dangers.

Which is ridiculous. We're in the Agency, which pretty much guaran-damn-tees a lack of demons and minions.

A shot of joy fires through my system, a fighting adrenaline rush vibrating the silver bracelet links. A dose of confusion follows, squelching the joy, the vibration. What is a minion doing in David's apartment? It's the same feeling I had the last time I was at the Agency. Maybe all that white noise confuses the *justitia*. Makes it think minions infiltrate the place.

"You know what you have to do." The voice's words warp, the distortion causing goosebumps across my skin.

"Dad?" Smythe seems to grow, aggression sparking red bursts around his head and shoulders. One hand held in front of him, he strides into the middle of the living room, turning toward the light.

I follow, a bit slower. Seeing as the *justitia* remains in bracelet form, I'm not too eager to jump into the middle of whatever is going on in the next room.

"Aidan?" David steps into the room at the same time I do, a remote control in his hand. He's wearing khakis and a white button down shirt, top button undone, sleeves rolled up mid-forearm. Behind him looks to be an office, complete with a hanging flatscreen TV over a cream colored marble fireplace. Oo-la-la.

"I heard voices. One of them was pretty creepy. Are you okay?" Smythe lowers his hand, the aggression surrounding him fleeing into the shadows.

David shakes the remote. "TV."

My *justitia* isn't convinced. But since nothing

moves in the room but shadows and an overall creepy feeling, I assign the unease to the white noise. Static makes me uneasy, so why wouldn't it do the same to some nerve-joining entity?

The fact I can think that thought with a straight face does not bode well for my sanity.

"Why is she here?" The remote points at me. Part of me wonders if by clicking it he'll make me disappear. Another part of me gets the impression he'd like to try.

"We have a problem."

"What's that?"

"That bitch Samantha tried to kill me." I take a step forward, stand closer to Smythe.

"Nonsense."

A tic starts in my jaw and I force my teeth to unclench, my hands to uncurl.

"I found her in a park in San Antonio fighting a league of minions." A hint of anger creeps into Smythe's tone.

"Son—" David points the remote at Smythe "—that's what she's supposed to do."

"Not without me, she's not. Samantha showed up at her house and took her to the park."

"And then left me there to die!" Anger releases the remembered fear of being setup, of fighting and losing, of thinking my death came sooner rather than later.

My innards react as if dunked in ice, a deep quiver low in my belly, the ice of near-death spreading throughout my limbs.

"Well, it didn't work, now did it. Really, Aidan. It's the middle of the night."

The tic starts again in my jaw. Or maybe that jaw-clench was due to the fear-chills shaking their way out of my body.

"Shouldn't you check it out?"

"Are you sure she didn't go herself?"

Was he smoking crack or something? If I could pull a stunt like portaling, I would not be standing here talking to David. I don't bother to smooth over my shocked expression.

"San Antonio is a five hour drive from Dallas." Smythe's arms cross, his eyes narrow. "Her purse was on the table. Her car was in the garage with the engine hot. And her brother was there hollering about her being hurt. I tracked the *justitia* to the park. Do you really think she can form a portal?"

David sighs, slaps the remote against his palm. Once, twice. "There has to be some other reason."

"Fine. Then you tell me how she got to San Antonio. Where I found her almost dead."

David's gaze rakes me from head to toe. "She looks fine."

"I called Eloise."

"You've got to be kidding me. Eloise?"

What's wrong with Eloise?

"She was happy to help. Ask her what she saw. She'll tell you Gin was hurt."

David points the remote at me. "So Samantha shows up at your house, takes you to a park, and leaves you."

"Yep. After telling the lead minion to remember their deal."

David freezes, eyes popping wide, his arm with the remote stretched out in front like he's a conductor made of wax. His lips turn in a grin that would make Lucifer proud. A fine tremor flows south before I can stop it.

"Did she now?" His arm pulls back, drops. "And what was the deal?"

I shrug, swallow, try to get enough saliva in my mouth to form words. With that too proud for the Devil expression on his face, I almost feel sorry for Samantha. Almost. "I don't know. I was too busy fighting off minions."

"How many did you kill?"

"About six." He nods. Looks pleased. "Then Smythe came along and blew them up and took me home and called Eloise."

"Blew them up?" David faces Smythe, the pleased expression covered by white lines forming around his lips. "What the fuck were you thinking? You can't weaken a demon by blowing up the minions. You know that. What were you thinking?"

Smythe plants his feet, keeps his arms crossed. But a faint tint of color sweeps across his cheeks. "It just happened."

"Just happened? An accident just happens. Blowing up minions does not just happen. It's planned. Damn it, son. If I said it once, I'll say it a million times. Stabbing a minion is the only way to hurt the demon. This is starting to sound like Jennifer's situation."

If Smythe's jaw got any tighter, he could etch metal with his teeth.

Ignoring his son, David turns to me. "What do you want me to do about this? Call Samantha?"

I'd like to beat the snot out of her, but suppose I'll settle with questions. And him believing me. "Please."

He walks back into his office, comes back out sans remote and with a phone in his hand. Hitting a couple of buttons, he soon has Samantha on video chat, Smythe peering over his shoulder.

"What's wrong, David?" Her voice comes across as clear as if she stands in the room. Isn't technology grand?

"Aidan and Gin claim you left her at a park to be killed by minions."

"That bitch! That's why you should never allow someone not of the bloodlines to wear the *justitia*!"

"Samantha, you know as well as I do that no one not of the bloodlines can wear a *justitia*. Now quit throwing barbs and state your side of the story."

She pauses, clears her throat. "There was a minion attack in San Antonio that Micah needed help with. I couldn't find Aidan so I went to Gin's house, waited for her to get home from work, which again, minion hunting should be a *justitian's* only job—"

"So you waited," David interrupts.

"When she got home I took her to the park and then left to get Micah. When I returned the minions were dead. I hardly think that's my fault. She's the one that killed them. Oh, wait. Most of those minions looked like they'd been hit by a blowtorch. Which means you need to speak with Aidan. Again." Her tone suggests she's fallen into a chocolate swimming pool. Judging by Smythe's glare and teeth clenching, he fails to feel the same.

"Thank you Samantha. Sorry to bother you."

"I'm happy to help, David."

Lying bitch. Sure, she returned to the scene of the crime, but only to try to find my dead body. But why? Was she that big of a purist that she'd want me dead?

"See?" David taps his phone screen before slipping

it into his pocket. "I told you she wouldn't set you up. It was a misunderstanding."

He's got to be kidding. He believes her? Of course he does. He knows her. He doesn't know me.

Righteous anger trumps helpful self-talk. "I think I know when I've been set up, and it was no misunderstanding. She meant for the minion to kill me!" Smythe steps to my side, puts a hand on my shoulder, tugs. Yeah, yeah, he's probably right, I shouldn't be yelling at my new big boss.

I step back. David's lip twitches as he sighs.

"Let's say you're right. Why?"

"I don't know! She's crazy?"

"She's not crazy. If you come up with a valid reason, come back and speak with me. Until then, I bid you good-bye." He gestures toward the front door.

He can't throw me out! He hasn't even taken me seriously. Whether good or bad, I say the first thing that pops into my mind. "She's jealous. She wants Smythe and thinks I'm in the way."

David looks at me, blinks, then starts laughing. "You have got to be kidding me! She's the one that broke it off with him. I doubt she's jealous. Now run along. And son, practice on your training. And hers. Good night."

"Sorry to bother you, Dad."

"Stay out of trouble, son."

He didn't believe me. Not at all. Thinks I'm a liar. An ache stabs into my chest, a serrated knife wound. I know I speak the truth. I know she set me up.

Didn't she? Did I misunderstand her?

I did not misunderstand. David doesn't want to believe me. A sense of frustration like a foreboding slams into me, spreading the chest ache across my torso, burying it deep into my soul.

Injustice. He's never going to discover the truth. Doesn't care to know. Would rather believe a lie.

Smythe grabs my arm. I look over my shoulder at David, glare at the man. His blue eyes narrow, start to submerse me in their depths, control my reactions, my thoughts. But Smythe yanks my arm, breaking the connection, forcing me to follow him as he pulls me out the door.

Did David really try to get into my mind, or was it a case of overactive imagination? Normally I'd side with the imagination, but Smythe had once before pulled me into the depths of his gaze, controlled my reactions. Who's to say his father can't do the same.

My favorite mentor hits the elevator button as if he's trying to push it off the wall. Tension rolls off him, a palpable wave of anger. When the elevator doors open, he shoves me inside, pushing the lobby button.

"I believe you," he growls.

"I thought you couldn't imagine her setting me up."

"I couldn't. But she lied. I can always tell when she lies. I want to know why."

"Stop at her floor. We'll settle this once and for all."

He shakes his head. "Fighting is not the way. We'll discover what she's doing, collect evidence, and put a stop to it." His smile looks every bit as evil as his father's do the Devil proud expression. Except his doesn't make me wary. "Then we'll show that evidence to Dad and let him choke on it."

Chapter 18

"A little aggressive, there, huh?"

"I wouldn't really hurt him. He just pisses me off sometimes."

"I understand." He has a normal relationship with his father.

Unlike me.

"You do? Your old man made you crazy, too?"

In more ways than one, sits on the tip of my tongue, but the words fade into nothing as the minion's face floats in my mind's eye, his voice a flaying whip to my soul.

You're nothing but a whore! A wasted piece of human flesh. You'll never amount to nothing. Useless tramp!

Whose voice spoke in my memories? The minion's from tonight? Or my father's? Past and present melds together, erasing Smythe and the wooden paneling of the elevator. Forcing me into the past with all the speed and gentleness of a tornado.

Sounds of flesh smacking against flesh splat against my ears, each noise bringing a burst of pain. The pungent odor of under-bathed man mixed with cheap whiskey assaults my nostrils as spittle beads on the sides of his lips. The coppery taste of blood fills my mouth as I lay on my back, carpet fibers burning into my skin.

My hand reaches to the side, fingers scrabbling until they grasp cold metal.

A brush of air. A meaty thunk.

Quiet.

The chirp of insects. The feel of grass beneath my battered body.

The sound of Smythe screaming unholy rage at my attackers.

Past swims into present swims into past.

I reach my hand out, smack it into wooden paneling. Wooden paneling of an elevator. An elevator with Smythe.

Present. Not past.

"Gin?" A touch on my arm. A concerned voice.

My eyes open. I'm slumped against the side of the elevator, mostly upright, totally embarrassed.

No one can know what happened. It's a secret T and I promised to share forever.

Ding! The elevator sinks into place, doors opening to a hallway.

"I'm sorry. I'm tired, worn out, hyped up, and frustrated. I must've blacked out." My voice sounds weak, so I paste on what I hope is a happy grin. Fake it until you make it.

Smythe's brows slam down as his gaze pierces through my lie. He knows. He just doesn't realize the reason.

Damn it. I used to be a much better liar.

Or maybe I never met anyone who saw through my defenses.

Freaking scary.

I step into the hallway, looking both ways. Which way to the white room, or as Smythe likes to call it, the landing area?

Doors snap close on a whoosh behind me as Smythe steps to my side.

"You should go home."

"Great idea. Thank you."

I'm silent as we walk down the hallway, push through a door into the white room. Silent as Smythe opens a portal, grasps my hand, pulls me into frigid coldness.

What can I say? I completely freaked out on him back there. He asked an innocuous question. One I've answered in some form or fashion before.

Doesn't everyone want to know about your family? Your parents? Of course they do. Of course I've answered his question before.

So why the hell did I freak out on him this time?

And of all people to lose it on, I chose Smythe. *Smythe*. I mean, why couldn't I chose someone like Jackie who wouldn't think anything's out of the ordinary if non-ordinary smacked her on the ass?

Instead I freak out on Mr. I-can-hack-into-the-police-internal-website-and-find-out-anything-about-anyone.

Good going, Gin.

I'm so caught up in my own drama, the outcome of our little trip through the land of freeze doesn't hit until we arrive in my living room. Until T's curious gaze lands on me.

Until he speaks.

"How was it? Did they arrest that bitch?"

My emotions snap from freaked out to frustrated in under a millisecond. Must be some sort of a record. And I have two of the three F's covered.

If Blake shows up I'll have all three.

Just not in the way the saying meant.

"He didn't believe me."

"Why not?" T's fingers curl as he faces Smythe.

"He's known Samantha longer and is more likely to believe her side of the story."

"What about you?" T challenges Smythe with a glare.

Smythe's lips flatten. "She's lying. And I'm going to find out why."

"Just not tonight," I interject. "I'm tired." And emotionally drained after my journey through the land of the past. And frustrated. And let's not forget disappointed that Blake forgot to show.

"You work tomorrow?" Smythe asks.

"I work from three to eleven."

"We'll train before you go to work."

"What kind of training?" T asks.

"Learning fighting stances. How to access her powers. That type of thing."

"Can I watch?"

"No." No way. I could just see it now, T landing a punch to the side of Smythe's head for some fighting move he tried on me.

If I wanted to learn, T needed to be nowhere around.

"Why not?"

"She needs to learn without any interference."

As usual Smythe has a point. But do I want to learn? What good am I really? My bracelet was forged to have the advantage over minions. And how did I show that advantage?

By getting my ass kicked.

But you're just learning, my inner voice notes.

Doesn't matter if I'm a newbie. Why am I even bothering fighting? Not to say the minion was right—I know I'm not worthless—but why have I bought into this super-slayer gig?

Do I really want to save the world?

Do I really care?

What do I want?

For once, the bracelet remains silent, as if it knows I need to grasp things on my own without its help.

A smart nerve-joining entity. Just what a girl needs.

"I'm going to bed." The male testosterone contest comes to an abrupt stop as both men stare at me. "What? It's after midnight. It was a long day at work and it doesn't help knowing someone wants me dead and the big boss doesn't care to find out who. See you tomorrow."

Ignoring the stunned looks, I give them my back. Two good-nights follow me down the hall as I make my way to my bedroom and close the door.

Emotionally drained barely touches the surface of how I feel. Where is Blake when I need him? It's not as bad as seeing Will lying in a pool of blood, but knowing Samantha wants me dead and the Agency's top man chooses her side evokes the same reaction as watching bullies pick on a kid and being unable to help.

Memories replay in my mind of the fight tonight. Of losing. Of remembrances conjured from the minion's words.

All of which make me itch for a slip out of reality. To become dependent upon things I've learned to do without. Which is why I need Blake. Since he said he'd try to come over tonight, calling him was out of the question. No use in guilting him for not doing something he hadn't planned on doing.

Maybe T was right. Maybe I've put too much stock in a relationship that's going nowhere fast. Or not going at all.

Being friends with benefits was not a relationship.

So why do I feel like I've fallen hard for him?

My life is such a mess.

I want things I can't have. I have things I don't want. Itches bite.

I drop my clothes over the chair, pull on my nightshirt, and turn out the light.

Footsteps thud against wooden floorboards before T's door squeaks closed. I imagine Smythe sitting on the couch, laptop in hand, pouring through the internet, trying to figure out why Samantha wants me dead.

At least he believes me. Even if he disregards the reason I gave.

I walk to the bed, sit on the edge. Memories loom in my mind, a rash of poison ivy, an endless itch threatening my sanity.

When younger I controlled them the only way I knew how, through drugs and alcohol, both of which in large enough quantities counteract my empathic abilities. Give me the ability to forget, if only for a moment.

I swallow, a memory forming, this one more pleasant. Another way of applying anti-itch lotion for the addict.

A deeper, darker, more powerful hit.

Forbidden pleasures.

My fingers stroke across the silver links of my

bracelet. It also possesses the power to shut down my emotions, to render me powerless, a slave to its bliss.

But it remains quiet. Respectful of my decision.

If I even have one.

Darkness beckons, a pull I've never been able to resist. My feet slide cool against waxed wood as they walk to the window. One hand pulls the cord, raises the blinds, the other unlocks the window.

I stare at the pane, swallow. Yes, I can conqueror the inner demons by opening the window. But do I want Smythe to know my secret?

Letting loose a sigh, I lock the window, lower the blinds. Walk back to the bed and remove my nightshirt. Cool sheets brush against my back as a knot forms in my stomach. Air from the vent above the door blows across my bare skin, puckering my nipples with a lover's caress. My breath hitches.

I roll to my side, reach into the nightstand drawer, pull out my vibrator. The darkness inside howls, wanting the better fix, the one that soothes my soul. But I can't always get what I crave when I crave it. Past experience proves my battery-operated BFF eases tension.

And I don't mind explaining its noise to Smythe.

Giving the window a last glance, I flip a girl's best friend on and allow it to drown me in a wave of fake bliss.

Chapter 19

Light creeps through the blinds, mixes with the heady scent of fresh coffee and frying bacon in a wakeup call to my senses. I lay tangled in sheets, naked as the day I was born, reaching for something on the other side of the bed that eludes my grasp.

Probably because nothing is over there but the other half of the mattress.

The previous night's frustration disappears in a rush of sunbeams, conquered by a magic deeper than time. I feel relaxed. Whole. Ready to meet the world.

Curious as to why Blake never called.

I'm not sure what it says about me when I'm more concerned over him than Samantha plotting to kill me.

Coffee beckons. No use in thinking until I've had a cup. Or three.

One shower and some clothes later and I leave the bedroom, walk into the kitchen.

Smythe sits at the table, laptop open and running, a plate of bacon and eggs to one side, a steaming cup of tea on the other. A full pot of coffee sits on the coffeepot, steam circling a dance around the lid. The clock on the wall ticks off the seconds of my life. Nine in the morning.

Which means T has already left for work.

So has Blake for that matter.

I need to stop fixating on my friend with benefits.

"Oh, hey." Smythe turns, cracks a grin. "I made extras if you want it." One hand gestures toward the stove. Sure enough a couple of strips of bacon and a scrambled egg sit in a skillet. "Did you sleep well?"

My gaze snaps from the stove to him. Does he realize how I almost fed the beast clawing gouges in my veins? It's not a secret I'm willing to share.

Along with other things best left dead and buried.

Things are only suspicious if you make them appear that way. *Quit gaping and start talking, Gin.* "I did, thanks. You?"

Like a homing beacon, I head toward the coffee. Grab my extra-large mug out of the cabinet and pour a cup. Two sips later and I'm ready for some of that food. My stomach lets loose with a growl and I realize it's been since yesterday lunch that I've eaten.

It's a wonder I don't feel faint from lack of food.

After making my plate, I sit at the table across from Smythe.

"So, what's on the agenda today?" Sticking a bite of bacon in my mouth, I chomp down, release a moan of delight. Just the way I like it. Cooked through but not crispy.

Apparently Smythe knows his way around the kitchen.

At least as far as bacon and eggs are concerned.

"A bit of training before you go to work."

"This tastes good." I wave the half-eaten strip of bacon his way. "Where'd you learn to cook?"

He shrugs. "Got tired of eating takeout when I moved into my apartment so I taught myself. Glad you like it."

"What else can you do? Hack into the police

website, save my ass, cook. Pretty talented there, Smythe."

"Yeah? I'm pretty good with my hands, too." He waggles his fingers, eyes crinkling at the corners.

And before I can blink, my libido fires off, locked and loaded, ready for action. I just bet he's good with his hands. I can imagine a dozen places those talented fingers can dance across my skin before he drops them back to the keyboard.

Gulp. "Nice to know. I'll keep it in mind."

"I've been trying to learn why Samantha set you up. It's not going well."

"Oh?" I speak around a mouthful of food. Nothing like demonstrating good home-learned manners.

"She didn't leave a traceable trail. No emails, texts or calls. Probably contacted the minion on a prepaid cell phone."

Swallow. Food always tastes better cooked by someone else. "Can you trace that?"

"Not unless I find the phone. Since I haven't been able to find evidence she set you up, I've started to look at why."

"She's a bitch and hates my guts."

"Lots of people hate others and do nothing about it."

"Most people aren't able to call up minions and have them do their bidding."

"She shouldn't be able to either." His fingers drum a word-punctuating rhythm against the table. "Guardians don't talk to minions. We help our wards kill them."

"So how did she manage it?"

"I don't know. But I'll figure it out." The

drumming morphs into a single tap, a wordless promise.

"I'm telling you. She thinks I'm white trash and shouldn't be wearing the *justitia*."

"The *justitia* has a right to choose who it wants to wear it. It chose you. At that point it ceases to matter what she thinks of your...background. You and it are one. She knows that."

Maybe not. But arguing the point with him seems like a lesson in futility, so I let it drop.

"So why is burning minions bad? David mentioned it last night."

Smythe pauses. Swallows. "You don't harm the demon. Only the swords can hurt a demon. Burning minions just roasts flesh."

My nose wrinkles, an involuntary reaction to the thought of burned minion. Good thing I'm finished eating.

Pushing my empty plate aside, I give Smythe my best thank-you grin. "Breakfast was great. You're welcome over here any morning you want. Provided Blake isn't around."

One of his brows does a meet and greet with his hairline. "Tell me about him."

"What's to tell? We're friends." Plus some.

"You care for him." A statement. Not a question.

"Yeah. We've known each other since college."

His gaze shifts to the wall behind me, grows distant before dropping to his laptop screen. "Must be nice."

"Come on, now. You can't tell me you don't have a friend."

"Of course I have friends." His gaze meets mine, offense bristling the edges.

"Well, I didn't mean you didn't. You just sounded

jealous there for a second. Wait. You are jealous." I point a finger at him. "You miss having a friend with benefits, dontcha?"

It's almost comical watching emotions play across his face. Embarrassment. Surprise. Shock.

"How'd you know that?"

"Magic. So, did you have one and lose her, or never have one and want her?" Asking if it's a him instead of a her never enters my mind. Tension-charged touches and hormonally induced electrical zingers took away that query. He swings the same way as my bedroom door.

Cha-ching.

As if that's going to happen. Work rule number one: never get involved with your boss. Or mentor.

Smythe blinks like he lost a lash in his eye. Red tints his cheeks, fades as he swallows and looks at the screen. He pauses long enough for me to think he's not going to answer.

Which of course makes me wonder what he's hiding.

When he speaks, the words lump together like cold oatmeal. "Had one."

"I'm sorry. What happened?" Old flame? Broken romance? This is going to be juicy.

"She died."

Or not so juicy. Which is the problem with digging up gossip. Sometimes the oopsy factor flies back in your face.

"I'm so sorry." I reach across the table, touch his hand before I think better of it. Emotions assail me, bitter, dark, a damp hiding place.

And then he blocks me out.

But flips his hand over so his fingers curl around my palm.

The silence in the room thickens, spreads, dampens the ticking of the clock, the hum of the fridge. The scent of rich soil fills the air as the taste of damp dirt clogs my mouth, pours down my throat. I cough, gagging on his emotions, the bitterness of his sorrow.

With a squeeze, he releases my hand, taking away the sensation of choking. A couple of breaths later and the feeling of being buried alive dissipates.

Looks like I'm not the only one in the room with secrets.

Or battling to keep my emotions out of the friends-with-benefits relationship.

"So." Smythe clears his throat. "Training. Put your plate away and let's get started."

Okaaay. One share session coming to an end.

"Let me brush my teeth and I'll be right back." Toothpaste with a chaser of coffee might sound disgusting, but I've learned to like it.

Besides, it gives me a chance to check my texts without Smythe noticing what I'm doing.

Grabbing my plate, I stick it in the dishwasher and mosey back to the bedroom. The cell phone lays on the bedside table and a quick peek shows Blake has not texted me. Or called. Or stopped by.

It shouldn't bother me.

So why does it?

I stare at the phone in my hand. A couple of weeks ago I wouldn't have called. After all, that's what being a friend with benefits meant. No strings attached. Dating whoever we please.

Not bothering each other with texts born of

insecurity.

But something changed in the last few days. Something drastic. We clicked.

For more than just a night.

Therefore sending him a where the hell are you text seems a logical next step in our new relationship.

Rationalize, rationalize, rationalize.

Multi-tasking is the work of a moment. Toothbrush in one hand. Phone in the other. Swype rocks, best invention ever.

Where R U? Missed U last night. I hit SEND.

Set the phone on the back of the toilet. Take a peek at the screen.

Nothing.

I spit and rinse. Still nothing.

Maybe he's in a meeting.

Or doing other lawyer-ly things. Yeah. That's it. Meeting time.

He's not ignoring me. Nope. Not at all.

I stare at myself in the mirror. Light brown hair, shit-brown eyes. Smooth skin. No beauty, but not fugly either.

But god, I'm such a mess. Why the fuck can I not deal with things like normal people? Why do my inner switches require certain substances or action items to shut off? Why do I touch people and get readings off them?

I'm beginning to sound like a petulant two-year-old.

Stuffing the toothbrush back in its holder, I grab the phone. Do another check.

No text.

Definitely a meeting. And as a no doubt impatient

Smythe sits in my kitchen, checking the phone every five seconds is not an option.

One last glance in the mirror.

Still me. Gin the fuckup.

Who has a wicked cool bracelet. I can't be that much of a fuckup for a bracelet like this one to choose me. Right?

Right. On occasion, self-talk becomes a great motivator.

At least to get my ass out of the bathroom and into the kitchen. Where training will hopefully take my mind off all these things.

Smythe leans against the counter, watching me walk into the kitchen, arms crossed over his chest. His black T-shirt, jeans and shitkickers don't so much scream fashion statement as badass. Unlike earlier, his face projects a business-like persona, no excess emotion to be found.

Unless one counts that gleam in his eye.

Approval? Or expectation of kicking my ass on the training field?

"What's on the agenda, boss?" I pick up my mug from the table, pushing past Smythe to the coffeemaker. Hot steam brushes my nose as I sip.

"Defense tactics." He reaches for my mug, but I twist, evade his grasp.

"Hey, now. A girl needs her caffeine."

"It's time for training." He holds out his hand, palm up.

As if I'm going to give him my mug. Something is wrong with the man. He clearly has no respect for a filled coffee mug.

"Smythe, Smythe, Smythe." I punctuate each word

with a head shake. "What do you have against coffee?" The liquid sears my throat as I swallow several gulps, knowing I fight a losing battle and determined to get in as much get-up-and-go juice as possible.

"You slept in late—"

"Because you kept me up half the night." Along with other things best left unsaid.

"And now you want to waste time drinking an addictive liquid."

"It's better than other things I could be drinking." I swallow a couple more sips, letting the dark wonder work its alert-giving way through my veins. Hello world.

"Are you aware of your addictive tendencies?"

"Lots of people drink coffee in the morning. Or tea. Ask around."

"It's not lots of people I'm responsible for. Just you." He steps closer, the heat from his body caressing my skin in a warm embrace. His blue eyes catch my gaze, reel me into his control, under his spell. One hand wraps around my mug.

"Release it." His words sink under my skin, a command I'm all too eager to follow.

Damn it. I really need to learn how to fend off his spell.

As soon as he turns to put the mug on the counter, the spell breaks, freeing me into bitch-land.

"What the hell?" I try to take a step toward my mug, but he grasps my upper arm and turns me toward the back door. His emotionless touch after the earlier sharing session tears into my awareness.

"Training. Now."

Train this buddy. I jerk my arm, simultaneously

trying to stomp on his foot. My sneaker hits steel-toed leather with the force of a car running into a brick wall, while my arm gyrations do nothing but crack my shoulder.

"Ouch! What the hell? Let me have my coffee already!"

Ignoring me, he swings open the door with his free hand and drags me onto the back porch. For half a second I fear he'll pitch my complaining ass down the three steps onto the grass, but instead he pulls me against his hard chest, lifts and walks down the steps. My feet swing against his shins, my chest flush against the warmth of his upper abs and pecs, my eyes even with his ear.

I'm being carried by Smythe.

And my damn traitorous hormones spark to life like a Fourth of July firecracker.

Only to fizzle when he drops me to my feet in the middle of the backyard.

"No fair. And I still want my coffee." I give my best glare, the one used to strike the fear of God into non-compliant patients, and turn toward the house.

Only to find myself staring at the underside of the oak tree's canopy while trying to draw in a breath. Blue sky peeks through gaps in the leaves as I suck down air into shocked-still lungs. Did I slip on a stone or did Mr. You-Don't-Need-A-Caffeine-Hit just sweep my feet out from under me?

Judging from that twinkle in his beady blue eyes, I vote for the latter.

The son of a bitch enjoyed taking me down and watching me lay there like an overturned crab. Humph, he wants to see a crab, I'll show him crabby.

Taking a deep breath, I fake a wheeze and watch as the twinkle disappears into brow-knitted concern.

He bends, one hand reaching toward my face. "Gi—"

Before he gets my name out, I twist toward him, hands locking around the back of his leather-clad ankles. A quick yank coupled with a roll and Smythe's arms windmill in classic oh-shit fashion. I drop my grip, continuing my roll until I land on all fours.

As soon as I push to my feet, I break into a run, heading for the backdoor. Coffee here I co—

A six foot five hunk of muscle appears in my path, blocking my escape route. I feint right, dodge left, but he sticks to me like a used car salesman on the scent of a sale.

I take off running to the side, heading for the side gate, when a heavy weight hits me from behind, knocking me face first to the ground. Hands grab my shoulder and hip, forcing me onto my back. I yank fistfuls of grass and dirt so by the time Smythe has me turned and sits on my thighs his face is in my line of fire.

The double-handed pitch lands on the side of his face, tiny pieces of grass and dirt stick to his skin with sweat. He lets loose with a curse and grabs both my wrists in one hand, his other wiping across his face in an effort to dislodge excess grass and dirt.

A rush of fear-spiked adrenaline dances through my system and I twist, trying to escape his hold.

No such luck.

Will he hit me? He can't be too happy with dirt in his eyes.

Most of my brain trips along memories of Smythe

rescuing me. Of how his temper snaps in a second, but never his fists. At least not in my direction. My brain might negate my question, but my body refuses to get onboard the not going to happen train and shoots out another dose of flee-adrenaline.

In the time it takes for those thoughts to run through my mind, Smythe finishes wiping dirt out of his eyes. I tense, then force myself to go limp.

But instead of rage, his eyes leak pride.

Relaxation edges its way out of hiding.

"Nice job. You caught me unaware with the ankle grab."

"It seemed appropriate." I swallow, continuing to watch for signs he's faking his not-angry stance.

None appear. Not even when he releases his grip on my wrists and stands, holding out a hand to help me up.

My gaze holds his—watching for the almost imperceptible twitch of facial muscles coupled with tensing of biceps that telegraph a change in intention—while he hauls me to my feet. His eyes narrow, a probing intent less painful but equally as scary as what my instinctive reflex fears.

Get a grip, Gin. He's not going to hurt you. You might not know him well enough to know his favorite food, but you know damn well he won't hurt you.

He drops my hand, gestures toward the backdoor. "Go on. You've deserved it."

I no longer crave the coffee, but it's the principle of the matter. Sticking a smile on my face, I walk past him, not hurrying for I am not scared.

Really. I'm not.

But I don't relax until I'm out of arm's reach, until

I make it up the steps to the tiny back porch and I don't release the breath until the mug is in my hands.

It's no longer hot.

I don't care.

Smythe shoves open the door, his presence filling the kitchen like smoke from a fire. After he closes the door, he takes a couple of steps to the table and slides into a chair. His eyes focus on me as I stand by the sink, nursing the coffee mug, trying to keep the liquid from sloshing over the side.

How am I supposed to fight big, bad minions if I can't even hold it together during my first training session with my mentor?

"Wanna tell me what's wrong or am I supposed to continue tip-toeing around the proverbial sleeping giant?" His fingers drum an inpatient rhythm against his jeans, a dull throbbing against my nerves.

"Is it that evident?"

One raised brow answers.

Okaaaay. Guess that's a yes.

I sigh. Holding his gaze—which means I'm really not scared of Smythe, right?—my mug and I walk to the table and sit across from him.

This ingrained behavior of mine is so silly. I should be over it. I try and usually succeed in not regressing to learned behaviors. But being around Smythe erases all my hard work.

Well, dammit, I'm going to have to work harder at stomping out those reactions.

His fingers stop their annoying drum. "Who was it? Father or mother?"

I choke down the lump of liquid. "What makes you say that?"

"Stop it, Gin. You think I don't have eyes?"

I drop my gaze, focusing on the grains of wood running lengthwise on the table. Whispered words leave my lips like a catharsis. "Father. He was a mean drunk. Mom was just drunk all the time. Neglectful but not harmful." Unless one counted children having to scramble to find food in the trash bins at school harmful. Some might think it built character.

"What happened to him?"

Meeting his gaze, I cock a brow. "Couldn't find it on the computer?"

He stares at me, a silent reproach.

I shrug, telling him the same thing T and I told the police all those years ago. "He came home one night, beat the shit out of Mom, and walked out the door. Never saw him again."

"No idea where he went?"

"Nope."

"Think he'll return one day?"

"Nope."

"Why not?"

"He took his stuff. Clothes, deodorant, razor. A man's not coming back when he takes off like that."

"And your mom?"

Pain bursts against my sternum, regret, remorse. "She drank herself to death a couple of years later. Came home from college and she was dead on the couch. Had been that way for days." The stench of death invades my nose, a memory so strong it still overwhelms to this day. I bring the mug up to my nose, inhale the rich scent of coffee, my own personal smelling salts.

"I'm sorry."

"Yeah, well. A body can only take so much before it falls apart." Something I learned the hard way. "What about your mom?"

White lines form around his mouth. "She's in a nursing home. Had a stroke."

"I'm so sorry. When did that happen?"

"When I was a teen."

"Seriously? She must've been awfully young to have a stroke."

He swallows, recites his words in that flat way people do to hide a deep-seated agony. "Passed out after a binge. Had a stroke. They revived her, but couldn't reverse the damage. She has to have round the clock care."

"That must be hard on you."

"Harder on Dad. But yeah."

"Could Eloise not help?"

"She wasn't available in time. We couldn't get in touch with her until several days later. By then it was too late."

"I'm sorry."

"Not your fault. Anyway." And he changes the topic faster than a menopausal woman gets a hot flash. "You did pretty good earlier with the element of surprise. But while a fistful of grass might work on a human, it won't have much effect on a minion. Are you finished with that coffee?"

He nods toward the mug, and I set it on the table. Drinking it no longer seems as important.

"Good. Let's go again with some defense moves."

Chapter 20

Hours later, after learning jujitsu moves and a few karate kicks, Smythe calls a halt to the beat up Gin session. Thank goodness. No more lying on the dirt/grass mixture otherwise known as my backyard gasping for air while waiting for his next move. Which usually resulted in a return to my bruised and dirty prone position staring at the underside of leaves.

No more of that today. Now I have the joy of getting dressed for work.

After a quick brush on my shorts and legs to knock off any remaining dirt and grass, I lead the way into the kitchen. Smythe follows, stopping by the table as I open the pantry.

"I'll be back after my shower. Help yourself to whatever."

"Thanks."

Not bothering to watch what he does, I grab an apple, the half-empty jar of peanut butter and a stack of saltines and carry the lot back into my bedroom. One shower later and I stand in front of the mirror, eating and dressing in a disorganized dance I've perfected since taking the job at Blue Forest.

My face bears none of the hits taken today. That privilege goes to my wrists, where the beginnings of bruises redden the skin. Nothing a scrub jacket won't hide, but I dab cover-up over the marks to be on the safe side.

Answering are you in an abusive relationship questions are not my idea of a good time. I'm usually the one asking the questions, not the one giving the reply.

I'm pretty certain I'll have bruising on my hips and butt from being thrown onto the ground, but those are easily hidden. It's my face I'm worried about.

Apparently for no reason.

I slip on my scrubs and sneakers, make a date to see Smythe tomorrow—more training, oh the joy—and dart out the door, locking it behind me. Smythe can wave a hand, form a portal, and leave my house without unlocking the door.

Pretty nifty trick.

Shame he can't use it to get me to work on time.

Especially since he's the reason I'm running late.

Traffic runs smoothly, my drive easy and quick. And on time. Amazing that. The shift is the exact opposite, it being a Friday evening and a full moon to boot.

Which explains why I don't hear my phone ringing, even though it sits in my pocket. It's not until I clock out an hour after shift ends that I bother to check the thing on my walk to the parking garage.

I don't recognize the number. But lucky for me they obeyed the leave a message command. I push the voice mail button and a slurred female voice booms through the speaker in a failed effort to shatter my eardrum. I yank the phone away from my ear in self-preservation.

"Hey!" It's a tone only the seriously drunk can pull off, a loud, almost screaming twang, delivered that way since she seems to have trouble hearing her own voice. I pause in the hallway leading to the garage, leaning against the wall. She might be stumbling drunk, but something in her tone sends a chill chasing through my vertebrae, a prelude of the coming message.

"Hey!" She starts again, apparently believing I didn't hear her the first time. "I got your number from Cecily." Cecily? I rack my brain as she pauses for breath, or another sip of her drink. The answer comes to me as she speaks, bringing with it the sensation of a ball of slithering snakes squirming in my stomach. I'm no longer leaning against the wall. I'm slumping with terror.

"Yeah, anyway. She said maybe you'd know? So, like, Blake never came home last night. She said you're friends, but I bet you're fucking my boyfriend. You can't do that, you know. Fuck him, right? He's mine. But he's gone." Sobbing fills the line, followed by a swallow. A deep inhale. I can almost smell the smoke as she exhales into the receiver. "Do you know where he is, bitch? Because I'm going to find him, or you. Mainly him. No you. Whatever. Call me."

The line goes dead.

Please press 1 to listen again, 2 to save...

I hit END with shaky fingers. Blake didn't forget to stop by last night.

He never made it.

So where did he go and how do I find him?

Maybe trace his route from his office to my house? Of course, that would entail me knowing what office building he worked in. But while I doubt Jordan thinks clearly enough to call the police, I'm certain she contacted Blake's mother, Cecily placed the call.

Which means the police are out looking for him, even if he hasn't been missing long. Cecily with her old Dallas money can pull more strings than a puppeteer. Unfortunately, unless he's possessed by a minion, there's nothing I can do the cops can't.

So the real question becomes whether or not I'll return Jordan's call.

I vote no. Reason being, I'm not in the mood to talk to the girlfriend of the man I'm having an affair with while she calls me names and insults my parentage.

Not that I don't do a little parentage insulting myself, but I'm not about to take it from some bottled-blonde boob-job bitch with a drinking problem.

Maybe Smythe would know what to do. As I walk to my car in a mind-fog, it dawns on me Smythe always shows up at my house. I have no idea where he lives—yeah, yeah, Boston in the Agency high-rise, like that tells me anything—or any idea how to get in touch with him.

I could call T, or send him a telepathic message, but it's after midnight and I know without asking he lies in bed with Jackie. Asleep. And what would he do? Tell me I'm better off without my FWB who has turned into way more than a friends with benefits relationship should? Yeah, I can do without that.

An intersection pops in front of me, light flashing red. I blink. Talk about autopilot. Somehow I got from the hospital hallway to my car, and halfway home, so lost in thought I didn't realize what I was doing. A quick glance in the rearview mirror shows no flashing lights behind me, only a stretch of dark road punctuated by street lights and the occasional car.

Damn. I haven't done anything like that since my younger, wilder days.

The rest of the drive goes without incident, as I'm now paying more attention to the road than my whirling panicked thoughts. I half expect to see a cop car parked in front of the house, sleepy detective ready to ask me questions about Blake, but there's nothing there except a dark blob of oil staining the asphalt.

The garage door pulls open, STOP HERE sign hanging down. Vines out of jojo, pops into my mind and I chuckle as I hit the garage door clicker. Out the garage side door, onto my back porch, key in hand. Open the door, close and lock it, turn around. A lone light shines from the living room, streaking across the tiled kitchen floor like a killer's scaly fingers searching for a throat.

I sure as hell didn't leave a light on.

Clutching my purse as if it were a weapon, I take a step closer to the table, peer around the fridge into the living room. The lamp on the end table next to the couch lights up the room with its energy saving bulb, a shining beacon of hope. Big black boots rest toes up over the end of the couch. Snores greet my ears in a calming in-out rhythm.

Smythe sleeps stretched out on my couch, open laptop performing a balancing act on his chest.

Air rushes out of my lungs on a sigh of relief. I release my white-knuckled grip on my purse. Well, that solved my how to get in touch with Smythe problem. Thank god it wasn't Samantha back again for round two.

I set my purse on the counter and grab a beer from the fridge. Which I then proceed to drink in long swallows until the thing runs dry. Naturally gulping down a beer like that makes me burp.

Not very ladylike, but it can't be helped.

Smythe jumps, boots slamming against wood as he goes from horizontal to vertical in under a second, hands fumbling to keep the laptop from crashing to the floor. "What—"

"Sorry. Beer." I hold the empty bottle, shake it a little.

He places the laptop on the coffee table, runs a hand through his hair, and blinks like a rousing dragon. "Bad night?"

"Blake's missing."

I could almost see him processing it, the wheels of his mind turning with the speed of a slug until they kicked into gear. Blue eyes narrow, laser sharp.

"How do you know he's missing?" *Maybe he just didn't want to stop by last night*, went unsaid, but still plastered across his face like words in a book.

"His girlfriend called. Drunk. Said he never came home last night and wanted to know where he was." I walk so I stand in the doorway between the two rooms, lean against the wall.

"What did you tell her?"

"I didn't. She left a message. Didn't think I wanted to call her back."

His mouth opens, closes as he decides not to speak his thoughts. But I see them on his face. He disapproves of sleeping with someone who has a significant other. Yeah, well. Circumstances and all that.

Maybe I should try having after midnight conversations with Smythe more often. I seem to know what he's thinking without touching him or watching his lips form words.

Or maybe I'm just that good at reading faces.

"Did she call the police?"

"She didn't say."

"Are you sure he didn't go away to work on a case?"

"He's an estate lawyer. Not criminal."

"So no one would want him dead?"

"Not for his job. At least I can't imagine why any client would want a hit on him. He does estate wills."

His fingers drum against his leg. "Maybe he wanted to get away from it all."

"Not without telling his mother, he wouldn't. Jordan implied Cecily didn't know where he was."

"Jordan being the girlfriend and Cecily the mom?"

"Yep. What do you think? Can we find him?" I shove off the wall. Take a step forward.

"Not tonight."

"But he's been missing for over twenty-four hours!" I swallow back the screech clawing its way out of my heart. How can I do nothing? How can I do anything?

He draws in a deep breath through his nose. "Gin. It's one in the morning. We're not doing anything tonight but sleep. If it was a kidnapping, then Jordan or his mother would've already received the note and alerted the police. She would not have called you asking where he is."

"Can't you work your magic and hack into the police website again?" I wave a hand at his going-blurry computer.

He sighs, shoulders dropping. "Okay. Come have a seat." He pats the couch cushion next to him before reaching for his laptop.

Still holding the empty beer bottle, I walk to where he sits—laptop balanced on his legs, fingers flying across the keyboard—and take a seat, close enough so my thigh brushes against his.

For once touching him brings no electric zingers.

Thank God.

Pages flash on the screen, confidential data accessed at will by a hacker. After asking me for his last name, Smythe types Blake Calder, hits enter and waits until the site loads the info.

Watching him hack the police website forms a twinge in my chest. Nerves or exhilaration? After years of working in the ER as a nurse, trying to make like I'm an outstanding citizen, I've forgotten how much fun it is to take a walk on the illegal side.

Provided the cops don't track the hack to my IP address and come arrest me.

"See—" Smythe points at the screen "—they've started a missing person's report, but haven't gotten very far on it. I don't see your name as a potential contact."

"Okay. So what do we do now?"

"Go to sleep." At my I-don't-think-so look he amends, "I'll sleep in here."

"You can borrow T's bed. I'll give you fresh sheets. He's not coming over tonight."

"You sure?"

"We'll change out the sheets again tomorrow. He'll never know."

"Okay." Smythe shuts the laptop, stands.

"Unless you'd rather do the portal thing back to your apartment?" Good manners dictate I ask.

"Would that make you feel better?"

"Whatever. I don't care." Liar. I need the security of his magic, the magic of his touch. Bleh. Where the hell do I get these thoughts? I might want him to stay, but definitely not for that reason.

He tucks the laptop under an arm and heads for T's room. "If it's all the same to you, I'll stay the night."

Whew. Mission accomplished. Just knowing he'll be in the house loosens the knot in my chest. Does he know his presence is a tangible comfort?

Probably not and it wouldn't do to tell him either.

Big head and all that.

"Sleep tight. Bathroom's down the hall."

I'm not sure if he heard me since the door closes on my words. No matter. He probably already knows where the bathroom is.

I snap off the light, double check the doors, grab my purse off the counter, and go into my bedroom. Close the door. Do the nighttime routine of clothes change, toilet and face wash. Brush my teeth for good measure. Turn off the light and crawl under the covers.

Light from the full moon creeps around the blinds, mixing with shadows of branches and leaves to form designs on the walls. Thoughts twist through my mind, questions of Blake's location, the bracelet's usefulness in tracking him, Smythe.

Finding him still in my house is a bit strange, after all, he claims to have an apartment. Not that I'm complaining. But is he staying for me? Or is forming a portal when tired harder than I think?

What do I know about magic anyway?

My thoughts circle around to Blake. I see his smile, the gleam in his eye when he wants me, smell the scent of his cologne as if he's lying beside me. My body remembers his touch, the feel of his skin on mine, the way the fine hairs on his chest tickle my breasts as he moves within me.

Where is he?

Unlike last night, where I craved and needed, tonight I'm too drained to crave anything, my needs reduced to finding Blake, to ensuring his safety.

What will I do without him?

Think positive, Gin. You'll find him.

I can only hope wishes come true.

Chapter 21

Sleep comes in snatches, dressed in dreams unremembered but nonetheless causing a sense of unease after waking. Or maybe all that unease came from watching the room grow lighter while knowing I needed more sleep. A groan escapes as I roll onto my side. The red numbers on the clock shine 8:00AM in a manner guaranteed to cause insomniacs to pull out a hammer and shatter all those happy freakin' numbers into small pieces.

I'm not grumpy at all after a night of little sleep.

Nope, not me.

Since lying around hoping sleep will smack me upside the head proves useless, I sit up, run a hand over my eyes.

Maybe Smythe ran another computer search and found Blake.

Desperate hope lives eternal.

Slipping into a tank top and shorts, I stop by the bathroom on my way into the kitchen. Clearly I'm the only one in the house with sleeping issues. T's door remains closed and the house has that sleepy, hung-over, not-yet-ready-to-rise feel to it.

After starting a pot of coffee brewing, I slip outside to pick up the newspaper. Enough humidity slams me in the face to curl my hair into ringlets in the under thirty seconds I'm outside.

Gotta love a Texas summer.

A bead of sweat runs between my breasts, pooling in the tank's built-in bra as I walk into the pleasant coolness of an over-worked air conditioner. Taking the paper into the kitchen, I hear the coffeepot crackling cheerfully as it makes my wake-up juice.

It's not until I pitch the paper on the table that I see the note. A small, white envelope sits on top of yesterday's paper, unopened. My brain cranks with all the speed of a cold engine, trying to process an occurrence before I've had a caffeine hit. It takes a couple of tries, until I realize T must've gotten the paper yesterday along with the note and put them both on the table for me to read. But Smythe's breakfast and ensuing training lesson interrupted my normal paper reading routine.

Which meant the note sat right there all day Friday.

Wonder what my paper carrier wanted now. The bill, maybe?

Join the crowd.

I grab the envelope, ripping open the seal, pulling out the card.

Thinking of You in calligraphy scrawls across the front, the crease at the top. Since when do bills come with that sentiment stamped on the front?

I open the card, blink at the picture inside. It takes longer than it should for the picture and words written on the card to register. But when they do, oh god, when they do...I crumble like a puppet with its strings cut, legs surrendering to gravity, fingers functionless. The card flutters to the floor, a silent landing with the force of an explosion.

A noise fills the kitchen, rattles the windows, strips

skin from my soul. Me screaming, "No!" in one long cry, loud enough to frost the room with my rage, my fear.

Footsteps pound a race as Smythe runs into the kitchen, clad in nothing but boxer briefs. My scream turns into hiccups, little breaths of refusal. One finger points at the offending card, the other slaps over my mouth as if to hold in another screech.

Smythe squats, yanks the card off the floor, and opens it, his jaw tensing as he stares at the picture. As he stares at a trussed-up and bleeding Blake, the picture Photoshopped onto the obviously homemade card.

"We have under four hours."

My lips refuse to form words, only allowing a moan to escape. Why? Who would do this to Blake? Why didn't I see the card yesterday? We could've started looking for him then. Now, he's been gone for over twenty-four hours. What kind of a friend, of a lover, am I not to notice the card? I'm worthless. Worthless.

And now he's been captured and hurt.

Pain explodes in my chest, a scalpel performing open-heart surgery minus the anesthesia. My stomach churns while the taste of bitter acid fills my mouth. Smythe blurs as I try to swallow around a boulder the size of a whale lodged in my throat.

Someone took Blake.

How dare they? They can't have my friend. He's mine. The invisible scalpel sears a resolve into my soul, forges a promise. I will find him.

"Gin?" Smythe's hand touches my forearm, a gesture meant to console. "Did you hear me? We have four hours until the meeting."

A swallow followed by a sniff. Then a hand wipe across my cheeks. Smythe remains blurry around the edges each time my eyes run through the open-and-shut routine, but the boulder in my throat moves, allowing some other noise besides the hurt-animal moan.

"What meeting?" Never scream, sob and then try to talk. It makes your voice sound like a ninety-year-old smoker.

Another hand pat on the forearm. "On the card. Noon Saturday. Then the address. We'll get him back."

I want to believe him so badly it forms a taste in my mouth. A citrus-y taste of hope congealing shock and grief into a rage hot enough to consume.

I will get him back. And whoever took him will pay.

****

"Cops." The word cracks through my raw throat. I swallow. Try again. "We need to call the cops." Look at that, words can come out of a grief-constricted throat.

"They can't help. This is the work of Jezebeth or her minion."

"Jezebel?" Wasn't that some Biblical queen with a bad reputation?

"No, not Jezebel. Jezebeth. A lower-level demon. This is her work. Or her minions'."

I clear my throat, hope for a non-raspy voice. "A minion took Blake?"

"It looks that way."

"What the hell? Since when do minions kidnap people?"

He gives me a get-real look, like I'm half-brained.

"I mean, kidnap people I know. Don't we, the *justitians* I mean, don't we fight them? How often does this happen?" Is T at risk?

"It's a bit unusual for a minion to go after a *justitian's* friend."

I clear my throat. Bye-bye rasp. "Like how unusual?"

"I've never heard of it before."

"Then how do you know that's who has him?"

"Because of the symbol on the corner of the card. See?" He points to the barely-there symbol. "Your average kidnapper wouldn't know that symbol. And you're unlikely to be the one who gets the ransom note in a normal kidnapping."

True. But the fact that a minion—or worse, a demon—kidnapped Blake makes the situation more horrific than when I thought some mobster grabbed him.

"Okay, I believe you. So why wait? Form a portal and let's go get him."

"First off—" he stands, puts the card on top of the newspaper "—I don't know where this address is." Both his hands turn palm up. "You can't just go portaling into someplace you have no idea where it is. Who knows where you'd land."

"But that's what you did with the minion when you portaled us into his car."

"No, my spell tracked the minion. I knew exactly where he was. I wouldn't have formed a portal if I didn't know." He offers a hand to me, pulling me to my feet when I grasp it.

Huh. Spells as GPS. Who knew? "Then why don't you form a spell now?"

"Too many unknown variables. We need to go to the address and see what's there."

"Google it then. Hurry up." Why is he just standing there holding my hand?

"And I doubt he's there."

"What? Where else would he be?"

"Think about it. Why would they give us the address where he is being held in advance? They'd expect us to come get him. But if they give us the meet address, then even if we show up early, we can't find the package."

I drop his hand as my back teeth snap together hard enough to knock off enamel. "Blake is more than a package."

His brows jerk up, hands raise chest-level in a classic back-off gesture. "It's a figure of speech. Don't you watch TV?"

"TV shows are fiction! This is real!" I point at the card, tapping it with my index finger.

"Okay. Okay." He spreads his hands in that gesture men give to calm down a hysterical woman. "The real issue is what they want in exchange."

Nope, not calm. Not yet. I draw in a deep breath, hold it, hold it, release the air on a long sigh. Still not calm, but at least I can talk without screeching. "The note doesn't say anything about an exchange."

"Well, they didn't snag him for shits and giggles. While demons usually use people with deviant tendencies to turn into minions, that doesn't mean they choose idiots to do their bidding. Most minions posses intelligence. They just don't use it for the betterment of mankind."

"Then why would they take Blake?"

"It has to be something with you, but I'm not sure what. As I said, minions don't normally mess with the friends of *justitians*."

"So what changed?"

"I don't know!" His palms crack against the table and I jump, heart cracking against my ribs.

He's not mad at me. Really. He's not.

"No cops." One finger points at me, before he strides out of the kitchen.

My breath releases on an exhale. I wipe my palms down the front of my shorts, trying not to glance at the card, trying not to remember the terror in Blake's eyes, the blood streaked on his face.

Not looking at the card means not reading the paper for distraction since the card lays on top of the paper, so I pour a cup of coffee and stare out the window. Watching the sun bake the grass into shriveled tendrils allows my mind to churn. Rather like my stomach. A burning no amount of hot, bitter coffee can soothe.

Shitkickers tap a rhythm down the hall until Smythe appears in the kitchen fully dressed in jeans and a tight black tee that highlights the muscles of his chest and arms. I'm beginning to think the man needs a serious wardrobe overhaul.

I take a swallow of coffee, letting it burn my already raw throat, hoping the heat burns away the damp taste of death clogging my throat.

Smythe places his laptop on the table, yanks out a chair, and smacks his butt into the seat. The computer whirs to life as he raises the lid, images flashing across the screen as the familiar start-up music plays.

I continue to stare at the window, gathering my thoughts, stuffing my emotions into a hiding place deep within my mind. I need all the clarity I can get for the upcoming rescue mission. No wayward emotions allowed.

My heart pounds a nervous rhythm. Good thing I don't have a stress test today. I'd probably flunk it. Unless having a stress level off the charts counts as a winner.

Thoughts are another matter. A barrage hits me, questions popping as fast into my mind as they leave, a constant stream of queries bringing on another round of heart pounding.

Xanax anyone?

"Okay," Smythe says, oblivious to my climbing stress level. "I found where the address is."

"Yeah? Where?" Cradling my mug, I walk to his chair, peer over his shoulder at the online map.

"Empty warehouse in Dallas." He points at the screen, drawing my attention to the little bubble marking the location of the address.

"That's not a good area of town."

"We'll portal in. Behind the building. Then we'll check it out before they arrive. You ready to go?" He snaps the laptop closed, pushes his chair back.

I step to the side as his chair misses my leg by inches. Coffee jostles over the rim, its heat stinging my fingers. "Watch it!"

"Sorry. Are you ready to go? We can go check out the lay of the land."

"Yeah. Just need my shoes. And something to eat." I put the mug on the counter. Rinse the coffee off my hands. Then it's off to the bedroom where I pull on a pair of socks and my sneakers. Back to the kitchen. Open the pantry. Grab a package of peanut butter and crackers, which I stick into my pocket.

Smythe holds out his hand to me, palm up, and I pitch him a package of snack crackers, too. Like me, he stuffs them into his pocket.

He speaks his portal-forming words, one hand held before him, the other reaching for my hand. As soon as my palm clasps his, I'm pulled into the iciness of the in-between, only to be spit out onto pavement half a second later.

I suck in a breath. Bad idea. Apparently abandoned means the city trash collectors refuse to come close to the building.

Or the city morgue dumps unclaimed bodies in this alley.

Smythe joins me in the hide-nose-behind-hand routine.

"Can't you wave a hand and get rid of the smell?" I fan a hand in front of my nose. I'm no longer hungry. Trying not to gag tends to make that happen.

"Magic doesn't work like that."

"Why not?"

"You really want to get into that now?"

"Point taken. Open the damn door. Hopefully the stench isn't inside, too."

Pulling something from his pocket, he walks to the alley door, keeping a hand over his mouth and nose. I follow behind him, holding my hand over my face. Isn't one supposed to get used to an odor, thereby rendering it less smelly?

Apparently my nose never got the memo.

Smythe drops his hand from his face so he can use both hands to work the tool. Excuse me, lockpick. A real lockpick. Just like they use in the movies when the thief wants to get into the locked building.

Bitchin'.

"So why aren't you using magic to poof open the door?"

"Wastes the magic."

"Huh?"

"I'll explain later."

Okay then. Later. One lesson on magic coming up. Once we rescue Blake and kill all the minions.

Provided I can kill one. What if they all talk to each other and learn about my weaknesses? What if they all speak the same words as that minion in San Antonio? What if they're right? Maybe I am worthless. After all, I did nothing to stop Blake from being kidnapped.

I didn't even find the damn ransom note until this morning. Twenty-four hours of reconnaissance wasted.

I am a worthless friend.

The door squeaks open, interrupting my wallow into the swamp of self-loathing.

"I'm in." Smythe's voice comes as a whisper, a breath of air spoken for only my ears. "Stay close."

Close. Check. As if there's another option.

Surely he doesn't think I want to continue standing in the smells-like-death alley.

I walk close enough for his body heat to warm my chest.

"I said stick close, not become one with me."

"Keep walking. I'm almost out of that alley." Once I cross the threshold, I swing the door shut, underused hinges squawking a protest.

The snap of the latch lessens the odor from the alley. Lessens, but not extinguishes. We stand in semi-darkness, surrounded by looming shadows. Dim light filters through high windows coated in a layer of grime.

Smythe exchanges the lockpick for a penlight similar to the one used at the hospital. *Click-click.* A beam of light stronger than any penlight I've ever used streams through the building's twilight, turning the shadows into large pieces of forgotten machinery.

"You sure this building's not one of those dump sites the EPA needs to cleanup?"

Smythe peers over his shoulder, shakes his head. Faces forward, walks toward the closest metal object. "It's an old metal shop." The beam of light dances across the metal contraption. "Company moved to a newer building."

"They apparently left their trash behind." I gesture toward the alley as I drop the protective shield of my nose-covering hand.

"They moved over twenty years ago. Anything they left behind shouldn't smell like that. It's probably dead rats."

"That's a lot of dead rats to produce that kind of stench."

"We can either find the stench or find your friend."

When put like that..."Good point. Lead on, fearless leader."

He snorts, a grin playing against his lips. The expression fades as he focuses on bouncing the light beam across the floor. Over the walls. Up to the ceiling.

We stand inside a large room, graffiti covering the walls, dirt and a chalk-like powdery substance coloring the floor dusty white. A set of wooden stairs ventures upward toward the ceiling. No, not the ceiling, a room hidden in the corner of the warehouse. Probably at one time a supervisor's office.

Now it's an accident waiting to happen.

Not walking up those stairs.

"We need to see what's up there." Smythe's light-beam hits the rickety stairs. I half expect them to collapse under the light's weight.

"Have at, buddy. Those things look too dangerous. Besides, that white powder covers the stairs."

"Good observation. Doesn't look like they've been used."

"Yep. Not even by the spray-can-wielding gangster." The wall of the upper room gleams with a distinct lack of graffiti.

Goes to show even a vandal possesses a sense of safety.

Walking through the building doesn't take long. One story, with the exception of the upstairs supervisor's office and a destroyed restroom, the oversized room lies deserted of human activity.

"Activate the *justitia*. See if there're any minion trails around."

"Aye, aye, captain." I stare at my bracelet, trying to remember how I saw the minion trails before. Did I ask it?

Minion trails activate!

Nothing.

Please, please, please?

Okay. So asking and begging don't help.

The answer slams into my mind, the memory a plea for release. Asking and begging don't help because the *justitia* wants a joining. It wants me to allow its abilities to fuse with mine. To allow an entity control of my body.

I'm not worthy. I can't do this. I can't.

But you can, floats through my mind. My thought? The bracelet's? Some other entity's?

Just when I think I'm not going crazy I realize it's all an illusion.

"Gin? You see anything yet?"

"Not yet."

"Try harder."

I squeeze my eyes shut. I can do this. I can save Blake. I can prove I'm not a worthless creature.

Shifting my consciousness to my wrist, I focus on the weight of the bracelet, imagining tendrils from the silver fusing to my nerves. A sharp bite of electricity zings up my arm igniting a kaleidoscope of colors in my mind. The *justitia* explodes with a song of joy.

It's ecstatic I want to work with it. Thrilled to once again be used. To be needed.

All the nerves in my body spring to life, a super-shot of energy pumping through my system ready for a fight. A fight with no minions, apparently. Instead of running loose like an uncontrolled infection, maybe the adrenaline rush should wait for the appearance of an actual minion.

And like a blast of dry air the energy evaporates.

Freaky. The damn bracelet actually heard my thought and responded.

Opening my eyes, I take a peek at the dusty room, expecting to see bands of red ribbons dotting the room. I know the *justitia* has activated the minion trail sensors in my eyes—oh my god, did I actually say that? I'm effing losing it—but there's nothing outside of a faint glow around the graffiti art.

Despite the obvious, I walk around the room, looking for the ribbons indicating a minion stood here.

Apparently minions avoid abandoned buildings like the rest of the human race.

It's not until I walk to the alley door, the one Smythe picked, that I see the trails. They remain by the door, venturing only a foot or so into the warehouse.

"The only trail in here is by the alley door." I point and Smythe shines his light over the door. "Do you see them?"

"Yeah, but I didn't earlier."

"You mean you looked?"

"Of course. You think I'd just walk on in without checking it out?"

"Maybe."

His brows slam into a vee. "What do you take me for? A fool?"

"So why didn't you see them when we came in?"

"I don't know. Maybe the lighting was wrong. Or my eyes hadn't adjusted."

"Or they came in while we were looking around."

"We would've heard the door squeak." But he runs the penlight around the door and surrounding wall. Even then I don't see the trails heading into the warehouse. Nope, they stay by the door.

Bam!

The door jumps, shaking in its frame like a seizing patient. Where's a spare pair of panties when you need them?

We stare transfixed and unmoving at the door as if it's the entrance for the second coming of Christ. Metal groans, the center of the door bending into the shape of a hand. A hand reaching toward us.

And then it starts to glow Hellfire red.

Chapter 22

A faint pulsing blush tints the door, gathering strength as wood feeds a fire, until the metal hinges crackle from the heat.

"Fucking shit! Get back, Gin!" Smythe clicks off the penlight, throwing his arm out as if to push me behind him.

The *justitia* springs to life. A burst of adrenaline surges through my veins with the roar of an engine opened full-throttle. And this time I welcome it, embracing the energy like a long lost friend, absorbing its strength until I'm filled with its power.

Vibrations rattle the door, a subsonic blast echoing inside my bones. A stench of heated sulfur slams into the room, singeing the hairs off my nose when I make the mistake of breathing.

What the holy hell is out there?

But I know the answer even if my mind refuses to believe it.

A soul-deep answer. One imbedded in every human since the dawn of time. An instinct geared toward survival. A nervous system response guaranteed to make you flee, not stick around and fight.

Some things need no explaining. Some things are known deep inside even if we modern humans refuse to believe such things exist.

They exist all right.

And one of them comes for me.

Bam! The door flies open, the squeaking hinges protesting the movement with a dying scream as they pop, leaving the door hanging like a human with a broken neck. Three minions walk inside, swords strapped to their backs, eyes scouting the perimeter of the room.

Guards.

A long, coal-black shadow precedes the demon into the warehouse. I'm so focused on the shadow I fail to see its entrance. Blood runs like a winter waterfall through my veins as I try to swallow with a tongue made from sand. Air, thick with sulfur and smelling like death, slams into the room, filling the warehouse with an indescribable stench.

God in heaven. How am I supposed to fight this...thing? I can't breathe. I can't tear my gaze from the shadow, let alone bother to look at the damn demon. How many of my fellow *justitians* fought one of these things and won?

Anyone? Anyone?

Or is it only me dumb enough to try?

No, that's not true. My first night wearing the bracelet, when Smythe took me to the Agency, a demon appeared in Austin, and Samantha the bitch was sent with her ward to kill it. Since I saw Samantha afterward, it's a pretty good assumption one can survive a demon attack.

Provided the blonde bitch didn't ditch her ward like she did me.

No doubt about it. I have to survive this fight because I owe that bitch some payback. And I never renege on a promise.

Besides, I want Blake back. Demon has Blake, I'll fight the demon.

Enough said.

Even if the air clogs my throat with the damp taste of loam.

Despite a sword thrusting from my bracelet, Smythe stands in front of me, a six-foot-five muscular wall of protection. At least I like to think of him as protection. Frankly, I'm not sure how much protection he offers against three minions and a full-fledged demon.

"You're early." The minion's voice snaps my gaze off the demon's shadow and onto the walking evil in human flesh.

I only see the minions. The three virtually identical minions who look like a cross between ex-military and Viking. Short blonde hair, tatted muscular arms and, I'm assuming, blue eyes, although it's hard to tell in this light. A shadow, a long, dark, gotta-be-evil shadow, stretches across the white-coated floor, but the creature stands back several feet from the door, out of my line of vision. I don't see Blake or his shadow. Where is he?

"So are you." Smythe responds by shifting his stance, his hands hanging loose against his legs.

"And you're trespassing."

"I can say the same for you."

"Yeah, but unlike you, we own this place."

"Then maybe you can figure out what smells." I step to Smythe's side, giving the minion my best glare.

And the evil-looking shadow disappears like it never existed, taking with it the stench of sulfur. Did I imagine the thing?

Maybe, but I'm definitely not imagining Smythe's

hand clasped around my wrist like a pair of handcuffs.

Shut the fuck up! screams through my mind.

Oh my god. Smythe knows telepathy. His words have their desired effect, speaking being a little hard to do with my mouth hanging open. Surprise masked as obedience. When did he learn telepathy? And how for that matter? Silly me, thinking T and I were the only ones with the ability.

What other hidden talents does he possess?

The lead minion laughs. "Hear that, boys? She thinks we don't know what the smell is." One finger points at the minion to his left, jerks to the open door. "Show her."

In the time it takes for the minion lackey to step out the door and return with a roll of carpet under his arm, a gamut of emotions dances the foxtrot through my system. *Surely he doesn't mean to bring the smell in here* turns into *why does he want me to see what the dead thing is* which morphs into *nonononono*.

It dawns on me I'm not breathing. I draw in a breath, but it refuses to move past the lump in my throat. Which means no help for the nausea building in my gut. I'm only vaguely aware of Smythe's grip loosening. All my attention focuses on the door, on the minion's shadow as it elongates in the slash of sunlight. On the lumpy roll of carpet he lays on the ground. On his boot-covered foot as it kicks the carpet. On the carpet as it rolls open, exposing the cause of the stench.

Blake.

I clasp my left hand over my mouth. But the cry escapes, rattles the grimy windows, finds an echo in the shaking of my heart. My chest explodes with an ache so encompassing it swallows me in pain. Nothing exists in the room. Not Smythe. Not the minions. Not the disappearing demon.

Nothing but my friend, my lover, and me.

I want to run to his side. To breathe life into his swollen, pale body. To let him know I came for him.

But I remain where I stand, one hand clasped against my mouth. It's too late to breath into his mouth, to perform chest compressions until he wakes. He will not wake. Ever.

And he'll never know I came for him.

Blake's body wavers in my sight as I blink.

He lays stiff on the carpet, face-up, blood dried in rivulets across his face. A wide gap forms a wicked smile in his neck. The grin of death.

Son of a bitch. They slit his neck.

Next thing I know, I stand in front of the minion who carried in Blake's body, my sword slicing a matching line across his throat. He drops to the ground, surprise written around his widened eyes. He's not the only one surprised. I have no idea how I got from Smythe's side to the minion's.

None.

Maybe I portaled. Maybe I lost my mind with a potent mixture of grief and anger.

Maybe I need to get out of my head and into the game seeing how Lead Minion's sword points my direction.

I let out a battle cry that would do a Kung Fu master proud and charge. My sword scrapes against LM's, metal screeching a protest as our swords fight for dominance. Pain explodes against my cheek, a backhand that sends me flying like a speeding missile. Just like it did in my house the first night I wore the *justitia.*

What is it with minions and backhands?

And why can't I remember not to fall for the trick?

It dawns on me mid-flight this minion is stronger than the one who showed up at my house. Stronger. More determined. Hits harder too. And if I slam into the concrete floor after flying, I can kiss my life good-bye.

Oh fuck.

Instead of concrete, I smack against the soft cushion of an overstuffed gym mat. The kind used by stunt people jumping off buildings.

Yet nothing lies between me and the floor outside of my clothes.

Not like I'm complaining. Invisi-mat just saved my last thought from being a cuss word.

I sit up, notice Smythe dropping his hand, relief etched across his face.

"Nice work, man." Lead Minion nods his head at Smythe. "But she's still mine."

"I'm not yours." A flash of ouch-ouch-ouch in my jaw dissipates the longer I talk. "You killed my friend, you bastard. You're my kill." Standing to my feet takes a bit of effort I hope the minion fails to notice. Despite nailing a landing on a non-existent cushiony mat, dizziness spins my vision. Best guess names backhand-to-cheek as most likely cause, but adrenaline fills me with such a rush the pain isn't even a blip on my radar.

The dizziness is a whole other matter.

Gin! Shut your fucking mouth! Stop egging him on!

Get out of my fucking head! I try to force Smythe out. To form the barriers learned over years of practicing with T.

Apparently barriers mean nothing for the man. He

remains in my mind like he owns the place.

These aren't your average minions. They're Demon Guards.

Demons need guards? WTF?

Watch out!

This time the cushiony mat doesn't materialize and I smack the floor with a resounding thud. Shit, that hurt. Now both sides of my face throb in unity with my heart.

But I've discovered how to forget about grief. At least for the moment.

Anger rides my veins, a boost of energy needing an outlet.

An outlet like a minion's face.

How convenient. I have two to choose from.

Pushing to my feet, I run at Lead Minion, sword extended. He meets my thrust with one of his own, and it's another round of screeching swords. The second minion jogs over, takes a swing, the flat of his sword whacking against my hamstrings.

It stings and will undoubtedly leave a bruise, but doesn't cut me. Smythe stands to the side. Why doesn't he burn these fuckers like he did the ones at the park? Why doesn't he lob a fireball or some other magic at them?

Clearly he's the reason a non-existent cushiony mat broke my fall. It's not like I magicked one of those up, and the minions sure as hell didn't. So why's he just standing there?

No time to think. Both minions engage me, and the moment becomes a blur of movement. Thrust. Evade. Kick. Duck. Gasp with pain as one of them gets in a hit.

Thank god the *justitia* overrules my pain receptors.

Unfortunately it can't do a damn thing about

swelling eyes.

Even magical bracelets have limits.

That still doesn't explain Smythe's reluctance to blow these minions to smithereens.

I'm wearing out. Not much training will do that to a person. Even if their *justitia* controls their nervous system. I might be moving faster than the average human, but the kicks and punches don't come naturally.

Something to work on when I get out of this mess.

Both minions use the flats of their swords to smack my legs, my arms. I'm covered in soon-to-be bruises. Why aren't they using the pointy tip of their sword? That would cause some damage. It's almost like they want me whole. Like they're herding me toward something.

The back of my ankle hits a step, and I fall backward, arms flailing. One arm slaps against railing and I grab on, preventing myself from landing on my ass. I recognize where I am. Up against the rickety stairs.

Those stairs I refused to go up earlier.

A stench of sulfur permeates the air, overpowering the decaying death odor. I glance toward the open door. See nothing but Blake's body lying in a wedge of sunlight.

"No!" Smythe yells, jumping forward, his hands moving as if signing to a deaf person.

Sparks explode from his fingers, fly over my head. I duck, but arms band around my waist, lift. I try to kick the shins of my captor, but a putrid grunt in my ear is all I get for my effort.

And then I'm airborne, once again giving my best flying-comic-book-hero impersonation. The minions duck and I sail over their heads, all loose limbs and broken strings. Right before I become one with the concrete, Smythe magicks another cushiony mat, breaking my free-fall.

Thank god for guardians.

I start to sit up only to have my head slam against the almost-deflated invisi-mat. Pinpoints of light blacken my vision. Something heavy crushes my legs. Smythe yells from a distance. Or what seems like a distance. He can't really be that far away, right?

Head injury. Probable concussion. Need a CT scan of the head to rule out bleeding on the brain.

Instead I get a wave of sulphur-laden death-breath blown into my face. Which oddly enough banishes the lack of vision.

Not like I'm calling that a good thing once my eyes start focusing.

An olive-complexioned woman sits on my legs, her model-perfect features marred by the evil smirk consuming her face. She's dressed in a charcoal gray long-sleeve pantsuit, white ruffled top poking out at the collar. Long hair parted to the side hangs down her back, not a strand falling in her face.

Definite sign of the supernatural.

Her outline blurs, courtesy of a mix of swollen eyes, concussion, and grief-driven rage.

Or her eau-de-rotten-egg perfume.

Yuck.

"You killed my regiment of minions!" Her voice resonates like a petulant toddler on the verge of a tantrum. "And now you must pay!"

Geez, how cliché. You'd think after millennia of stalking the earth a demon could come up with something cleverer before it annihilated my ass.

"Yeah, yeah, yeah. That's what they all say." All the cookie-cutter bad guys that is.

Smack! Her palm whacks against my cheek, snapping my head to the side. Ouch, ouch, ouch. I'm tired of playing punching bag for a demon.

Especially one not smart enough to pin down my wrists. Her loss, my gain.

Making a fist with my left hand, I punch her in the temple. She sags to the side enough for me to scramble out from underneath her deceptively lightweight-looking self. I squat beside her.

Light flashes in my peripheral field, drawing my attention away from the demon. Smythe fights the two minions using magic bursts of energy to halt their attack. Despite light knocking against the upper windows, little makes it in, so it's hard to see. And my eyes are swollen. But Smythe looks like he's tiring out. Although how the man who incinerated a regiment of minions with the same effort as breathing can look tired is beyond my comprehension.

All that I noticed in the time it took for my eyes to open and close. One blink. And my attention returns to the still pissed off and snarling demon.

Who should command all my attention.

"You dare hit me?"

Note to self: demons have god complexes.

"You got a problem with that?" The words hang in the air, droplets of a poisonous aerosol, as a jolt of oh-shit-what-did-I-just-do passes through me. I smarted off to a demon. A freakin' I-live-in-Hell-and-eat-children-for-lunch demon. Smythe stomps around my kitchen yelling, and my gut response leaves me frozen with fear. But a demon says something I don't like and I sass it.

Clearly something is wrong with me.

And it's not my bracelet.

She blinks a couple of times, and then again for good measure. And what do you know? Sass can stop a demon in its tracks.

For all of five seconds.

"You should bow before me!" She roars, her breath strong enough to stop a Mac truck, let alone a human. Apparently mouthwash is unheard of in Hell. "I am Jezebeth. I am powerful! I killed your friend, the one you love. And you're next, you worthless whore."

I might be sick and tired of being called a worthless whore, but the barb hits its mark. I freeze, squatting in front of the kneeling, enraged demon. She's right. I should be face-down in fright before her. I'm not worthy of this fight.

"Look at him!" Her hand gestures toward Blake's body. "You killed my men. I killed the one you love. Tit for tat. But I had more men so now you must pay."

"You killed him for revenge?"

"Are you deaf? Yes. You killed my minions. Do you know how long it takes to train a regiment of minions? You killed them! You and your thrice-blessed guardian."

Her words snap me out of my pity party. All I needed was a reason to fight, and she just gave it to me. Another reason to live. Revenge on Samantha. Not only did the bitch try to have a regiment of minions kill me, but now those minions' demon wanted me dead.

Samantha is going down.

I leap to my feet, arm drawn back for a blow. Only

to perform another flight routine. My breath gushes out on an oomph as I smack against the floor. Bursting lights dim my vision at the same time the demon jumps on top of me. How can such a petite-looking woman weigh the same as a horse?

This time her knees press against my forearms, trapping my wrists along with the *justitia*. Her nails on one hand extend into claws, her face a mask of insane glee. My heart trips, drumming against my ribcage hard enough to flutter my tank top. *Move, move, move, move, move* chants through my brain and I twist in vain.

Her other hand grabs my tank, lifts, pulling my shoulders off the ground, then slams me back. Everything flickers to static as my head bounces. The *justitia* dulls the pain, tries to force my body to move, to escape. But I lay there, a broken doll teetering on the edge of unconsciousness.

Fight, fight, fight! Like washing the grime off a window, my vision clears. Right in time to see death swinging forward in the shape of claws. I force myself to watch. To watch the demon Jezebeth take my life.

To watch her eyes widen, her hands reach for her stomach as the tip of a sword pokes out. Faster than I can blink, she slips off the sword and leaps up, spinning mid-air to land at my feet. With a roar that shakes my bones, she jumps at the one who attacked her, claws extended. I haven't a clue how she manages to fight after being stabbed in the stomach. Clearly stab wounds don't affect demons the same way they do minions and humans.

I try to see around her, to see her attacker, but my blurry vision coupled with the dim light of the warehouse makes that attempt useless. As long as I kill that bitch demon I don't care who attacks her.

Taking a breath, I roll to my side, pausing as dizziness spins my vision. Somehow I manage to draw my feet underneath my body, push upright. The room sways, nausea threatening an appearance. The taste of bitter acid fills my mouth and I swallow. My head throbs in time with my heart, a fast-paced dance of pain. Jezebeth continues to fight, back to me, her posture slumped forward as she protects her injured abdomen.

I suck in a breath, ignore the spots flashing along the periphery of my vision. Grabbing my right wrist with my left hand for stability, I draw my arm back like I'm swinging a bat, the ball in this case being Jezebeth's neck. The *justitia* slices through her neck in one stroke.

Which is a good thing seeing how the blow uses all my energy and I crumple to the floor, a puppet with its strings cut.

Black blood spurts in the opposite direction from where her head lands, covering me in spatter. Nausea presses against the back of my throat. With a flash of light her body and head turn to ash, coating the floor with a fine black silt.

Unfortunately her blood spatter remains on my tank.

A man stands before me, holding a sword dripping wet with black demon blood. Tall, Middle-Eastern in appearance with black, wavy, shoulder-length hair, he wears a blue polo shirt and jeans, both of which are tight enough to show off muscle definition even in the dim light.

Who the heck is this?

A smile brushes his lips and my skin prickles as if cold fingers squeeze my chest. The *justitia* stills its frantic plea for me to move as the man shifts his sword to his left hand and reaches out his right. His gloved right hand. As if he knows his touch will bother me.

Awareness fails to catch up to relief over still being alive. I grasp his hand, allowing him to pull me to my feet.

Bad idea. My head swims with the position change. The bracelet fires a warning at the same time Smythe yells an incoherent string of words. My gaze jumps to Smythe. He leaps over the two prone—dead or unconscious—minions on his dash toward me.

A breath of warm air caresses my back. A fear-laden jolt sprints a dash across my flesh, a warning of situation bad turning worse.

Warm air in an abandoned warehouse baking in the morning Texas summer sun should not send me warning-danger signals.

Time slows, the thought hanging in my mind like dust motes floating in the air. Smythe's legs pump faster as his eyes widen to saucers of terror. A flash of light sparks on the opposite side of the room, a portal forming. Samantha steps through, followed by whom I assume to be her ward. Both wear identical looks of this-can't-be-happening.

High-pitched ringing screams along my nerves, in my ears. The *justitia* sounding a warning a bit too late. No, not a warning.

A greeting.

What the holy hell?

Smythe stops several feet from us. "Gin, step away from him." His voice holds an edge of panic. I try to move, but the man tightens his grip, locking my hand in his grasp.

I twist. The man holds on, yanking me against him. His arm with the sword encircles my waist, pulling me flush to his body. Then he lifts so my feet dangle. My cheek presses against his chest facing Smythe.

Who fires a round of colored lightning flashes from his fingers, aimed at the man's head. The man leaps forward to avoid the blast. I hear a crackle as it hits the wall, feel small pings of plaster as the wall explodes. Samantha runs toward us, fingers colored in light like Smythe's. Both of them release their balls of energy in synchronization.

For a split second I believe all those colors hit us, swirling around like a drunken kaleidoscope. Then an icy blast of super-chilled air bites into my skin, stealing my breath, freezing my tears to my cheeks.

I haven't been hit by magical flashes of energy.

It's worse. I've been captured by a demon.

Chapter 23

Struggle! Escape! Oh yeah, right, self. I'm in a portal, a freakin' demon portal. Who knows what will happen if the demon releases me in the middle of a port. Dying via lost-in-portal is not on my bucket list.

But when we land...

I collapse on stone flooring like a deflated balloon missing its helium. Probably due to the knock-me-on-my-ass stench of sulfur as opposed to something more ominous like bleeding-brain-induced-dizziness. Real elegant, Gin. Way to look strong in front of the evil demon disguised as a hottie.

But then, it's a little hard to look strong and capable when you're huddled on the floor trying not to breathe through your nose.

Or puke.

How can I be dizzy lying on the floor?

"Greetings, *Justitian.* I have looked forward to this day." The demon sounds like an average man. Deep voice, but not too deep. Unknown accent. The stench of sulfur wafts from the stones, not the demon. Are demons able to turn the smell on and off? I didn't notice it on his skin in the warehouse, but then Jezebeth had played whack-a-mole with my head so the possibility existed I missed the odor.

Although how one can miss the stench of rotted eggs I don't know.

Wait a minute. Had the demon asked me a question? Or made a statement?

Definite head injury.

"Who are you?" And why did you drag me here, wherever here is?

Laughter rolls across the floor, a malicious echo against stones that creeps into my marrow. Trembling spreads from inside out, a rage of excitement begging for freedom.

Ecstasy floods my veins, the *justitia's* response to the demon.

As if meeting a friend after the passage of many years.

Try a millennia or two.

What the hell? Isn't the thing supposed to fight demons, not give them the metaphysical equivalent of a hug?

I give it a feeble whack against the stone floor. As if that will force it to work right.

Nope. Still ecstatic about the demon.

Shit.

"Ah, I see," and then he rattles off a word I could never hope to pronounce, "is pleased to be in my presence. It's been so long, old friend. Too long."

I raise my eyes to the demon, whose outline blurs the longer I stare. Wetness stains my cheeks and I sniff. I will not lose it in front of a demon. I will not.

But pain and grief paint my insides with a potent mix of unbelief. I cannot be lying on stones in a demon lair. Blake cannot be dead. I cannot be dying. I need to be fighting this thing, this demon masquerading as a man.

Isn't that what I do? Aren't I supposed to fight

demons?

How? How do I fight when all I want to do is curl up and hide?

Or admit myself to the nearest hospital.

I'm pretty certain Jezebeth knocked something loose in my head that should remain unbroken. Like an artery. How long until I stroke?

I can't remember.

Not good.

And the traitorous bracelet seems oblivious to my anguish.

But the demon's not. He walks to me, looming large as I stare up at him. Squatting, his ungloved hand hovers a bit above my head and red-hot power cascades over me, a gentle wave soothing away the ache.

My eyes close in bliss. Ah. His power feels similar to Eloise's, and I drift in the same cloudless ocean of healing she uses. I shouldn't allow a demon to heal me. I might have jumped off the turnip truck this week, but even I know that.

And yet, his power entices, soothes, heals. I'm helpless to push him away. I don't want to push him away. I don't want to die. I want to live.

Even if it means using a demon's power to do so.

With that thought something switches deep inside. Instead of absorbing his power to heal, it pools for future use, like I'm a reservoir for evil.

I jerk and he withdraws his hand.

"Better, *Justitian*?"

I clear away the dry, dusty lump in my throat. "Thank you."

"It's the least I can do for an old friend."

"Friend?" How crazy are demons?

Maybe I'm not as healed as I think if I have to ask.

"Expression of speech, I believe you say."

"You know the um—" Why can't I remember these things? Duh. You don't heal instantly from a head injury. "Um, the bracelet? I mean *justitia*?"

The demon's lips twist. A smile? A grimace? "My, my. You are new. They told me, but I did not believe them."

"Who's they?"

One eyebrow pops, condescension written over his face. Nice to know demons possess expressions.

Demons possess more than expressions. Have I picked up another personality, or is the bracelet talking to me? How can a bracelet talk? And if it is talking to me, why the hell would it rather jump for joy upon seeing this demon than kill it? *Answer that* justitia.

It doesn't answer. Maybe I am going crazy.

Or crazier.

I clear my throat. My *justitia* might be malfunctioning, but the rest of me is feeling better by the minute. Demon healing is a good thing. Really. "Why did you bring me here? Why not kill me at the warehouse?"

"Killing is so—" he waves a hand "—passé."

"Then why did you let me kill Jezebeth?"

"Sometimes killing is necessary."

"And you thought it necessary for her to die."

He nods. "She outlived her usefulness."

"She killed my friend." *Oh, great Gin. Sob on the demon's shoulder, why don't you. Stop crying and try to figure out how to escape.*

He stands, takes a step back. "Some things cannot be helped."

"Thanks for the sympathy." I sniff, run a hand under my leaking eyes. *Pull it together, Gin. Sooner rather than later.*

"I think I see why," another round of the tongue-curling word, "chose you."

Air I didn't realize I held escapes in a breath of noise. Unlike Jezebeth, he's not going to beat the sass out of me.

At least not now. "Why's that?"

"Eager for compliments, are we?"

"What's that word you keep saying?"

This time the bracelet reacts to the tongue-curling word, a fine tremor shaking the silver links.

"It is the name of what you call your *justitia*."

"How do you know that?"

"I have been around for many years and know many things. But this name," that I still can't pronounce, "is also written into the device itself. Have you not been taught how to read the runes inscribed?" He points at the bracelet.

I sit up, eyeing my wrist. The sword juts from the bracelet, runes dancing down the blade, across the silver links around my wrist. "Nope. Haven't had that lesson yet." Does Smythe know about the meaning of the runes?

"The symbols closest to your skin represent the original wearer—" he shivers "—the next set the name of the *justitia*, the set closest to the tip represent my name."

"Who are you?"

"I am Zagan, commander of legions, general to the ruler of Hell. And now captor of a *justitian*." Teeth flash white in his too-smug face.

"Why did you capture me?"

"Many reasons." He sniffs the air, circles around me, predator to my prey. I twist my upper body, trying to keep him in sight. "Scared of me?"

"What makes you say that?"

He chuckles, the noise scratching like fingernails against the chalkboard of my spine. "Ah, little *justitian*. I think I'll keep you. You make me laugh. And you smell good." Zagan leans forward, sniffs, invading my personal space, but not touching. What's his idea of smelling good?

Fear-laced sweat?

"I do?" My voice sounds more pathetic-squeak than strong and confident.

He takes a step back, gives a little hum. "Oh yes. Like peanut butter. I love peanut butter. Great invention, that."

"Peanut butter?" Seriously? Peanut butter? Where does he smell peanuts?

Then it hits me. The crackers in my pocket. My breakfast I no longer feel like eating. I'm pretty certain anything dropping into my stomach will do a u-turn out of there, so if the demon wants my crackers, more power to him.

I pull out the package. So much for six round cracker sandwiches. Crumbs held together by peanut butter are all that remain.

"Is this what you smell?" I hold the package to him, a peace offering.

His eyes widen. "You give your food to me?" The lights in his eyes warn of an underlying meaning, but if a demon wants to eat my food instead of me, I'm down with the idea.

"If you want."

He grabs the package. A rip later and he crams the crumbs inside his mouth. Chews. Swallows. "Mmmm. Delicious. Your gift is worthy."

"Worthy?" Of not eating me?

"I will spare your life. You will become malleable."

"Malleable?" I sound like an echo.

"Mine. Same difference."

Oh, I don't think so, buster. I might be a lot of things, but being yours is not on the list.

Note to self: demons are insane.

Play along, drifts through my mind. The bracelet's command? My own advice? Whichever, it sounds good. The game of pretend might just get me out of here.

Or dead.

"I'm yours?"

"Did I not just say so? You and I are much alike. Very much alike. More than I thought at first, you see. You and I can do great things. Great. Things. If you will let me. Will you let me?" Soulful black eyes lock my gaze, draw me into their depths.

I fight the pull. "You can't make me a minion. I am not evil."

"Ah, humans." He tsks, shakes his head. "Forever lying to themselves. But you should never lie to a demon." He runs a glove-clad finger along my jaw, the caress sending an unexpected—and unwanted—jolt straight to my core. "We can see your soul. And you don't have to be a minion to be my servant."

"I thought *justitians* were immune from demon influence."

Remind me, if nursing doesn't work out to go into stand-up comedy. I never thought of myself as all that funny, but the demon chuckles like I'm the next late night show host.

"Oh-oh-oh." He straightens, slaps his leg with each chuckle. "I am going to enjoy being your master. Stand up."

The command stings, electricity forcing obedience. I roll to all fours, pushing back until I squat in front of Zagan. The bracelet screams, no longer happy to see the demon, as it tries to overpower the command. But what can it do? I've been commanded. I want to stand.

But you don't have to! Don't listen to it!

I have to listen. I've been told to stand. Standing is what I want.

No you don't. Don't let it control you!

Maybe I want to be controlled.

No you don't. You've already let that happen once. Remember?

I don't want to remember. Don't make me remember.

"Stand!"

I shoot to my feet. I've done what my master wants. I'm pleased. My master is pleased.

The *justitia*, not so much.

Zagan circles around me. How could I ever have thought the expression on his face to be anything but joy? Beauty? He bends toward me, and I raise my face to his, a silent plea for his kiss. Which he grants me, firm lips moving over mine and when I open my mouth, his tongue thrusts inside, a lover's kiss.

At his touch, evil tangles of thoughts twist into my mind, show me a glimpse inside a creature I can never comprehend. It hurts. Agony blossoms, making a migraine seem pleasant in comparison. I should pull away. Instead I draw his tongue deeper into my mouth, run my hands across his shoulders. I am with my master. Why should I care about anything else?

I sense a pop, like a plug pulled out of an outlet, and the agony in my head disappears. Only my conscious exists in my mind. No more tangles of demon thoughts. The realization comes as a dull reflection, background noise to the all consuming kiss.

Pain slices through my mouth. Oh god it hurts! Barbs cover Zagan's tongue, and they cut my lips, my tongue, my gums and the coppery taste of blood floods my mouth. My blood, swarming thick as a flock of gnats into my throat, choking me, killing me.

And I want Zagan. I crave him. His kiss fills me like an aphrodisiac, a painful pleasure, a promise of coming delight. My nipples tingle, wetness floods my panties. My core throbs in time to my heart, a silent plea for his touch.

Blood clogs my throat and I swallow. Wetness above. Wetness below. Arms band about my waist, pull me against a rock hard physique, a leg rubs against my core. Oh, God, yes. Please. More pleasure. Until I drown in it. Until you fill me. Rid me of me. Fill me with you.

Goddamn fucking son of a bitch! T's voice roars in my head, his cry a sharp drop into reality.

Am I really getting off on a demon's leg? What. The. Fuck?

Before I can react, T shoves his way into my conscious, taking control of my body as if he owns it. His hands—my hands—shove away Zagan (nononono,

I want the pleasure, don't go, don't go!). Forces my legs to follow through with a kick that misses its intended crotch target. Blood coats Zagan's wide-eyed, brows-raised face, clotting around his lips like he overdid an application of hooker-red lipstick. As if T's possession allows an opening, the *justitia* fires along my nerves, following the path into my brain T forges each time he drops by for a "visit."

T no longer controls me.

Neither does the demon.

Gin? What's happening?

Not to sound ungrateful because I'm really thankful, but you have to go now.

I don't think so.

Bye, T. I—the *justitia*—slams the mental door on our conversation, thrusting my twin back into his own body.

All this happens in the time it takes Zagan to go from surprised to pissed off. And let me tell you, a pissed off demon is not a creature you want to cozy up to.

Unless you have an entity possessing you. Riding your nerves like it owns them.

Which, at the moment it does.

I'm one with the *justitia*, it's so deep within me I feel its thoughts, understand its dilemma.

It doesn't want to kill Zagan anymore than Zagan wants to kill me.

So why did the demon capture me?

I run a hand across my lip. Ouch, ouch, ouch. Blood pools in my stomach, threatens a bout of nausea. Where was Eloise when I needed her?

Something tells me Zagan won't be so quick to

heal me again after that missed kick to his crotch.

The pain disappears. Courtesy of the *justitia*.

Just like it blocked the demon's thoughts from rupturing my brain.

Clearly, being possessed wasn't so bad after all.

Since I know what to say to stop the oncoming demon annihilation session. "Master, it hurt."

Zagan's eyes narrow, relax as he draws in a breath, as he channels his inner yogi. His tongue—his barbed tongue—pokes out, runs around his lips, gathering my blood for one last swallow.

Yuckiness. But I, thanks to the *justitia*, keep my face schooled into a mask of passivity, the helpless servant, begging her master for aid.

And Zagan falls for it.

Score one for the *justitia*.

"My apologies for your pain, *Justitian*. It has been some time since I kissed a human, and I forgot your intolerance for my true form. It will not happen again."

You got that right, buster. No more demon kissing for me.

So why do I crave his touch? Want his hands touching my skin, calling my pleasure?

Note to self: demons transmit insanity.

"Thank you, Master." Gag, gag, gag. Being subservient wears me out, and I've only started the act.

"Now, where were we?" He runs a hand over his head in a gesture reminiscent of T. "Ah, yes. I was extolling the virtues of enlisting you as my servant. Not a minion, you learned correctly there. I cannot take you as a minion. But I can take a *justitian* for my servant. Especially when they are too inexperienced to understand how to use their shiny new bauble."

He's right. I don't know how to use the *justitia* correctly. Until minutes ago I believed all I needed to know about the *justitia* was how to turn it into a sword and stab a minion. Or demon. But now that it forged a connection into my mind, embedded itself along my nerves, I realize wearing the *justitia* means so much more than stabbing a minion. Do other *justitians* feel the same?

A question for another time. Like when I'm away from the demon's lair.

How do I escape? I can't port. I doubt asking Zagan to take me home will work. The *justitia* has no inclination to destroy the demon, its reasoning beyond my scope of understanding. Does it really think of the demon as a friend? How can demons and *justitias* be friends? Isn't that a conflict of interest?

So much for thinking its control of my nervous system meant I understood its thoughts.

And yes, it has thoughts. Scary, that.

The *justitia* wants me to play dumb. Literally. To convince Zagan I'm his servant. Maybe then he will mention why he captured me as opposed to fighting me.

Aren't demons supposed to fight the *justitians*?

Blake's death seems to have slowed my thought process to a crawl. Or maybe it was having my ass kicked by Jezebeth. Or being captured by Zagan. Or his healing. Or other rather embarrassing things that really shouldn't have happened between us. Yep, plenty of reasons to choose from for sluggish thinking.

"Come, *Justitian*. Let me show you my home. Then we can talk business." Zagan turns, heading toward a door opposite from where I stand.

Huh. So that's what he did with his sword. Back

sheath. Just like the minions in the park. Must be an evil dead type of thing.

And why did that thought pop into my mind? Talk about a case of nerves.

I follow him, ever the role-playing obedient servant. He holds the door open for me, allowing me to step through...

Into the cool comfort of a mammoth marble-tiled, Corinthian-columned, white-washed room. A mixture of antique and modern furniture gives portions of the room an eclectic feeling. Those were the nice portions. Other parts looked like a gaudy trip into a gigolo's boudoir crossed with a BDSM trade show. Last but not least, rising a good five steps above the floor, stood a dais, demarking that portion as a throne room. And yep, there stood the throne, a monstrosity of twisted iron in the shape of writhing humans.

How apropos.

Lesson in Demon Decorating Tips 101: how to look gaudy and disgusting while still maintaining a sense of awe.

"Wow." Are bespelled demon servants supposed to speak? Who knows? I decide to act like they can. The *justitia*—while telling me to act subservient— nonetheless treads away from the whole demon-servant thing. Maybe it doesn't know anything about it. Or maybe it knows and doesn't want me to know.

Deep thoughts for another time.

"You like? I decorated it myself." Pride drips from his voice.

"It's..." Awful? Gaudy? Frightening? "...wow."

"You will be comfortable here."

"Where's here?"

Okay, so servants can speak but not ask questions, judging by the expression on his face.

Thank god he relaxes after giving me a squinty-eyed look.

"My home."

Oh, right. That tells me a whole heck of a lot. I swallow the repeat question and opt for a nod.

"Come, come. Have a seat." He gestures to a modern looking overstuffed sofa in avocado and yellow plaid, a 70s flashback of bad decorating taste. I sit, watching as he removes his back sheath, fingers the hilt of his sword. "You will throw a kink in their plans. They will not expect you to work for me. They believe I am bound to their agreement." He slaps the sheath against the coffee table, lip pulled into a snarl. "I will tell you what to say, and then you will go to the Agency. You will tell them you are well, but since you are mine, you will gather all the information you can about the other *justitians* and report back to me. Understand?"

"Information on the others and report back to you. Check. How will I do that?"

"You do not know how to gather information?"

"How do I return?"

"I will find you. I wish I could see the surprise on their faces. They told me to take you, they made me promise."

"They made you promise?" The Agency made you promise?

"Shocking, is it not?" Zagan sits beside me, close enough for the heat from his leg to caress mine. One arm stretches across the back of the sofa like a lover on a date. I keep his hand in my peripheral vision. Hoping he won't touch me. Wishing he would. "They discovered how to make me promise and hold me to that promise. It has been many millennia since that has happened." He looks at my *justitia* and damn me if the bracelet doesn't do the invisible equivalent of a pride dance.

"How did they learn?"

"Curious little human aren't you?" Uh-oh. Maybe curiosity really does kill the cat. Or in this instance the human. "I do not know how they learned. You will find that out so I can prevent it from happening again."

"Yes, Master." Right after I stab your spiky-tongued hottie ass into oblivion.

"Good girl." He tucks a strand of hair behind my ear with his gloved finger. Does he know I'm an empath? Does he care?

"Why did they want me?"

One eyebrow rises, sliding a mask of cold smugness across his features. His hand drops to the back of the sofa. "Silly human. They don't want you. They want your *justitia*."

Chapter 24

Now I'm confused. With a capital C. Zagan claims the Agency wants my bracelet. Did Samantha do the supernatural equivalent of hiring the demon in order to take my *justitia* to give to someone she thinks more worthy?

Is that why she hired the minions to kill me? I thought that was because she was jealous of me and Smythe.

Although there is no me and Smythe. But still. Crazy bitches don't need a reason to go all crazy, now do they?

And while I wouldn't put it past her to try to kill me again, I also have a hard time believing she could bind a demon to her to do her bidding.

My memory replays the warehouse scene, right before the demon portaled me here. I see Samantha and her ward leaping out of a portal, fear in her eyes as she looks at me.

Fear.

If she asked the demon to capture me, why would she show fear? No, if she had supernatural demon binding abilities, she would have had the demon kill me, not capture me.

Unless she has something else planned.

If not her, who else? I don't really know anyone beside David, Smythe's father, and he seems to be in charge of things. Just because he took Samantha's side, doesn't mean he wants me dead.

I'm not such a fool to realize the only way to remove the *justitia* from my arm is by my death.

So who at the Agency wants me dead?

Smythe?

I discard him as soon as his name pops into my mind. He's spent too much time saving my ass to want to kill me.

Unless he's sick and tired of playing white knight to my damsel in distress.

Who else? I don't know anyone else, but apparently knowing me is not a prerequisite for wanting me dead.

"They want my *justitia*?" I can't sound anymore shocked if I tried. And trust me, I'm not trying.

"It's the most powerful one, you know. Or maybe you don't, being new and all."

"I didn't realize that."

"Oh, yes. Most powerful. Given to the least powerful." His eyes gleam, mirth crackling the corners with spider webs of glee. "You are a mystery to them."

"Yeah, I know."

"How you came to have the *justitia* is a mystery. Where it disappeared to is a mystery."

"It disappeared?" Smythe mentioned this before, but as Zagan seems to have a penchant for sharing information the Agency won't, maybe he will be more forthcoming if I play ignorant.

At the moment, playing ignorant is not hard.

And my *justitia* refuses to mention where it disappeared to or how it came to be in Will's possession. Which means I can't be choosey about gathering intel from the demon.

Zagan shakes his head. "I cannot believe the poor quality of training the esteemed Agency has done for its newest recruit. Have they not taught you anything besides killing with the pointy end of your sword?"

"Of course, Master. I've been learning defense moves and some basic history of the *justitias*." Along with a dose of smartass and a sprinkle of making-demon-believe-you're-his-servant for good measure.

He waves his hand as if my words emitted a foul odor. "It disappeared. They wanted it found, of course, but searching high and low did not find it. Then you appear with it on your wrist. How was that?"

"It appeared in my pocket one day at work."

"How? Who had it?"

"I don't know, Master." Looky there, I can tell the truth. I have no freaking idea how the bracelet appeared in my pocket.

He sighs a whiff of blood-tinged air. My blood. A shudder starts at my nape and performs the shimmy through my body. I kissed Zagan?

Gads, what was I thinking? Oh, wait. I wasn't.

A wave of disgust roils through my gut. I kissed a demon. Did more than kiss him. If T hadn't chosen that moment to invade my being, I would've stripped and fucked the thing.

Whore! You are nothing but a worthless whore!

I hear his voice as if I stand before him, cowed, my head hung in fearful obedience. Memories slam into my mind, old memories overlaid with newer ones from the minion fight. Shivering racks my limbs as the memory squeezes me in its grip.

"...cold?"

Yes, it's cold in my memories, cold in death. Cold skin on my lover's face.

"...you cold?"

Yes, cold runs like ice inside my veins, turning me purple with chill. I don't want Blake to be dead. I need him.

"Are you cold?"

A touch accompanies the words, words I realize Zagan spoke several times. My gaze meets his black-souled one. And something sparks between us.

It's not me who looks at my lap. It's the *justitia*, but I'm glad it broke the connection. Glad too Zagan broke the trance of memories.

I swallow. Getting lost in memories while trying to pump a demon for information and figure out how to get away from here was not good policy.

Mind in the game, Gin. Mind in the game.

I need all the brainpower I possess to escape.

Along with a dose of luck.

"I'm sorry." I rub my hands along my arms in hope the friction would chase away memories.

"Sorry does not answer the question. Are you cold?"

"No, Master." Just wallowing in marrow-chilling memories.

"As you wish. Now, I will prepare you for your trip to the Agency."

"No you won't." Smythe's voice booms from behind us, from the door where we entered the room. Both Zagan and I turn to face my rescuer.

Yes, I'm saved! I do a mental victory dance while forcing my body to remain still, ever the obedient servant.

"Step away from her."

He came for me! He really came for me! And then I see Samantha standing behind him.

Fucking bitch.

Who also jumped into a demon's lair with Smythe to save my ass.

What's wrong with this picture?

Who cares? Not I. For the moment anyway.

Zagan stands, a snarl written on his face like grooves in sand. "Ah, little whelp. You are too late. She is mine."

He grabs my arm, yanking me to my feet, his ungloved palm tight against my flesh. And ohgodohgodohgod the tangles of evil slam into my mind, a bursting agony. I can't move. I can't think.

Like before, the *justitia* slams my empath connection shut, locking the demon's emotions and thoughts out. I sag. System overload. But the pain in my head fades, my vision returns. Thank god.

Zagan still holds my arm, remaining in the same place he was before I blacked out. Smythe, though, has moved into the room, Samantha and her ward behind him, playing sheep to his shepherd.

Footsteps sound behind me and I turn, watch as a regiment of minions steps into the room, lining the dais like a row of needles. When I look back to the trio, Samantha's ward wears a pale but determined face, her eyes wide as she stares at the row of minions. Smythe and Samantha only have eyes for Zagan.

"One last chance. Let her go."

"Or you'll what? Get upset and burn me? You can try, but you won't succeed. Demon flesh is impervious to flames."

But not to a stab from a *justitia*.

"Gin, step away from the demon. Remember what I showed you."

Oh yeah. He had taught me how to escape from someone holding my upper arm. The problem was I failed to remember it. *Think, Gin, think.*

Zagan barks a nerve-grating laugh. "Little whelp, you failed to listen to me. She. Belongs. To me. Kill the guardians, *Justinian.*"

And he releases my arm right when I remember what to do. Oh well. "No."

"Excuse me?" Surprise and anger fight a war across his face.

"It's a simple word. Two letters." I hold up two fingers. "N and O. No." Which apparently no one ever said to him.

Anger wins the battle, the air dropping several degrees. "You dare to say no to your lord and master?"

"You're not my lord and master." I swallow a lump into my churning stomach. "I faked it."

"Impossible."

"Believe it." I swing my sword as a warning to step back, aiming for his stomach.

But Zagan moves faster than I do, leaping out of the way before I track his movement. The minions run into the fight as do the Agency trio. Within seconds swords sing as metal crashes together.

The demon glares at me, eyes narrowing. "You have given me your blood, your food. You cannot disobey me."

His words give me pause. So that's what the warning lights in his eyes meant when I handed him the crackers. Clearly the *justitia* blocks the demon influence, allowing me to think on my own.

"My apologies, Zagan." He reaches for me and I slash the air in front of him. Like my *justitia*, I find it hard to want to kill him. I should want to rid the world of his presence and yet, I don't.

Conflicted much?

"This is not the way it works. You are mine!" He throws a wave of energy at me, a red ball of Hell's power. Without thinking about it, my arm comes up, blade blocking the pitch. Correction: absorbing the pitch.

Well, whatdaya know? I'm a poster child for a glow stick. Licks of color stream up my arm, cover my torso, before being sucked inside as a sponge absorbs blood. It takes my breath away. The power. The energy.

The evil.

What does that say about me? That I can absorb a demon's power? Turn that power into my own?

I flick the sword like I'm shaking water off my hands. Power slams into Zagan, driving him back a foot. Talk about giving someone a dose of their own medicine.

Except my shot acts like a red shirt to a stampeding bull, turning it into a raging madman. Or mad-demon in this case.

The *justitia* fails to block the next shot, and I rug-burn my way across the red shag carpet like a go-go dancer's boot. Ouch, ouch, ouch. Before I have time to recover, or assume a defensive posture, Zagan leaps on me, hips straddling mine.

And sex is not on his mind.

Murder, however, rises to the top of the list.

"You are mine!" His screech echoes off the stones,

fading the fight around us into the background.

Note to self: do not make demons mad.

The thought barely registers before sharp pain claws my nape. His talons gouge stripes down my neck, over my collarbone, slicing through the cotton of my tank until his palm rests over my heart. My breath catches, refusing to move past my larynx.

He's going to rip out my heart and eat it for a snack. He's going to kill me. He's going to...have me stab him through the neck.

What the hell?

The *justitia* moves my arm, drives the tip of the sword through Zagan's neck all the way to the other side. What happened to not wanting him dead? I don't want him dead. What the hell did I just do?

The sword hisses a searing burn as I yank it free. Zagan screams, shuffling off me like a crab, while I roll to a sit. On a minion that would've been a killing blow. The demon just howls, hands clasped against either side of his neck. Blood trickles through his fingers, but his screams shake the mortar loose between the stones. Dust coats the room in a fine silt.

The other *justitian* runs toward Zagan, sword drawn back for a killing blow. Keeping his gaze locked to mine he slams his hand against the shag carpet hard enough to ripple the floor like waves from an earthquake. Mid-swing, the *justitian* flies backward, landing hard on her ass, head smacking against an uncarpeted area of the marble floor with a meaty thunk. She lays immobile, the sword disappearing into the bracelet. Was she dead?

Instinct honed over years in the ER has me jumping to my feet, taking a step toward her. Zagan staggers into my path. The exit wound on his neck holds clotted blood, diminishing even as I stare. He holds a hand over the entrance wound, a look like a wounded puppy shining from his eyes.

"You hurt me."

"I'm sorry. I'm so sorry. It was an accident." Why am I apologizing to a demon? Especially since it's my job to destroy them. "I thought you were going to kill me."

His head cocks to the side. "Silly human. I cannot kill you. But I can try to turn you." He pulls his hand away from his neck, looks at the blood, returns it to the wound. "You are mine. Even if you have managed to avoid being ensorcelled."

A portal forms around Zagan, warm air rushing out in a fake greeting. He raises his gloved hand, palm toward me.

"Until we meet again, *Justitian*."

With a burst of colors, Zagan disappears.

I sag, my breath sawing in and out like I ran a marathon.

Or almost lost my life.

But the fight with the minions rages on and the other *justitian* lies injured.

A minion runs toward my downed sister-in-fighting, sword extended, clearly seeing an easy kill. Not on my watch he doesn't.

I dash toward the *justitian*, hoping to reach her in time to block the minion's blow. The minion sees me, narrows his eyes as he puts on a burst of speed. I arrive first, almost tripping over my feet to avoid stepping on her.

And then I'm flying through the air, crashing into a

table with handcuffs and chains. Pain explodes in my ribs, my breath refusing to enter bruised lungs. I slump against the table, a chain narrowly missing my head as it falls to the floor.

What the hell just happened?

Tears blur my vision. I'm pretty certain the chain lies immobile against the floor, but I'd never know it by looking at the steel links. Which seem to sway in and out with every thump of my heart. A couple of blinks later and my vision clears. Please not another head injury. I've had enough of those in one day to last a lifetime.

Samantha strides toward her ward, hand glowing with energy. The minion sprawls several yards from the *justitian*, an obvious victim of Samantha's energy ball.

My brain turns over with all the speed of a winter-chilled engine. Samantha holds her ward in her arms by the time I realize the bitch tried to kill me. Again.

She really shouldn't move her ward. Possible spinal injury. But my lungs continue their protest against breathing, which makes speech a bit difficult.

Right when I swear I'm going to pass out, the lungs remember their purpose, expanding with a wheeze. No wonder they didn't want to work, breathing is freaking painful.

Samantha screams, a frustrated cry of grief that slams against the stone walls with the force of a tornado. It looks like she's trying to form a portal, holding her hand palm out away from her body. Or maybe she just missed hitting a minion.

"Aidan, it's a trap! We can't get out!" Uh-oh. That doesn't sound good.

How can they not get out? Why can't she form a

portal and leave?

I push to my feet, using the table as leverage. Dizziness slaps me across the face, turning the room into a swimming tableau of sounds and colors. I draw in a breath. Whimper. Try another breath. Let out another whimper. Lurch toward Samantha like a drunk zombie with a broken ankle.

Minions break away from where they cluster around a figure I assume to be Smythe, forming a semi-circle with one sword-wielding minion fighting my guardian. Smythe holds his own, his sword crashing against his opponent's as the minion presses him backward. The entire semi-circle steps forward as Smythe steps back.

Herding him toward us.

The sword hangs limp at my side as I stumble toward Samantha. Part of me wants to beat the hell out of her, the other half wants to crawl back into bed. Both parts want to help the *justitian*. It's not her fault her guardian is a bitch.

I think.

Smythe locks swords with his minion opponent. Bracing his hand against his arm, he shoves the minion into the semi-circle of walking evil. Then he turns and hauls ass straight for me, boots barely making a sound against the shag carpet.

The pack of minions follow, running after him like a pack of wolves on a hunt. Smythe grabs my wrist, yanks my arm half out of the socket in his rush to get to Samantha.

Pain swells, disappears like makeup covers a bruise thanks to the *justitia* blocking nerve endings. Somehow I manage to stumble faster. Probably in self-defense of my arm.

Samantha grabs her ward under the arms. "I can't lift her!" Her eyes pop wide in her face, whites rolling like a spooked horse.

"I'll take her." Smythe hands his sword to Samantha and swings the downed *justitian* into his arms.

"You need to stabilize her head. She might have hurt her neck." I step toward her, but my *justitia* remains a sword, making it a bit hard to touch without slicing through her skin.

Samantha glares a go-die wish, which I return with one of my own. Just you wait, bitch, just you wait.

"They're gaining on us." Smythe's words have me glancing at the minions.

Who draw closer, boots thudding in unison. Why haven't they attacked?

"Don't just stand there. Move." Smythe shoves past Samantha, ignoring my warning about stabilizing the *justitian's* neck. Okay then. Why listen to the ER nurse?

Samantha's eyes narrow, and she points a finger at me. I roll my eyes. Whatever. I can live with her attitude problems. The minions' attitude of not attacking bothers me more.

Which goes to show I clearly have a case of one too many whacks on the ole noggin today.

"Move!" Samantha gestures toward Smythe, as if I'm supposed to walk in front of her.

Fine. Hoping she won't push me or send me flying across the room again, I do as she wants.

Metal and leather jingle a funeral dirge behind us as the minions pick up their pace. Boots slap a rhythm against the marble. A grunt sounds behind me and I whirl, only to see a minion engage Samantha in a fight.

She twirls Smythe's sword like a baton, all flash and no contact. The minion steps back, raises his sword.

Before I can blink, Smythe's sword flies out of her grasp, spinning through the air to land with a metallic clatter against the floor.

"No!" Smythe yells, but what can he do with his hands full?

Dashing to her side, I raise my arm, block the minion's blow. My ribs screech a protest. Broken or bruised? The *justitia* shuts down the pain, working overtime to keep me pain free.

But I can still feel the injury.

And my body reacts accordingly.

I block the minion's blow, but the force drops me to my knees. Yet another owie. His shadow falls over me, dark and ominous. Air whistles as he swings his sword toward my neck.

Throwing myself to the side, I land on the marble floor. Owie number...what is the count now? Two? Yeah, two too many.

A blast cracks above me, lightning flashes striking the minion in the chest, throwing him backward, his sword flying from his hand.

Samantha stands with her glowing left hand held toward the minion. Her right stretches in my direction. The air vibrates around me, static forms along a path shooting from her fingertips. Metal scratches along the marble floor followed by a whoosh of air over my head.

Smythe's sword lands in her outstretched palm like a homing pigeon.

I meet her gaze. "Thanks."

She nods.

Teamwork. Putting aside your grievances to get the job done.

"Go, go, go!" Samantha waves at Smythe, urging him into the room Zagan brought me to when we arrived, the two of us following at a run. Or in my case a lurch.

It's the same room Smythe, Samantha and the *justitian* landed in. Maybe they can form a portal in the smells-like-fire-and-brimstone room and get us out of here.

Minions cluster around the open door like nuts on a chocolate bar. Samantha holds out her hand and—praise all that's holy—a portal forms.

"Where?" Smythe turns to her.

"The Agency. Go!"

Apparently guardians don't need to touch the portal creator to enter. Since I trust Samantha about as far as I can throw her—and right now that wouldn't be an inch—I grab Smythe's arm hard enough to leave a bruise.

"Omph." He sucks in a breath at my grip, raising a brow as he looks down at me.

I don't trust her.

He shrugs, steps into the portal. Maybe he read my mind, maybe not, but the end result is the same. Freedom.

The cold steals my breath, freezes tears on my lashes, my cheeks. And then we land in the white room, stumbling forward as if pushed.

Or I stumble. Smythe shakes free of my grip and strides across the room, places the injured *justitian* on the floor.

"Call the medics!" He snaps at the young geeks sitting at the row of computers.

One of them picks up a phone, rattles off the request into the mouthpiece. The other two act like injured *justitians* and battle-worn guardians popping into the room happens so often it's not worth a second glance.

I melt into the floor, legs refusing to hold my weight, collapsing into a boneless mass reminiscent of the wicked witch of the west. Samantha helps my descent into oblivion by shoving my kneeling self over in her rush to get to her ward. I should be mad, but the marble floor leaks a cooling salve across my bruised body. My *justitia* responds by disappearing the sword into the bracelet.

Samantha drops to her knees beside her ward, dropping Smythe's sword like it burned her hand. The sword clatters against the marble floor. Smythe gives her a go-to-hell glare as he picks up the sword, cradling it in his hands as if it were his beloved child. He runs a palm over the blade, across the hilt as a shudder shakes his shoulders. When he stands to sheath the sword in a back harness I'd never noticed before, he catches sight of my dissolved ice cube impersonation.

His face morphs into lines of worry, lips part, eyes widen. "Gin?"

I lift a hand off the floor, wave it back and forth. "Hey."

It takes him less than a second to reach my side. Another second and he kneels, fingers grasping mine, white lines forming around his lips like cracks in dry earth. "You're hurt."

"Hello, Mr. Observant."

"But still a smartass. Guess it's not as bad as it looks?" The white lines of his lips ease, although concern continues to bleed from his eyes.

"I've been better."

Crash! I about jump out of my skin as the door leading out of the white room slams into the wall. White-clad personnel of what I assume to be the paramedic type dart into the room, swarming around Samantha and the *justitian*, ants surrounding a treat.

"We need someone over here!" Smythe hollers, gesturing toward me.

One of the medics leaves the swarm, lands by my side, rolls me onto my back. Pulling a penlight from a pouch, he shines it into my eyes in the classic check-the-injured-for-a-concussion move performed daily by thousands of medical providers.

"Doesn't look like you've lost a lot of blood. Minion sword catch you?" He rummages through his pouch on a search for who knows what.

"Demon claw." The medic and Smythe stiffen, hiss in a breath. My gaze darts between the two white-faced men. Surely they've seen a demon claw a *justitian* before. I doubt I'm the first in however many millennia this fight has been raging. And I doubt Zagan's claw was poisoned. If that was the case, I'd be dead.

But my heart-rate picks up speed, hammering against my ribs with breath-stealing accuracy. "What?"

"Which demon, Gin? Jezebeth or the other one?" Smythe's fingers tighten around mine.

"The other one. Does—" I try to ask, *does it make a difference*, but Smythe drops the f-bomb like he wants to blow apart the room.

Guess it makes a difference.

Thud-thud! My heart smacks against my sternum, panicking in spite of my mental command to calm down.

"We're going to have to move her to the infirmary. I don't carry the potion for a demon scratch in my pouch."

Way to be prepared, medic. "Why not?"

"It needs to be made fresh." The medic gestures to his buddies, who have moved Samantha's ward to a stretcher, and are strapping her down for transport. "We need another stretcher."

"I can walk."

"I'll carry her." Smythe reaches an arm under my knees, behind my back, and lifts me. My ribs scream a protest as he shifts me in his arms. A fine tremor runs through him, into me, as the muscles in his face tense.

"I can walk." Because I'd rather lurch along as opposed to having him drop me. And did I mention the rib pain?

Which vanishes at the thought, relegated to a corner like a child in timeout. Still there but being quiet. For the moment.

"No." His tone brooks no argument, the final say-so in the matter.

Okey-dokie then. But if he drops me on my ass, I reserve the right to chew his to pieces.

The medic walks a fast pace behind Smythe, trying to keep up with his long strides. We get to the elevator right when it arrives for the stretcher. Smythe crams us into a small sliver of space between the stretcher and the side of the elevator, turning sideways so my head doesn't smack against the wall. Samantha holds her ward's hand, her face as leached of color as her hair.

She looks as if she pulled an all-nighter three nights in a row and then ran a marathon. Exhausted circles play raccoon around red-rimmed eyes. She strokes the back of her ward's hand, a gentle gesture meant to calm, to show support.

Her ward lays oblivious, face pale against the white sheets of the stretcher. The elevator rattles a hum as it rises, counting floors with a subdued ping. Sweat and blood overlaid with chemical cleansers form an odor unique to hospitals.

I try not to gag. It's completely different when it's my sweat and blood as opposed to one of my patients'.

The elevator glides to a stop, pinging our floor with a tone reminiscent of a funeral. When the doors swoosh open, the medics run the stretcher out, dashing to the area opposite from the elevator.

The room reminds me of an old-fashioned infirmary. Beds line the sides like tired soldiers, forming an aisle to the opposite side of the room where a steel exam table sits like a beacon for blood.

Or injured *justitians.*

Medics rush the stretcher to the table, shielding the view with a privacy curtain that hangs from the ceiling on a track. White-coated professionals yank aside the curtain, pulling it closed behind them.

Smythe carries me to one of the beds, sets me down with all the awkwardness of a large man holding a baby for the first time. My ribs squawk in pain, fade to background noise. The same medic who attended me in the white room steps to my bed, pulling a curtain around us.

"We need to prep the demon antivenin potion to prevent the poison from spreading."

"What poison? Am I going to die?" I don't feel poisoned. Injured, sure, but not poisoned. But not all poisons make you foam at the mouth or have convulsions or bleed out.

Some are silent killers.

No, no, no. Please God, don't let me be poisoned.

"I'll be right back." He leaves, the clack of the curtain's track beads on the ceiling swallowed in a burst of noise from the opposite side of the room. From the sound of it, things aren't going well for the other *justitian*.

Or, apparently, for me.

"Am I going to die?" I grab Smythe's hand, squeeze for all I'm worth. A tremor starts in my chest, forcing my heart to gallop as if I ran a triathlon.

He eases onto the edge of the bed, looking almost as bad as Samantha. Black circles form half-moons under red-rimmed eyes. Lines play etch-a-sketch in his pale face.

No wonder his arms tremored when he lifted me. Why didn't I notice how exhausted he looks when we were in the white room? How can I call myself a nurse and miss that level of tiredness?

"Not die. Not exactly."

"Are you okay?"

"Used too much magic. It's draining."

"I appreciate it."

His lips twitch. "You're welcome. But I'm not sure I helped." His free hand passes over the slice in my skin left by Zagan's claws.

"Lesson learned. Never piss off a demon."

"Yeah. Good luck with that. They come pissy."

"Get the elevator! We need to get her to surgery.

Stat!" One voice yells directions, interrupting my about-to-be-asked question. Both Smythe and I focus on the action behind the curtain, holding our breaths as if that helped the *justitian* improve. A ding sounds as the requested elevator arrives.

"It's here! Hurry, hurry, hurry!"

The squeak of rushed stretcher wheels hurries through the room, disappearing into elevator, doors swooshing shut behind it. I swallow. I could have been on that stretcher instead of her. Sobering thought.

I take a deep breath. Nothing I can do to help her. Might as well learn what Smythe's cryptic words mean. "So how do I not exactly die?"

"When a demon scratches a *justitian*, the poison released can separate the bond the *justitia* has with the wearer. Permanently."

My gaze falls onto the *justitia*, onto the silver links of the bracelet. Was this my chance to get away from the thing? Do I even want away from it?

While my nervous system leaps into a the-sky-is-falling-run-run-run mode, my mind remembers finding the bracelet in my pocket. The joy when it bonded. The fear my tentative grasp on normality ended with its discovery. Being possessed by an entity. Self-doubt over my skills as a *justitian*. Worry about whether or not I am worthy enough to wear the *justitia*. The rush of killing evil. The knowledge I can help others. The ecstasy when the *justitia* forged new pathways along my nerves, when it bonded with me in a way it hadn't bonded in hundreds of years.

When I knew it hadn't truly bonded in hundreds of years.

And in that panic-stricken moment I realize I don't

want to live without my *justitia*. Mine. I belong to it as much as it belongs to me. Oneness. Possession.

"Where's that potion?"

Chapter 25

"They have to mix it. But one of the medics should be back to tend the rest of your injuries. What happened?"

I assume he means how I got hurt as opposed to how I let a demon capture me. "Samantha threw me."

"What?"

"A minion was heading toward what's-her-name? The *justitian*?"

"Micah."

"Yeah. Zagan threw Micah—"

"Wait a minute. Zagan?"

"The demon who captured me. Anyway—"

Smythe's grip on my hand hurts. "Zagan was the one who captured you?"

"Yes. Did you want to hear how Samantha blew my ass across the room for trying to help Micah or not?"

"Zagan?"

I take that as a negative on the flying act. "What part of his name do you not understand?"

"The part where he captured you. Are you sure it was Zagan?"

"That's who he said he was. Why would he make up something like that?"

"Zagan is a deceiver, a liar. And a demon. Who knows why he'd make up something like that."

"He explained the runes on my *justitia*."

"Runes?"

I flop my wrist onto his leg, twisting it back and forth so he can look at the runes etched into the metal.

"See? There're three sets of them. The first set is the name of the original wearer. The second set is the name of the bracelet. Which, by the way, is completely unpronounceable. The last set is Zagan's name. He said this *justitia* was made for him."

Smythe holds my hand, peers at the bracelet. "Are you sure he spoke the truth? I've never heard the runes meant anything."

"The *justitia* reacted like it was the truth. I believe him, Smythe. He said someone at the Agency hired him to take my *justitia*. Said the Agency wanted it." I whisper, not wanting a prying set of ears to overhear our conversation.

"You can't hire a demon." Smythe shakes his head. "You bind them to you, and it's a stupid thing to do. Even if you're stoked with magic."

"Well, that's what he said."

Smythe rolls over my words like they don't exist. "And why would the Agency want your *justitia?* It's useless by itself, and we thought the line died out. Why would we want it?"

"I don't know! I'm just telling you what he said." I yank my hand out of his grasp, giving him my best what-the-hell glare.

"What else did he say?"

I open my mouth, intent on telling every word from Zagan's mouth, until I remember the light in Zagan's eyes as I gave him my crackers. His kiss. How part of me enjoyed it and wanted more.

No way in hell am I mentioning to anyone—with the exception of T since he was, in a way, there—Zagan's kiss and my resulting whacked out feelings for him.

"He wanted me to come back here and gather information for him about the Agency and the *justitians*. Figure out how whoever it was knew how to bind him."

Smythe's eyes pop wide. "What the hell made him think you'd do that?"

"He said I was his servant."

"What a bunch of shit. See what I mean about being a deceiver? You can't become a demon's servant unless you give them some of your blood and a gift in exchange."

Your gift is worthy. Oh, fuck. I gave the big bad demon a gift. And a bloody kiss. And let him heal me until I soaked in his power.

A million and one shits.

These thoughts shoot through my mind in the time it takes me to realize a guilty look sits on my face and I need to do something about it.

Unfortunately Smythe notices.

Shit.

Smythe crosses his arms, his face a mask of you-did-what under a layer of smoldering rage. When he speaks, his voice growls a warning. "Tell me you didn't give him a gift."

"Okay," the curtain yanks back, showing the original medic and a couple of his friends, who push a portable X-Ray machine into my area. Original Medic closes the curtains. "We're going to take some pictures of those ribs. See if they're broken. Your potion is being mixed and will be here as soon as possible."

"Thank you." And a special thanks for interrupting Smythe's shocked growl.

Maybe he'll forget about our conversation by the time the medics finish with the X-Ray. It could happen.

Yeah, right. Let's face the facts here.

I'm screwed.

In more ways than one.

They position the machine over my bed, which means Smythe moves to lean against the wall next to my head. He sways in my peripheral vision.

Or vibrates with rage. Either way a chair would do him good.

"Hey guys." The medics pause in their machine set-up, look my way. "One of you needs to get him a chair before he falls over." I gesture to Smythe.

"I'm not going to fall over," Mr. Over-confident growls.

All three medics stop the machine set-up to take in Smythe's exhausted face, tensing jaw and clenching fists and one of them darts out the curtain for a chair. Smythe takes the offered chair, swinging a leg over it so his arms rest against the back. His glare frosts my cheek, but I ignore him, focusing on the medics and their machine. What's an icy cheek when demon poison courses through my veins?

I have more to worry about than his glare. Apparently my bid to save my ass from becoming the next demon snack meant I set myself up to become Zagan's servant.

So why wasn't I? If Smythe spoke true, how did I manage to stab Zagan? No wonder the demon looked so surprised.

The answer sifts through guilt and panic. My *justitia* prevented Zagan's mojo from enthralling me. So what will happen if the potion doesn't work against his poison?

Will I become his servant?

The medics hit the bed with the machine, moving it enough to cause me to groan. Broken or bruised ribs scream a complaint against the movement. The pain fades. Not as much as before, but still a reduction.

Does that mean Zagan's poison isn't working?

I try to talk to the *justitia* and get hit with a whole lot of nothing. Is my connection to it dying? Or is it just silent?

So many questions, not enough answers.

But one thing I know. It's a damn good thing OSHA doesn't make an appearance. Apparently Agency folk aren't too concerned about radiation safety. Neither the medics nor Smythe puts on a lead vest while they snap films of my ribs.

Lying with my eyes closed against the pink blush of the humming florescent bulb gives time for another thought to rush through my brain. One I've been trying to avoid.

How am I going to live without Blake?

I see his bloated face as if he lies before me, the blood-red gap in his neck where Jezebeth clawed him a new mouth. Why? Why did it have to be him?

All the tension of the day releases, an avalanche of sorrow held in check by instinctual survival mechanism. Now that I'm safe, the stress holding me together releases and tears leak from the corners of my eyes.

"We'll get these processed. Jason here'll bandage

up that scratch." Original Medic wheels the machine away, taking one of his buddies with him.

I sniff. Run a hand across my cheeks. Hope no one notices.

Gin? T's voice drifts into my head, the panic in his tone a slap to my psyche. Why didn't I try to tell him I was okay before he had to ask?

Blake's dead.

A long pause. *I'm sorry. How are you?*

Banged up. But alive. I'll be fine. Physically anyway.

You sure? Because you've never thrown me out like that before. What the fuck did you do?

I didn't. The justitia—*my bracelet*—*did.* So if the *justitia* blocked T's access, why is he talking to me now?

A cold dread clogs my lungs. Demon poison. Obliterating the *justitia's* influence. No, no, no. I want it back. I want to be one with my *justitia*, with the entity inside. I don't want it to go away.

Gin? What's happening? What's wrong?

I open my mind, shove my memories into T, allowing him to see what happened. His shock, the rage belonging to him alone, slams into my conscious.

You need to get rid of that thing. It's dangerous.

I can't. I don't want to.

Gin. Take. It. Off.

No.

I don't like you wearing it.

It's not your choice.

What if you die? Have you thought of that?

Death happens to all of us. You can't stop living.

I don't want you to die.

I don't want to die either. Trust me.

I feel him take a breath, run his hand over his head. *How long until they let you go?*

I don't know. They have to patch me up first. Maybe tomorrow?

Jason touches my neck, throwing me out of the conversation. I feel T hovering in the back of my mind, a silent shadow of observation.

"That's a nasty cut, ma'am." His southern drawl makes me feel right at home. Or as at home as one can feel lying in an infirmary ward.

I hear the sound of paper tearing.

"This is going to sting a bit, but we need to clean this up." He's right, it stings a bit. Make that a big bit.

Ouch, ouch, ouch. At least he wears gloves. No wayward thoughts.

"Hmm, looks like it's healed. How long ago were you hurt?"

I look at Smythe. I have no idea how long it's been. Time flies when you're having fun, or not having it as the case may be. He shrugs.

"How healed are you talking about?" Standing, Smythe peers over my head at my neck. Lets out a low whistle. "That's almost healed."

"Then why does it sting so badly?"

"It's still cut," Jason says, running another round of the alcohol swab over my skin. "Great healing ability. Are you sure it was a demon's claw?"

"Yep. Why?"

"Demon's claws have poison which cuts off your connection to the *justitia*. The *justitia* is what causes you to heal quickly. So it seems like the demon had no effect on your *justitia*."

"That's good, right?"

"Yep. Just a little unusual. Never seen it before."

"How often do you see a *justitian* clawed by a demon?"

"Happens whenever a *justitian* meets up with a demon. We're quite efficient at preparing the potion. Luckily demons don't like to appear on earth."

"Are you done here?" Smythe's fingers tap a foxtrot against his leg.

Jason pauses, swab resting against my skin. "Guess it doesn't need a bandage after all." He removes the swab, pitches it in what I hope is a biohazard bin by the bed. "There you go. All clean."

"Thank you." I give him a grin as he gathers his things.

"Anytime, ma'am." With a nod, he slips out the curtain.

"Did you give Zagan a gift?" Smythe all but growls the words, his voice a warped vibration.

I swallow. I am not scared of him. Not scared. At all. He's all bluster, no bite. At least toward me. "Um. About that. How was I supposed to know giving him my crackers bound me to him? I was trying to save my ass from being eaten by the big bad demon."

Smythe lets loose with enough f-bombs to sink a ship.

I don't like the way he's talking to you. T interjects.

What the hell? Get out of my head already! I give a shove and T disappears.

The curtain yanks open, track balls screeching a metallic yelp at the force. David storms into my little area, the air around him crackling with anger.

"What the fuck just happened, Aidan? We've got

one *justitian* undergoing surgery to remove pressure on her brain and another one clawed by a goddamned demon. What the hell were you and Samantha doing? Day-fucking-dreaming?"

Smythe's out of his chair faster than a rocket liftoff, exhaustion disappearing under the smoke of rage. Why can't men just say 'I'm worried' as opposed to getting all irate?

Pesky Y chromosome.

"Fighting our asses off is what. Don't speak on matters you weren't there for."

"I can speak on any matters I goddamned well please." David's hand smacks the footboard of the bed and I jump. "I'm on the board. That makes me your boss. Now what the fuck happened."

"It's not his fault." Both sets of glaring eyes turn to me as I push to a sitting position, gasping at the pain in my ribs. I suck in a breath through my nose.

"Dammit, Gin, stop moving." Smythe grabs the controller for the bed, raising the head until it supports my upper body. Then he props the pillow behind my head and helps lower me against the mattress. Nurse Smythe. Ahh. Discomfort taken care of, I can turn to more important matters.

Like giving David a piece of my mind. "It's not Smythe's fault. I killed Jezebeth after Zagan stabbed her. Then he grabbed me and opened a portal before Smythe or Samantha could do anything about it. They tracked me to his lair and saved me." Or Smythe tried to save me, Samantha blasted me across the room. But she did help me at the end so I decide to be magnanimous and not mention my flying act to David.

"Zagan grabbed you?" For a second I wonder if a

ghost stands behind me glaring at David. When he speaks Zagan's name, his face pales, eyes frozen wide, a statue waiting for animation.

"And stabbed Jezebeth," Smythe interjects, his jaw a jutting line.

"Zagan stabbed Jezebeth? What the fuck did you stumble into, son? A demon pissing contest?"

"He said she'd outlived her usefulness. But she'd already killed Blake then." I sniff. Look up at the ceiling. Close my eyes against the florescent light.

"Blake?"

"Her friend."

"Jezebeth captured and k...killed him." *Him* breaks off on a sob, as a crushing pressure sits on my chest. Tears cut a path down my cheeks, returning as fast as I can dash them away.

A tissue appears in front of my face, dangling from David's fingers.

"Thank you." At least that's what I try to say. It comes out garbled and nasally. When I grab the tissue from David, our fingers touch, electricity spilling up my arm.

I drop the tissue. "Oops." Pick it up.

"Sorry."

What just happened? Why the electrical zing but no emotional thoughts? My *justitia* unfurls like a plant awakening in the spring, a subtle vibration under my skin, along my nerves. It's alive! Zagan's poison didn't kill it after all.

Now I'm sobbing happy tears.

Until the feeling dissipates.

"Care to tell me why Jezebeth killed your friend?" David's tone holds none of the anger he showed earlier.

Instead, it calms me, makes me want to confide in him.

"Dad." Smythe's tone growls a warning, but to what? What's so bad about me telling David what Jezebeth told me?

I blow my nose. Dash my fingers across my cheeks. Sniff again for good measure. "Jezebeth was upset I killed her minions, so she killed Blake." I clear my throat, blink as David's outline blurs. "Then she tried to kill me. That's when Zagan stabbed her and I killed her and you know the rest."

"Zagan released you?"

"I stabbed him. He portaled away."

"But he scratched you? Or was that Jezebeth's work?"

"Zagan's. Why?"

"Jezebeth is, was, a lower level demon. Zagan is a commander of legions. The more power a demon has, the quicker the poison in their claws works." Smythe taps his fingers against his leg, eyes narrowed as he stares at me. As if he's trying to look inside, to see whether or not Zagan controls me.

Damn. Guess our interrupted conversation isn't over yet.

"The healers are working on your potion. They've done this before. Don't worry." A muscle kinks between David's brows. "Did Zagan tell you anything?"

"He talked." I shrug. "Not sure how important it was." Liar, liar, pants on fire.

His fingers drum against his leg for a five count. "Go on, now. Don't keep me waiting. Spill it."

I don't want to spill it. I don't want him to know what Zagan told me. I want to keep it all to myself.

But I'm not going to let the demon control me. Even from a distance.

I feel like a traitor.

"He said someone at the Agency bound him to capture me."

"He said what?" David's eyes pop wide.

I repeat it.

"I heard you the first time. I'm having trouble believing he said that."

"Well, he did." Along with a lot of other things I'm keeping to myself.

"Well, now, don't you believe a word that demon says. I'm sure my son here has told you all about him. The Deceiver. That's what Zagan is. Lies. Can't believe a word he says. You hear?"

"Yeah, but shouldn't the threat be assessed?" Smythe asks. "What if he told the truth?"

A tic beats a rhythm in David's jaw. "Why would we want her captured? She works for us."

"He said the Agency wanted my *justitia*."

"Oh, now that's a load of horseshit. While I admit it's a shock to have it bond to someone we knew nothing about, why would we want it off you? Doesn't it make more sense to leave it where it is and train you?"

When put like that...his logic made sense.

But I still believe Zagan.

"See? He's lying to you. That's what he does. Sometimes the *justitias* pick up demon's lies. Did yours react to him?"

"Nope, it was too excited over seeing him again." I clasp both hands over my mouth. Why the heck did I say that? I didn't mean to say that. I didn't mean to say anything more than I had to about my encounter with Zagan. What's gotten into me?

Mouth shut from here on out. No way in hell am I saying anything about kissing him. Or the potential for me to be his servant. At least not to David.

I'm surprised Smythe hasn't interjected that little tidbit of good news. Maybe he's too embarrassed to admit his mentee gave a big bad demon a gift.

Not that I'm complaining.

"What do you mean?"

"Excited?" Smythe and David speak a duet, both pairs of eyes wearing identical brow raises.

No way out of this now. Me and my big mouth. Since when do I have a big mouth? "They seemed to know each other."

"Makes sense," David says, "The *justitias* were made to fight demons. Zagan's a demon. No worries."

"Why would I worry?"

He waves a hand, a dismissive flip of the wrist. Opens his mouth. But before he can speak, Original Medic steps around him, a mug in his hands.

"Good news. Your ribs are just bruised. They'll be painful until they heal, but at least they aren't broken. And your potion is ready." He offers me the mug.

A thick brown liquid swirls inside. Something tells me it's not a chocolate milkshake.

"Be sure to drink it down all at once."

With those words, I know it's going to taste horrible. I stare at the brown sludge. Suck in a deep breath. Bring the cup to my lips. Maybe it'll taste like a milkshake.

It doesn't. Thick, chalky paste slides across my tongue. Yuck, yuck, yuck. If the bond with my *justitia* wasn't on the line, I'd spit the drink in Original Medic's face. Instead I swallow. Gag. Swallow again. The potion tastes like dead vegetation, dirt covering a grave.

A blurry grave solidifies in my mind, damp earth bowed outward, an image from the past. I shudder, swallowing away the remembrance.

My stomach cramps and I double over in pain. Pain shoots through my limbs, fires my nerves into a jitterbug. The mug drops from my trembling fingers, caught by the medic before it hits the floor. Smythe and David act as if a seizing *justitian* is a common occurrence in the infirmary and nothing to worry about.

Their attitude only slightly relieves my panic. Since when do seizures mean anything good?

The *justitia* roars to life, the potion a rush of adrenaline to the entity residing along my nerves. I'm pretty sure I've stopped seizing, too enthralled by its race up my body into my brain.

And then I'm lost in its memories. Lost in the past. Lost as it fuses its consciousness to mine, as it solidifies the bonds it started to build in Zagan's lair. For a moment it's an open book, a book with its pages flipping in the wind. Images and thoughts appear, only to disappear on a breath of air. I see but don't understand. Its memories a vast ocean with currents moving through time.

You'll learn. I'll help. Together we'll overcome.

Its thoughts echo a deep timbre through the recesses of my mind, a promise, a vow.

Hands shake my shoulder, voices call my name. I hear, but don't want to obey. I want to remain lost in memories, separated from reality.

Go! The *justitia* commands.

Its voice I obey.

My lids pop open, focusing on the face in front of my mine. White lines bracket Smythe's mouth, worry bleeding into the corners of his red-rimmed eyes. David stands behind him, eyes slits of icy blue. The medic holds my wrist in his gloved hand, fingers against my pulse.

"What happened?" Smythe asks, propping a hip onto the bed.

"That potion was god-awful is what. You ever heard of flavoring to make the medicine go down better?" A rasp thickens my voice.

A corner of the medic's lip turns. "Yeah, I've heard that before. How do you feel?"

I clear my throat. "Full of bumps and bruises, but alive. The bond with my *justitia* is still alive. Thank you."

"You're free to go home. Keep an eye on that gash. It's healed enough to close but could give you some problems. Let us know if you need anything. And no strenuous lifting until your ribs heal. Nothing over ten pounds."

"No problem. Thanks."

He nods, leaves my area, closing the curtain behind him.

"You heard him. Portal me out of here so we can go get Blake." A lump builds in my throat and I swallow. "He deserves a decent burial."

"The cleaners are taking care of your friend," David drums his fingers against his leg. "Aidan's staying right where he is. He's burned through magic today like a rich bitch on a shopping spree."

"Yeah, well at least I got Gin back."

"So you did, son, so you did. Now rest up." He points at the bed next to mine, the bed hidden by the privacy curtain.

"What are the cleaners going to do with Blake?" I catch David's gaze. "He deserves a proper burial."

"I'm sure they know that."

"So what are they going to do?"

David sighs. "I don't know exactly. My guess is make it look like a mugging. That's what they usually do to bystanders caught in the crossfire of our war."

"How often does that happen?"

"Too often. Now if you'll excuse me. I have some matters to attend to. I expect to see you rested and healed, Aidan."

Smythe jerks his chin at his father, one of those male nods of affirmation. David shuts the curtain as he leaves.

"You gave a gift to Zagan?" Smythe hisses. Damn. And here I thought he forgot.

"I didn't know what it meant! I was trying to discourage him from eating me."

"Dammit Gin." He shoves a shaking hand through his hair. "I assume he took some of your blood too? You had cuts when he captured you."

Heat slaps my cheeks. Hopefully Smythe will think Zagan licked the blood off my skin. Which is gross, but not as bad as him knowing what really happened.

"Yeah. I was out of it when he first took me, but I'm pretty sure he took blood." Like a hundred percent sure, but hey, what Smythe doesn't know, doesn't hurt. Right?

Smythe's brows slam together. "Out of it? You mean worse than when I found you?"

Uh-oh. Me and my big mouth. I thought I swore to keep it zipped close. "I think I was dying. He healed me."

"Goddamn it!" Smythe throws his hands in the air, stalks to the foot of the bed. Oversized hands slam against the footboard as he leans forward, lips flattened. "You exchanged blood and a gift with a demon and then let him heal you?"

Not in that order, but yeah. My gaze slips to the cotton sheets covering the bed. "I'm sorry. I didn't realize what I was doing."

He runs a hand across his head, stares at the ceiling, chest heaving deep breaths. I pull my legs toward my chest. The movement sends pain through my ribs, but it makes me feel a bit safer.

I'm no longer so sure Smythe won't smack me upside the head.

The hum of the pink-hued florescent bulb echoes in the silence, punctuated by Smythe's deep breathing exercises. His head lowers, eyes piercing me with the heat of his ire.

"Okay. You swapped blood and a gift. Technically that makes you his to control. Although I've never heard of a *justitian* being controlled by a demon. I don't sense the demon inside you and you fought him off. Servants can't do that. Maybe the gift and blood exchange don't work on *justitians*."

"I don't feel controlled by him." Although I want to see him again. Geez Louise. Talk about having issues. I store the thoughts away in case Smythe tries his telepathy talents again. "And my *justitia* is alive and well. And I just swallowed the worst tasting potion ever, which guarantees no demon poison in my veins. I think I'm clear." I can only hope.

Smythe's nostrils flare. His eyes narrow to slits. "Don't ever do that again."

I look at my hands. Meet his gaze. "Don't worry. I know better now."

He nods, anger leaking from his pores like a punctured balloon. "I don't want to lose you."

"Yeah. I don't want to lose me either."

His lips twitch. "You're going to be the death of me."

"It's not like I'm trying. I just...don't know things."

"I know. I'll do a better job of teaching you. Starting with what not to do with a demon."

Something tells me I have that lesson down pat. But I nod anyway.

What if I'm wrong? What if I'm really controlled by Zagan? I don't feel controlled by anything but the *justitia*. And I took an antivenin potion. And I'm almost certain Smythe performed some sort of super secret guardian scan on me to verify the lack of demon presence in my body.

All of which means I'm demon free.

Hopefully.

Smythe appears to need a change of topic. He's not the only one. Questions pop into my mind. Questions having nothing to do with Zagan and everything to do with Blake.

"What is the cleaning crew going to do with Blake?"

He blinks a couple of times, clearly thrown by the topic change. "Want me to find out for you?"

"Do you mind?"

"Nope."

"Do you need to rest first?" The circles under his eyes seem deeper, darker, threatening.

"Nope." He grabs his phone from his pocket, punches a number. After a brief question and answer session, he pushes a button on the screen, replaces the phone in his pocket. "It's as Dad said. They're making it look like a mugging. The police have been alerted to the location of the body so he'll be found. I'm sorry, Gin."

I nod. Close my eyes against the press of tears. Smythe walks to the side of the bed, rests his hand against my forearm, a warm comfort soothing to my soul. The *justitia* hovers in the background, its presence a buzz of energy watching, recording my thoughts, my actions.

Having the *justitia* hiding out seems...natural. As if I've found my place in the world. As if nothing else matters but our relationship.

Which is a lie.

Other people matter. A lot. Or did.

I dash a hand under my eyes. I want to go home. I want to be comforted by holding T's hand. But I'm stuck here until Smythe recovers.

Unless I trust another to portal me home.

Which I don't.

"I'm going to my apartment."

"Didn't your dad say for you to rest in the bed next to mine?"

"I'll heal faster in my place. Not here."

"Why? They can't make you a magic potion?"

"You don't replenish drained magic by drinking more magic." He shakes his head, a smile edging up his lip.

"Then what do you do? Because, no offense, but you look worse than a stoned drunk."

"Gee, thanks." He runs a hand over his eyes. "Rest helps. But there are certain...rituals I need to perform."

"Oh? What kind of rituals?"

"Magical ones." His lips twitch. I think he's trying to be funny, but his grin fails to reach his eyes.

"No shit, Sherlock. Elaborate."

"Secret magical rituals."

I roll my eyes. "Really? So how can you perform magical rituals when you're drained of magic?"

"Carefully."

"You're pulling my leg."

He pats my leg. "Let me take care of things. Rest here and I'll come get you when I'm ready to take you home."

"Can I walk around?"

"I suppose. Why?"

"Don't want to stay here." Samantha being in the vicinity and all. I don't think she'll try anything but don't want to risk my life on that assumption. You know what you get when you assume. "Are you sure I can't come with you?"

He sighs, runs a hand through his hair. "All right, but you'll need to stay where I tell you to. You can't disturb my ritual or it might not work right."

"Okay. Promise no disturbing."

"Can you walk?"

"Sure." And even if I can't, I'm not asking him to carry me. This is an infirmary. A wheelchair is bound to be lying around somewhere.

I swing my legs over the side of the bed, stand. The room spins a whirling dervish. For a moment I fear I've been inadvertently portaled, but the motion calms after a couple of deep breaths. By the time I regain my balance, Smythe has the curtain pulled open, one hand held toward me. I grasp it and together we make our way toward the elevator.

Chapter 26

I snap awake, the footrest of the recliner clicking into place, propelling me upright. My heart trips an unsteady rhythm, pounding through the fog of sleep. What woke me?

A fan hums a whirl of air, the only noise in Smythe's apartment. The dim light over the stove casts its glow into the living room allowing me to see furniture and shadows. Nothing scary.

The apartment consists of a living room/kitchen combo with a door to the bedroom and another door to the bathroom. Not big enough to hide a person. A quick glimpse at the front door shows it locked, the deadbolt in the same position as when Smythe turned it. For all appearances it's only me and Smythe in the apartment.

No light shines from under his bedroom door. None has the entire time I've been here. Or at least it hadn't before I fell asleep. According to the cable box clock I slept three hours.

Maybe a dream woke me. My dreams scattered to the corners of my mind when I woke, shadows visible but unremembered, settling with the cold touch of a shroud.

Pulsing brushes along my nerves, the *justitia* watching, waiting. The flatscreen TV shows my reflection, one hand clamped over my heart, head tilted to the side, listening for all I'm worth.

Beneath my hand my heart slows its frantic beat, relaxing as my tension subsides. A dream. A dream must have wakened me.

Breathing a sigh of relief, I lean the recliner back and close my eyes. A heavy pressure sits on my chest, the knowledge I failed Blake. I should have checked the paper earlier. Should have listened to my instincts and looked for him when I noticed him missing instead of assuming he didn't intend to stop by. What kind of a friend am I?

Why did he have to die? Why did he have to suffer? Alone, with no one to offer him comfort? I roll onto my side, not bothering to stop the flow of tears. If history repeats itself, I'll fall asleep to the sound of my grief, tasting the salt of my tears.

Sleep coats me in a tattered blanket, coming to me in fits and snatches. Dreams, ever elusive, disturb before drifting away on a wave of unease.

And then I wake, eyes snapping open, ears listening for a threat. Light from the bulb above the stove blankets the room in a dim glow, elongating chair shadows into fingers. The hair on my arms stands at attention. Intuition as old as time freezes my lungs, sends my senses into hyperawareness.

Something, or someone, shares the room with me. Watching. Waiting. Prickles tingle my nape. I shoot out of the recliner, swaying until a bout of dizziness passes.

No one is in the room. Nothing but me and the flatscreen TV. And the furniture. A quick peek at the front door shows the bolt locked.

So what's up with the prickles?

Light flickers under Smythe's door, a rhythmic pulsing that pushes against my flesh. *Magic*, whispers along my nerves as the *justitia* recognizes the source.

Magic woke me? Is that even possible?

I take a step toward his bedroom door. He told me to stay out of his room while he performed some ritual to restore his power. Curiosity killed the cat might be an overused cliché, but it describes my current stopped-in-the-middle-of-the-living-room situation.

What would he do if I opened the door? What if the ritual goes astray like some wayward bolt of lightning, striking me dead?

Lights flicker under his bedroom door, thin fingers dancing to a silent rhythm. Beckoning. Warning. Pulsing streams over my body, warm hands stroking fire through my veins.

I take a step back. Curiosity be damned. He can tell me tomorrow what this ritual involves. At least I know what's waking me.

The recliner welcomes me back like a long lost friend, its soft cushions pillowing my body. It takes longer this time to fall into sleep, my mind twisting a dance of torments.

Unconsciousness beckons, a dark pull of anxiety, and I grab hold, letting it drown me in its depths.

"Gin!" Someone shakes my shoulder, but I fight him off. He can't have me. I won't let him.

"Gin!" He's still there, persistent.

I cry out, try to escape. Zagan can't have me, I need to rescue Blake. But hands grab me, shake me.

My lids flip open, optic pathways try to make sense of the face before mine. What is Smythe doing here? Oh, yeah. I'm in his apartment. No one chases me—at least not now. A dream. Only a dream.

Tell that to my running-a-marathon heartbeat.

"You were having a bad dream."

Ya think? I suck in a breath, release it on a sigh. "One of those chase ones where you never get the target."

"I hate those. How are you feeling?"

I take another deep breath. A deep breath. So much for bruised ribs. "Really good. My ribs don't hurt."

"That's good. You heal fast now that you wear the *justitia*."

"I know. But it's still weird. My ribs should be sore for some time. I should have a concussion. And a big open gash on my neck."

"That's healed, too." One finger follows the path of Zagan's claw-mark, the warmth of his touch a pleasing distraction from the lingering dream shadows. "Only a red line. It might not even scar."

"That would be nice. Scars are much hotter on men than women."

He chuckles. "Would you like some breakfast?"

"Breakfast?" I glance at the digital display on the cable box. Eight in the morning? I slept all night on a recliner? No wonder everything feels stiff.

Oh, wait. That has to do with used-to-be bruised ribs and a minion fight. And demon scratch.

"I have eggs and bacon if you want." He gestures toward the kitchen and the aroma of fried bacon smacks me in the face. Yummy.

When we got back to his apartment last night, he fed me a frozen dinner, which was my only meal of the day. Needless to say, I'm hungry. Stomach growling starving.

"Let me do the bathroom thing, and I'll be right there."

After my bathroom trip and unsuccessful attempt at ridding myself of bed-head, a plate of food sits at the bar. I grab the accompanying fork, plop down on the barstool, and dig in. Smythe is a great cook.

At least with bacon and eggs.

When I finish stuffing my mouth, Smythe has the kitchen spotless, dishes in the dishwasher, cabinets wiped down. Wow, a man who can cook and clean.

What are the chances?

"Thank you for breakfast." I rinse my plate, add it to the dishwasher. "So, what did that super-secret ritual last night involve?"

"Secrets." A grin teases his lips. I roll my eyes, cross my arms. Give him my best spill-it look. "It's not that glamorous. I draw energy from the surrounding area and drink an herbal tonic to help replenish my strength. Then I go to sleep. Sleep's the best thing for it."

"I saw flickering lights from under your door. Felt something drawing on my energy. So I got back in the recliner and the pull went away."

"Lights?" He cocks a brow. "What time was this?"

"Around midnight."

"You must've been dreaming. I was asleep then."

"I wasn't dreaming. Something kept waking me, and the last time I got up to see what it was, but that weird pulling feeling made me decide not to open your door."

A muscle knots between his brows. "I was asleep, Gin. I didn't even use candles for the ritual. You sure you weren't dreaming?"

"Yeah, I am." Right? I did wake up in the middle of the night, didn't I?

"Well, I don't know what to say. I'd tell you if I did some sort of midnight voodoo." His grin returns, but his eyes seem wary. "I bet you want to go home. Change clothes."

"Sounds like a great idea." I took a shower last night, wiped the blood off my skin, but had to borrow one of Smythe's tee-shirts and a pair of scrub pants from the infirmary. The shirt hangs to mid-thigh, and the only good thing about the pants is the drawstring that keeps them from bunching around my ankles.

And carrying my underwear instead of wearing it puts me in the same trend-setting class as certain celebrities.

Smythe opens the door, lets me walk through first. A real gent. He probably just wants to stare at my ass as I walk in front.

"Did you hear how Micah's doing?" I face him while he locks the door behind us.

"She's recovering from surgery." He walks toward the elevator and I fall into step beside him. "Since she hasn't wakened, they're not sure how she's going to be."

"Why didn't you call Eloise? Isn't she the Agency healer?"

Red flushes his neck, tinges his cheeks. "Eloise doesn't always come when called."

"She always came when you asked her. Maybe you should've called."

"Micah's not my ward. Me calling her wouldn't have had any more effect than whoever tried calling her. She does what she wants, when she wants."

"So why has she healed me twice? Micah's been with the Agency for longer than I have."

He pushes the call button for the elevator. Clears his throat. "She likes me."

"Geez, Smythe, did you sleep with her, too?"

"We're friends."

Ding! The elevator doors slide open and we step inside.

"Friends? I know how that goes." Intimately. Or I used to. Pressure crushes my chest, a soul deep pain leaving me sobbing. I slap both hands over my face, trying to hold back the tears.

A heavy weight slips around my shoulders as Smythe draws me into the warmth of his embrace. One hand strokes my hair, offering comfort. In return, I blubber all over his shirt, dampening it with my tears.

Until I have the absurd thought that if he wore a ring, it would get caught in the tangles of my hair. Then I'm laughing, snorting tears like a lunatic.

Ding! The elevator doors open. Good thing no one but Smythe hears me laughing my head off. He probably thinks I'm crazy.

He's not far from the mark.

"You okay?"

I dash fingers under my eyes, as try to calm the laughter. "I had a silly thought."

"Sometimes those help when you're grieving a friend's loss." He catches the door, holding his arm out to keep it from closing. I walk through and lean against the wall, trying to pull things together. I refuse for the young 'uns in the white room to see me fall apart.

Smythe steps into my line of sight. One hand runs down my arm, grabs my hand, gives a squeeze. "I won't insult you by saying things will be okay. But do know that life goes on. It's up to you to stand still or hop onboard."

I sniff. "I'm a hopper. You got a tissue?"

"Just a minute." He squeezes my hand before walking off down the hall, disappearing into a room.

I sniff, run my fingers under my eyes, down my cheeks. Good thing there's not a mirror around, I might scare myself. The elevator pings a warning before the doors slide open. I give the occupants a half-hearted smile and hold my hand between my cheek and them. No reason to scare others with my tear-stained blotchy cheeks.

How long does it take to get a tissue? Does Smythe have to run to the drugstore for one?

"Who're you?" A snap of gum joins the voice beside my ear.

I drop my hand. A young woman in her late teens stands before me, purple hair punked into a Mohawk, cherry-red lips smacking a wad of gum like a horse chewing hay. Knee-high leather platform boots hit several inches below her red polka-dot miniskirt. Her eyes narrow on me like I'm some bug needing to be squashed.

I sniff. Politeness insists I offer a handshake, but I doubt she wants one of my tear covered ones. "I'm the new girl on the block."

"Cute accent. Where'd you pick it up?"

"Hey, Laurel. What are you doing up this early?" Smythe holds a box of tissues in his hand as he walks toward us.

Laurel flutters her lashes at him. Oh geez. "Who says I got up? Maybe I'm just coming home."

Smythe hands me the box. No more tears coming up. I grab a tissue and start dabbing at my cheeks.

"If you were coming home, you'd be headed the other direction. Come on, Gin, let's go."

Ignoring Laurel's huff, Smythe half-drags me down the hall and into the white room.

"In a rush to get away?"

"She has a crush on me. It creates problems."

"Problems?"

He waves a hand, clearing my question as he would a foul odor.

"Who is she?"

"A potential *justitian*."

"And that puts her off limits?"

"Her age puts her off limits. Do you want to chat or go home?"

"Home Jeeves."

He shakes his head, eyes closed as if asking for patience. Holding one hand toward the special portal-forming corner, he mutters under his breath until the portal appears. As he grabs my hand, leading me into the icy depths, I offer a quick smile to the computer geeks. Who ignore me. Not that I blame them. I'm not looking my best.

The portal drops us in my living room. Warm air rushes across my skin from the ceiling air vent. It takes me a moment to realize the air only feels warm after the icy depths of the portal. Sunlight peeks under the blinds, bathing the room in a dull gleam. The air conditioner wheezes a needs-repair-work tune.

Smythe heads for the kitchen. I start to follow until Blake's picture on the card pops into my mind. I can't go in there. I can't see that picture.

As if he reads my mind—which he probably does—Smythe picks up the card, folds it in half and slips it into the pocket of his jeans. Then he picks up yesterday's paper, shakes it to get my attention.

"Trash or recycle?"

"Recycle. Out the back door."

Despite the kitchen's current newspaper-less state, I can't go in there. My feet freeze in the doorway, my heart hammering behind my ribs. Not good if I ever wanted to eat again. The food is in the kitchen.

"Everything okay here?" Smythe picks up his laptop, turns to face me. "I need to take care of some things if you don't need me."

"I'm fine." Liar, liar, pants on fire. "T's coming over." Or he will be once I ask him to.

"Good. I'll come back tomorrow. I need to do a better job of training you."

"You're doing fine."

"You have a lot more to learn. It's hard to know where to start when you weren't born into it."

"You're telling me." I lean against the wall, hoping to look nonchalant as opposed to fearful of my own kitchen. Hopefully he won't notice. Stranger things have happened. "I work tomorrow. Don't stop by until after eight. Okay?"

"We're going to need to do something about that. *Justitians* don't hold other jobs."

"Either rig the lottery or pay me what I currently make. Until then stop by after I get off work."

"All right." He forms a portal to the side. "Rest up. I'll see you tomorrow."

"Okay. And Smythe?" He pauses, turns to look at me. "Thank you. For saving me."

"That's my job. See you tomorrow." He steps through the portal, disappearing into the icy swirls.

Chapter 27

I walk backward, until the backs of my legs hit the arm of the couch. Still can't go in the kitchen. Damn. I hate panic attacks.

Leaning against the couch arm, I open the connection between our minds and call T. Once he promises to come over, I walk into my room. My tank top is torn and bloody, my shorts not much better. The shoes, though, look okay. I drop Smythe's shirt and borrowed scrub pants on the bed. Stripped naked, I walk into the bathroom. Brush my teeth. Comb my hair. Pull it into a knot and hop into the shower.

T's sitting on my bed when I get out of the hot, humid bliss. My feet freeze in the doorway. But only for a second. Then I'm darting back into the bathroom to grab the towel, yelling over my shoulder.

"What the hell? Did you learn to portal?"

"I've been here for ten minutes. Thought you heard me holler."

Towel firmly in place under my arms and held there by both hands, I give him a glare as I head for the dresser. "You scared the crap out of me."

"You want me here or not?"

"Dumb question. Turn around." Once he faces the other way, I pull out a pair of panties, slip them on while holding the towel in place. "Where's Jackie?"

"Probably at work by now."

Oh, yeah. I forgot she's a cashier at one of the big chain super-stores. Good thing the cash register tells her how much change to give.

I pull on a pair of shorts, keeping the towel in place until they sit on my hips. Then I put on a bra and stick a tee-shirt over my head, pulling it into place as I drop the towel. Dressed and ready to go.

Go sit in the living room that is. Not sure I can make it into the kitchen. The whole thought of walking in there speeds my breath and heart rate until I sound like an overheated dog.

"You okay?" T runs a hand over his head, watching me towel-dry my hair.

I shoot him a glance, walk back into the bathroom. "Yeah."

Floors squeak as he follows me. I hang the towel on the hook and start combing my hair.

"Liar." Nothing like having a mind-reading twin. "You wouldn't have called if you were okay."

"Then why did you ask?"

"Give you a chance to speak about it."

"You know what it is."

"Yeah, but it helps to talk about it."

"What are you now? Sigmund Freud?"

"You're the one that called me over."

I toss the comb on the counter, eyes tearing. "I'm sorry. It's not your fault. He's dead, T. What am I going to do without him?"

T gathers me into his arms, holding me as I sob on his shoulder. I'm a mess. An ugly mess. A rotten friend. Despite my fancy new bracelet, despite my bond with the *justitia*, I couldn't even save the one person that meant so much to me.

"You still have me, Gin. You'll always have me."

Peace flows through me, quieting my sobs, calming my self-loathing thoughts. I did all I could to save Blake. Yes, I should've found the note the day before, but could we have saved him?

He was already dead.

T's voice or my *justitia*? Or my own realization? By the time I saw his body, he'd been dead for at least a day. Was probably killed after they took the picture. Keeping him alive had never been the goal. Causing me to suffer like Jezebeth suffered was the end result.

Am I going to let a demon win?

A dead demon at that?

I sniff, snuffle a hiccup. How do I grieve but not let her win?

"Let's get a bite to eat." T strokes my back, my wet hair.

"Not hungry." Not to mention the kitchen thing. I can't go into the room where Blake's picture was. I can't see his bloodied face, the fear in his eyes. I can't.

Which in a way is letting Jezebeth win. I'll fight that battle another day.

"Well, I am. Let's go." Still holding me, he backs out of the bathroom, crosses the hall, aims for the kitchen.

I dig my heels into the floor, trying to halt the progress. My breath hitches in my throat, my pulse floods my ears, eliminating noise. T tightens his grip around me, lifting me up so my feet dangle.

I try to shove against his embrace, try to run, try to fight, but I'm caught, a mouse in a cat's jaws. He sets my feet on the tile floor of the kitchen, his grasp firm around my waist.

I know what he's trying to do, in the back of my mind I understand, but the kitchen holds memories I want forgotten. I don't want to look at the table and see the paper. Don't want to see Blake's face on the card. Don't want to remember how I felt upon seeing it. How I still feel now.

T holds me. Always holds me. Always comes for me. Always loves me.

The kitchen still frightens. It holds memories I'll never forget. Maybe I'll never be able to nonchalantly walk into the room to grab coffee, or cook a meal, but I'm not going to die in here either.

At least not today.

The peace of his touch streams through me, calming my runaway emotions. My heart-rate remains high, my pulse singing a tune of fear in my head.

"It can't hurt you, Gin. You know that, right?"

Swallowing, I close my eyes. How many times in my past has this happened? Granted, not for years, not since I cobbled my life together with will and drive, but enough times for me to recognize, this too will pass.

I refuse to open my eyes. The panic attack might pass, but it might also return if I pay attention to where I stand. T's grip on my waist relaxes, as if he senses the switch in my emotions.

"Better?"

"Maybe."

"Stand here," He leans me against the wall, drops his arms. "I'll get me something and we'll talk in the living room."

"Okay." Not opening my eyes though. Drawing a deep breath through my nose, I focus on pulling the air down, down, until it hits below my navel. Then I release it, imagining the air traveling up my spine, throwing bad spirits out of my body. As I continue to focus on my breathing, my muscles relax, calming my senses.

A whoosh of air passes me, followed by the scent of mustard, floorboards squeaking as T walks into the living room. He sets the plate on the coffee table, stoneware thunking against wood. More squeaking and his touch, feather-light against my arm.

"Come on. Open your eyes and talk to me while I eat."

I can do this. I can open my eyes and see the kitchen. I can.

Forcing my lids open, I stare into T's eyes. And keep staring as he leads me out of the kitchen. Once I'm in the living room I step away.

"Thanks. I'm better. I think."

"Sure you are. Sit down and tell me about things."

Somehow he managed to carry two glasses of water and a plate into the living room with only one trip. My brother, full of juggling skills.

I pick up a glass, take a sip. Hold it in my hands, rubbing a finger over the perspiration beading down the sides. "I'm not sure what's going on anymore, T. Neither's the *justitia*."

"Go on," he speaks around a mouthful of ham sandwich.

"I'm supposed to fight minions. And the occasional demon who appears on earth. Which is rather disconcerting when you think about it, but okay, whatever. But I don't think I'm getting the whole truth from the Agency."

"Why?"

"Zagan, the demon who captured me..."

"The bastard who was kissing you?"

My cheeks heat. "Yeah. That one." The less I say about that kiss the better. "Anyway, he told me about the runes on my *justitia*. The Agency claims they've never heard of it and that Zagan is a deceiver and I can't believe a word he says."

"Then why do you?"

"I don't know. My *justitia* feels the same. Zagan's a worthy opponent, but not a liar when it comes to certain things."

"You can't always go by feelings. Cold hard facts are what you need."

"The only way to get those is to figure out what's going on at the Agency."

"Get to know the others like you. What do you call yourselves?"

"*Justitians.*"

"Yeah, those. Ask around. Maybe Smythe knows something."

"I don't think he knows anymore than anyone else. He doesn't even know where my *justitia* disappeared to. Or how it disappeared. Or how I got it. He's still researching the matter."

"You sure you can't just take that thing off and return it to them?"

"Yeah. And I don't want to either. I like it right where it is."

"I don't."

"I know."

After wiping his fingers on his shorts, he leans over, traces the former gash from my neck down to my collarbone. Warmth flows from his touch, settling deep inside.

"He doesn't control you, you know."

"No, I don't. What if he does?" Cold creeps into my marrow at the thought, rattling my limbs like a seizure. T pats my shoulder, drops his hand to his lap.

"Look inside. What do you see?" He takes the last bite of his sandwich, chewing while waiting for my response.

I do as he asks, closing my eyes, searching inside for Zagan's influence. Nothing. I don't even notice the *justitia* and I know it lives along my nerves. I take a deep breath, try again. This time I see the purple glow of the *justitia* twining around my nerves. Creepy.

But I wouldn't have it any other way.

Nothing but the *justitia* entwines around my nerves. Nothing.

A flicker of relief flares to life.

I'm not controlled by the demon. Somehow, despite what I did and what should have occurred, I'm free of his influence. How did my *justitia* burn out his control?

Do I really care the how as long as the end result is me thinking sans demon-influence?

"Nothing but the *justitia*." My eyes open and I can't help the smile flirting with my lips. "He doesn't control me!"

"Glad you see it, too."

"Too?"

"I didn't notice anything but that damn bracelet inside you. Which is creepy enough. You just needed to believe you're demon free."

Smart man, my brother.

Except when it comes to choosing dating partners.

T sets his plate down. Drains his glass dry. Puts it back on the coffee table. "You worried me. I don't like to worry about you." He grabs my hand, gives it a squeeze.

I return the grip, squeezing as hard as possible, drawing his concern around me like a shawl. The peace felt from our clasped palms surrounds us, calms our hearts into one pulse, one union, one being. Like when we were in our mother's womb, protected from the world, safe from harm. A wave of peace rocks against my skin, pulling me into its depths. With a sigh, I relax, letting the wave pull me into the darkness of its embrace.

Chapter 28

I flash my hospital badge at the staffer whose job it is to allow no more than two family members at a time to pass into the ICU. Hospital staff don't count as family, even if we're the only family a patient has.

Take Will for instance. No family left. No one but his co-workers. Since he woke from a coma yesterday, we've been taking shifts sitting with him.

Today's my turn. Good thing he's awake from the coma. I have more questions than a reporter.

I poke my head into the room. Sally Ann sits beside a sleeping Will, chomping on a bag of vending machine cookies. She waves a hand in front of her mouth, exaggerating her chewing, her head tilting from side to side as she waits to swallow before talking.

Normally I don't mind chatting it up with Sally Ann, but today I want to wake Will and let the questioning begin. I only have so much time before I need to be back in the ER.

She swallows and stands, stepping beside me. "Gin, hon, haven't gotten a chance yet to say, I'm so sorry about your friend." Sally Ann pats my shoulder, her manicured nails scratching against my scrub top. "I saw it on the news last night. What a shame. He was such a cutie. I can't believe someone would do that to him."

"Me either." The police found Blake's body

yesterday morning, and the news splashed the find across the TV last night. Lawyer's body found, throat slashed. Mugging gone bad.

Little do they know. And it's my job—or the Agency's—to keep it that way.

"I can't believe it. Oh, honey, I'm so sorry. Here, have a tissue." A tissue box appears under my chin, tissue fluttering as she waves the box.

It amazes me how grief sneaks upon you at inopportune times, causing uncontrolled tears. I thought my mental deep breathing exercises on the drive in prepared me for questions about Blake.

So much for that idea.

On the plus side, Sally Ann is the only person at the hospital who's met Blake. Maybe no one else will comment on the find.

I can wish.

"I'm sorry." I swipe the tissue under my eyes, hoping to get things under control before speaking to Will. Hard to get answers while crying. "I'm having a hard time of it. It was a surprise."

"He was so nice. I loved talking to him at your party. I just can't believe it. And don't worry about the tears. If people don't understand, they can just go to hell."

Yeah, like I'm going to tell Nurse Hatchet to go to hell. I like my job just fine the way it is.

I offer Sally Ann a half-cocked smile. "Uh-huh. Thanks for the advice. So far I haven't lost it. Knowing Will is out of his coma really helps."

"And here's some more happy news for you. He's doing so good off the ventilator that they're gonna move him to the floor. Once they have a room. Can you believe? We all thought him a goner. Lucky fellow, eh?"

The tissue pauses against my cheeks as I glance at Will. Still sleeping. Not for long. "Yep. Lucky. Can't believe he's going to walk his happy ass out of here." Especially after all the blood he lost. I close my eyes and swallow as the memory of him shot and bleeding out makes an unwanted appearance.

"Yep. Can you believe how fast he healed? It's been what, like six days since he was shot? They said the wounds were healing twice as fast as normal. Maybe that's rumor but still."

"You're right." I drop my hand holding the tissue, tears disappeared into hiding. "That does make me happy. You're a good friend, Sally Ann. I think I'll keep you around."

She snorts a chuckle. "No problem, honey. Just come on back to Miss Sally Ann for some happy news. You can bring your brother too, you know. That'll make me real happy." She winks her over-mascara'ed lashes and I swallow a grimace.

T and Sally Ann? Breakfast threatens a second appearance.

"Well, gotta get back. Maybe he'll wake for you. He didn't for me." Giving me a little finger wave over her shoulder, she walks down the hall, disappearing from view.

Yeah, he'll wake for me. I sniff one last time, drop my tissue in the trash, and step to Will's bed, giving his shoulder a shake. "Will, wake up."

He moans. I shove the little voice telling me he needs his sleep into hiding and shake his shoulder harder. "Wake. Up."

Will cracks a lid. "Wha…?"

"Tell me how you got this bracelet." I hold the *justitia* in front of his face.

His eye shuts. Right when I'm about to give him another shake, he blinks open both eyes. Shuts them. Opens.

Yeah, I should let the patient be. But sometimes they need waking for their health.

Or yours.

"Gin?" Sleepy questions fill his tone.

"Hey. Good to see you awake." In more ways than one.

"Wasn't I asleep?"

"Not anymore." Curiosity stomps out my conscious concern. "Tell me about this bracelet. How did you get it?"

He shakes his head, gaze bouncing off mine. "I don't want to talk about it."

"Tough shit. I put it on, it won't come off, and all sorts of crazy things have happened since then." I'll wait until later to tell him about the demon-slaying abilities. Might give him a fright.

He closes his eyes and inhales through his nose. "Did you take it out of my pocket?"

"I found it in my scrub pocket after I found you. Maybe you put it in there." Telling him the thing suddenly appeared in my pocket without human intervention sounds strange even after experiencing it.

"Maybe." His lids pop open, gaze focusing on mine. "I just meant for you to keep it safe from my shooter. Whatever happened to him? Did they catch him?"

"He's dead."

Nothing like murderous news to wake up a sleepy patient.

Will's eyes flared. "They said he came after Lara."

"I'm really sorry." I pat his gown-covered shoulder. "Really, I am. But I need to know everything you know about this bracelet."

His eyes cut to the side. Close. Open. He sighs. "Dad gave it to Mom. Said it was important and for her to never give it away or lose it. Then he died and Mom stuck it in a drawer and never wore it. One day I found it and was playing with it. That's the day she was killed." He swallows. "She told me to take the bracelet and hide so I did. The man who killed her kept screaming about the bracelet so I always wanted to keep it safe. I must've slipped it into your pocket when you came to check on me. I don't remember much of that day. Just the gun firing. It's mostly a blur."

Great. Another case of localized amnesia.

"I'm sorry to have to ask you, but as I said weird things have happened since I slipped on your bracelet."

"What kind of weird things?"

Yeah, right. He'd really think I was nuts if I told him about minions and demons and the Agency. "I'll talk to you about it when you get out."

"Don't think I can handle it?" He raises a brow, a trace of a grin on his lips.

"You need your rest."

"You're the one who woke me up. Should've thought about that earlier." His smile twitches across his face, highlighting the tiredness lurking in his eyes.

"Yeah, well. Let's just say this bracelet is really special and leave it at that."

"Only because I'm too tired to get my ass out of

bed and make an issue of it. Just wait. I'm getting stronger every day."

My heart thumps a happy rhythm as I return his grin. "I heard. That's great news. Soon you'll be out of here."

"Not sure where I'll go. Knowing Lara was..." he swallows, choking on the word. "Was...was...you know, home seems violated. I'm not sure if I can go back."

After a panic attack over visiting my own kitchen, I can sympathize. I pat his shoulder. "It'll be okay."

"Yeah. That's what they say." His eyes drift close. Snap open. Drift close.

"Well, I better go." My conscious won its fight over curiosity. I really need to let the man rest, even if I didn't discover all I wanted to.

But I learned something. Will knew nothing.

Smythe won't be happy. Or maybe he will. Googling things on his laptop made my mentor about as happy as a puppy gnawing on a shoe.

Will's lids open, and he reaches a hand toward me. I lean down and give him a little hug, making sure not to touch his skin. When I pull away his brows are furrowed.

"Never pegged you as a tattoo type of person. What does it represent?" He points, and I slap a hand against the top of Zagan's clawmark. A mark no longer visible on my skin, thanks to my new set of healing powers. Smooth skin greets my questing fingers.

My brows furrow a painful squeeze, echoed in the speeding thump of my heart. "What are you talking about? I don't have a tattoo." Is he hallucinating?

"Go look." He points to the little mirror above the

sink in his room.

I obey, twisting my head to the side and pulling my ear forward, the tip of my ponytail brushing against my fingers as I stare at my reflection. The mark branded right below my hairline behind my ear looks familiar. I shove my face closer to the mirror. This can't be happening.

The same rune marks my *justitia*. Zagan's mark.

My stomach twists a tango as the color slides off my face like plastic melting in a fire. I'm not a fool. I know what the tattoo means. Zagan marked me as his. I'm not as free of the demon as I thought. Shit.

A word about the author...

Karilyn Bentley's love of reading stories and her preference for sitting in front of a computer at home instead of in a cube drove her to pen her own works, blending fantasy and romance mixed with a touch of funny.

Her paranormal romance novella, *Werewolves in London,* placed in the Got Wolf contest and started her writing career as an author of sexy heroes and lush fantasy worlds.

Karilyn lives in North Texas with her own hunky hero, a psycho dog nicknamed Hell Hound, a crazy puppy, and a handful of colorful saltwater fish.

More on Karilyn and her books can be found at: www.karilynbentley.com.